MW01674794

Walter K. Kelly

Curiosities of Indo-European tradition and Folk-Lore

SALZWASSER VERLAG

Walter K. Kelly

Curiosities of Indo-European tradition and Folk-Lore

Reprint of the original, first published in 1863.

1st Edition 2022 | ISBN: 978-3-37500-627-3

Verlag (Publisher): Salzwasser Verlag GmbH, Zeilweg 44, 60439 Frankfurt, Deutschland
Vertretungsberechtigt (Authorized to represent): E. Roepke, Zeilweg 44, 60439 Frankfurt, Deutschland
Druck (Print): Books on Demand GmbH, In de Tarpen 42, 22848 Norderstedt, Deutschland

CURIOSITIES

OF

INDO-EUROPEAN TRADITION AND FOLK-LORE.

CURIOSITIES

OF

INDO-EUROPEAN TRADITION AND FOLK-LORE.

BY

WALTER K. KELLY.

Popular tradition is tough.—DASENT.

LONDON:

1863.

PREFACE.

THE purpose of this book is to make known some of the most remarkable discoveries which have been achieved by the successors and countrymen of Jacob Grimm, and to indicate, in a manner not too abstruse for the general reader, the method and line of research which they have pursued, with a success in some instances surpassing all expectation. The labours of their great master have received due honour in this country: they have gladdened the hearts of our children, enriched the minds of our studious men, and nurtured a spirit of inquiry which has done not a little towards rescuing from oblivion the perishing remains of the old ways of life and thought of our forefathers. Learned and unlearned, we have all been delighted to sit as listeners at the feet of Jacob Grimm, but I am not aware that any attempt has yet been made to naturalize amongst us the admirable fruits secured within the last few years by German explorers of his school. Yet the attempt is surely worth making; for it may be truly said that it is only through the ultimate facts ascertained by these men that we begin to discern the true value and the mutual bearings of all the secondary facts collected by their predecessors.

The grand distinction of the new school is that they have worked with a new instrument—the Sanscrit language and literature—an instrument which has yielded in their hands, and promises to yield still more abundantly, results fairly comparable with those which spectral analysis has realized in physical science. They have made it their task to trace back the traditional beliefs and popular customs of ancient and modern Europe to their common source, and have found the object of their search in the crude conceptions of nature, and of the powers that rule it, which were entertained by a primæval race of nomades, the ancestors of all the chief European races. In this way not only have they succeeded in demonstrating what was but dimly surmised before—the radical unity of all the principal pagan religions of the West, but they have evolved a principle of order out of the seeming chaos of ancient and modern superstitions, and assigned an intelligible cause for many of its doctrines and practices apparently the most fantastic and unmeaning. What, for instance, could well have appeared more hopeless than any attempt to account for the origin of a custom so universal, yet apparently so whimsical, as divination with the sieve and shears, or for that of the belief that witches, like the weird sisters in "Macbeth," were in the habit of sailing over the sea or through the air in a sieve? Yet it has been ascertained that the custom and the belief were no arbitrary freaks of fancy, but normal deductions from primitive notions of natural phenomena and their supposed causes. So too all our legends of magic treasures concealed in lakes, swamps, or mountains, and coming to the light at stated periods, are found to have had a similar origin; and the invention of the divining-rod has been brought home to a people, among whom the more practical invention of a simple instrument for producing fire from the friction of two pieces of wood was regarded as a prodigious effort of superhuman genius.

In the foremost rank of the learned Germans who are worthily building up the edifice of which Grimm laid the broad and massive foundations in his "Deutsche Mythologie," stands Dr. Adalbert Kuhn, the author of many profound researches in comparative philology and mythology. His work "On the Descent of Fire and the Drink of the Gods" marks a new epoch in the history of the latter science. It has now been four years before the world, having been published in 1859, and the soundness of its surprising demonstrations has been acknowledged by the best judges in Germany and France. It is my chief authority for what will seem newest to English readers in the greater part of the following pages; and although the very different nature of my work has seldom allowed me to translate two or three consecutive sentences from Dr. Kuhn's elaborate treatise, yet I wish it to be fully understood that but for the latter the former could not have been written. I am the more bound to state this once for all, as emphatically as I can, because the very extent of my indebtedness has hindered me from acknowledging my obligations to Dr. Kuhn, in the text or in footnotes, as constantly as I have done in most other cases.

In not a few instances I have been able to illustrate Dr. Kuhn's principles by examples from the folk-lore of Great Britain and Ireland, and would gladly have done so more copiously had matter for the purpose been more accessible. My efforts in that direction have made me painfully aware how much we are behind the Germans, not only as to our insight into the meaning of such relics of the past, but also as to our industry in collecting them. The latter defect is indeed a natural consequence of the former, and it is to be hoped that our local archæologists will no longer be content to labour under either of them when once they have found what far-reaching knowledge may be extracted out of old wives' tales and notions. Only four years ago the editor of "Notes and Queries" spoke hypothetically* of a time to come, when the study of folk-lore (he was, I believe, the inventor of that very expressive and sterling word) should have risen from a pleasant pastime to the rank of a science. Already his anticipation has been realized, and henceforth every careful collector of a novel scrap of folk-lore, or even of a well-marked variety of an old type, may entertain a reasonable hope that he has in some degree subserved the purposes of the ethnologist and the philosophic historian.

Subjoined is a list of the principal works referred to in the following pages, with some of the abbre-

* In the Preface to "Choice Notes."

viations which have been substituted for the full titles :—

Amélie Bosquet, La Normandie pittoresque et merveilleuse.

Brand, Popular Antiquities, with additions by Sir Henry Ellis. Bohn's edition.

Choice Notes, from Notes and Queries. Folk-Lore. London, 1859.

Dasent, Popular Tales from the Norse. Edinburgh.

D. M.—Jacob Grimm, Deutsche Mythologie. 3te Ausgabe. Göttingen, 1854.

Hertz, Der Werwolf. Stuttgart, 1862.

Kemble, The Saxons in England. London, 1849.

Kuhn, Herab.—Die Herabkunft des Feuers und des Göttertranks. Berlin, 1859.

Kuhn, Westf.—Sagen, Gebräuchen und Märchen aus Westfalen. Leipzig, 1859.

Kuhn, Zeitschr.—Zeitschrift für vergleichende Sprachforschung.

Kuhn und Schwartz, Ndd.—Norddeutsche Sagen, Märchen und Gebräuche. Leipzig, 1848.

Liebrecht, G. T.—Der Gervasius von Tilbury Otia Imperialia. Hanover, 1856.

Mannhardt, Die Götterwelt der Deutschen und Nordischen Völker. Berlin, 1860.

Reinsberg-Düringsfeld, Fest Kalender aus Böhmen. Prag, 1862.

Robert Chambers, Popular Rhymes of Scotland. Edinburgh, 1847.

Schwartz, Der Ursprung der Mythologie dargelegt an griechischer und deutscher sage. Berlin, 1860.

Wolf, Beiträge zur Deutschen Mythologie. Göttingen.

CONTENTS.

CHAPTER I.

CHAPTER II.

CHAPTER III.

CHAPTER IV.

CHAPTER V.

CHAPTER VI.

CHAPTER VII.

CHAPTER VIII.

CHAPTER IX.

CHAPTER X.

CHAPTER XI.

INDO-EUROPEAN TRADITION.

CHAPTER I.

INTRODUCTORY—COMMON ANCESTRY OF THE INDO-EUROPEAN NATIONS—COMMON ORIGIN OF THEIR MYTHOLOGIES.

It is indisputable that the principal races of Europe who are known in history, as well as the high caste Hindoos and the ancient Persians, all belong to the same stock; and that the common ancestors of this Aryan or Indo-European race once dwelt together in the regions of the Upper Oxus, now under the dominion of the khan of Bokhara. The evidence upon which this cardinal fact has been established is of like kind with that which commands our belief in the ascertained truths of geology, and is in no wise inferior to it in fulness, consistency, and force of inductive detail. It is drawn from the analysis and mutual comparison of all the languages of the Indo-Europeans, in which they have unconsciously written the history of their race, just as the earth has written the history of the mutations which its surface has undergone, in the strata which now compose its outer crust.

The Aryans of Europe are the Celts, Greeks, Latins, Germans (Teuton and Scandinavian), Letts and Slaves. The only portions of its soil not possessed by them are those occupied by the Basques, Magyars, Turks, Finns, Laps, and some Ugrian and Tatar tribes of Russia.

In the act of tracing out the mutual affinities of the Aryan languages it was impossible to overlook the traditional beliefs, rites, and customs which those languages record. Hence the investigation gradually resolved itself into the two allied sciences of Comparative Philology and Comparative Mythology. Both sciences bear testimony to the primitive unity, mental and physical, of the whole Aryan family. Often is the same verbal root found underlying words and groups of words most dissimilar in appearance, and belonging to widely different languages, under circumstances that entirely preclude the hypothesis that it is in any one of them a borrowed possession. It is just the same with a multitude of beliefs and customs which have existed from time immemorial in Greece and in Scandinavia, in the

Scottish highlands, the forests of Bohemia, and the steppes of Russia, on the banks of the Shannon, the Rhine, and the Ganges. Take any of them separately, as it appears among a single people, and it will rarely happen that we can penetrate very deeply into its meaning or the causes of its being. We shall even be in danger of too hastily attributing its origin to some arbitrary caprice of ignorance and superstition, just as fossil shells and bones have by some been supposed to have been so formed *ab origine* by a freak of nature. But the mystery clears up more and more as we examine the subject on all sides by the light of kindred phenomena; and in this way we are led on to many surprising and pregnant discoveries of the common elements out of which the mythical traditions of Greece, Italy, and the Northern nations have been severally and independently developed. In this way also the most trivial maxim or practice of modern superstition may become an important link in the chain of human history, taking that term in its most comprehensive sense. For "popular tradition is tough," and there are still extant among ourselves and elsewhere items innumerable of an ancient lore, transcending that of the school-master, and now only succumbing at last to the navvy and the steam-engine; a lore which remains unchanged at the core from what it was some thousands of years ago, ere the first Aryan emigrants had turned their steps westwards from their old home in Central Asia. The dog had been domesticated long before that event occurred, yet watch him now when he lies down to sleep. Though his bed be a bare board, or ground as destitute of herbage, he turns himself round and round before he lies down, just as his wild ancestors used to do before him, when they prepared their couch in the long grass of the prairie. With not less tenacity does the popular mind hold fast by the substance of its ancient traditions, and also for the most part with as much unconsciousness of their primary import.

Previously to the dispersion of the Aryans, their condition, as revealed by the languages of their several branches, was in the main nomadic and patriarchal, yet not without some beginnings of agriculture, and, in proportion thereto, some rudiments of a higher form of social life, some approach to a municipal polity.* Their stock of knowledge was what they had gathered for themselves during their passage from the savage state to that in which we here find them. The growth of their vocabulary

* Kuhn, Herabk. p. 1, and in Weber's Ind. Stud., i. 321—363.

had kept pace with the progress of their observation and experience, and was in fact an automatic register of that progress. It was a highly figurative vocabulary, for that is a necessary condition of every primitive tongue. In all stages of language, even in that at which it has become "a dictionary of faded metaphors," comparison is the ready handmaid of nomenclature. A piece of machinery, for instance, is called a spinning-jenny, because it does the work of a spinning woman. "To call things which we have never seen before by the name of that which most nearly resembles them, is a practice of every day life. That children at first call all men 'father,' and all women 'mother,' is an observation as old as Aristotle. The Romans gave the name of Lucanian *ox* to the elephant, and *camelopardus* to the giraffe, just as the New Zealanders are stated to have called horses *large dogs.* The astonished Caffers gave the name of *cloud* to the first parasol which they had seen ; and similar instances might be adduced almost indefinitely. They prove that it is an instinct, if it be not a necessity, to borrow for the unknown the names already used for things known." *

In this way the primitive Aryans composed their vocabulary of things seen in the sky, and so it

* Farrar "On the Origin of Language," p. 119.

became for all succeeding generations an inexhaustible repertory of the raw material of myths, legends and nursery tales. The sun, for instance, was a radiant wheel, or a golden bird, or an eye, an egg, a horse; and it had many other names. At sunrise or sunset, when it appeared to be squatting on the water, it was a frog; and out of this name, at a later period, when the original metaphor was lost sight of, there grew a Sanscrit story, which is found also in German and Gaelic with a change of gender. The Sanscrit version is that "Bhekî (the frog) was a beautiful girl, and that one day, when sitting near a well, she was discovered by a king, who asked her to be his wife. She consented, on condition that he should never show her a drop of water. One day, being tired, she asked the king for water; the king forgot his promise, brought water, and Bhekî disappeared."* That is to say, the sun disappeared when it touched the water.

Clouds, storms, rain, lightning and thunder, were the spectacles that above all others impressed the imagination of the early Aryans, and busied it most in finding terrestrial objects to compare with their ever varying aspect. The beholders were at home on the earth, and the things of the earth were com-

* "Saturday Review," Feb. 23, 1861.

paratively familiar to them; even the coming and going of the celestial luminaries might often be regarded by them with the more composure because of their regularity; but they could never surcease to feel the liveliest interest in those wonderful meteoric changes, so lawless and mysterious in their visitations, which wrought such immediate and palpable effects, for good or ill, upon the lives and fortunes of the beholders. Hence these phenomena were noted and designated with a watchfulness and a wealth of imagery which made them the principal groundwork of all the Indo-European mythologies and superstitions. The thunder was the bellowing of a mighty beast, or the rolling of a wagon. The lightning was a sinuous serpent, or a spear shot straight athwart the sky, or a fish darting in zigzags through the waters of heaven. The stormy winds were howling dogs or wolves; the ravages of the whirlwind that tore up the earth were the work of a wild boar. Light clouds were webs spun and woven by celestial women, who also drew water from the fountains on high, and poured it down as rain. The yellow light gleaming through the clouds was their golden hair. A fast-scudding cloud was a horse flying from its pursuers. Other clouds were cows, whose teeming udders refreshed and replenished the earth; or they were buck goats, or shaggy skins of beasts dripping water. Sometimes they were towering castles, or mountains and caverns, rocks, stones, and crags,* or ships sailing over the heavenly waters. In all this, and much more of the same kind, there was not yet an atom of that symbolism which has commonly been assumed as the starting point of all mythology.† The mythic animals, for example, were, for those who first gave them their names, no mere images or figments of the mind; they were downright realities, for they were seen by men who were quick to see, and who had not yet learned to suspect any collusion between their eyes and their fancy. These "natural philosophers"—to speak with Touchstone—had in full perfection the faculty that is given to childhood, of making everything out of anything, and of believing with a large and implicit faith in its own creations.

The beings whom they first recognised as gods were those that were visible to them in the sky, and these were for the most part beasts, birds, and reptiles. Some of the latter appeared to combine the flight of birds with the form of creeping things,

* Nearly all the Sanscrit words for rock, stone, cliff, crag, &c., signify also cloud.

† Schwartz, U. M. 12.

and then the heavenly fauna was enriched with a new genus, the winged dragon. Glimpses of other human forms besides those of the cloud women were seen from time to time, or their existence was surmised, and gradually the divine abodes became peopled with gods in the likeness of men, to whom were ascribed the same functions as belonged to the bird, beast, and snake-gods. By-and-bye, when all these crude ideas began to shape themselves into something like an orderly system, the surplusage of gods was obviated by blending the two kinds together, or subjecting the one to the other. Thenceforth the story ran that the gods changed themselves from time to time into animal forms, or that each of them had certain animals for his favourites and constant attendants in heaven; and these were sacred to him on earth.

Let us not think too meanly of the intelligence of our simple ancestors because they could regard brutes as gods. It was an error not peculiar to them, but common to all infant races of men. The early traditions of every people point back to a period when man had not yet risen to a clear conception of his own pre-eminence in the scale of created life. The power of discerning differences comes later into play than that of perceiving resemblances, and the primeval man, living in the closest communion with nature, must have begun with a strong feeling of his likeness to the brutes who shared with him so many wants, passions, pleasures, and pains. Hence the attribution of human voice and reason to birds and beasts in fable and story, and the doctrine of the transmigration of souls. To this feeling of fellowship there would afterwards be superadded a sense of a mysterious something inherent in the nature of brutes, which was lacking in that of man. He found himself so vastly surpassed by them in strength, agility, and keenness of sense; they evinced such a marvellous foreknowledge of coming atmospheric changes which he could not surmise; they went so straight to their mark, guided by an instinct to him incomprehensible, that he might well come to look upon them with awe as beings superior to himself, and surmise in their wondrous manifestations the workings of something divine.*

The distinction made in historic times between gods of the upper sky, the waters, and the subterranean world, was unknown to the primitive Aryans. The horizon, where earth and sky seem to meet together, was the place in which the supernatural powers were most frequently descried. When they

* Herder, Ideen. Hertz, Der Werwolf.

were not there they were beyond the clouds, in their own world, which was common to them all, and which extended indefinitely above and below the surface of the earth. The origin of most water-gods and nymphs of the European Aryans may be traced back to the storm and rain deities of the parent stock; and the greater part of the myths relating to the sea are to be understood as primarily applying not to the earthly, but the cloud-sea, for no other great collection of waters was known to the first Aryans in their inland home. In like manner mythical mountains, rocks, and caverns are generally to be understood as clouds. It was in the clouds that men first beheld the deities of the under-world, whose abode was fixed in later times in the regions from which they might have been supposed to ascend when there was wild work to be done in mid-air.

Although, as we have said, the cloud-sea of the first Aryans has been generally transferred to the earth in the mythologies of the West, nevertheless the existence of an ocean overhead continued to be an article of wide-spread belief in Europe, down at least to the thirteenth century; nor is it quite extinct in some places even at this day. Agobard, Bishop of Lyons, fought hard against it in the ninth century. Many persons, he says, are so insensate as to believe that there is a region called Magonia, whence ships come in the clouds to take on board the fruits of the earth which have been beaten down by storm and hail. The aerial navigators carry on a regular traffic in that way with the storm-making wizards, pay them for the corn they have thrashed with wind and hail, and ship it off to Magonia.*

Gervase of Tilbury† relates, that as the people were coming out from a church in England, on a dark cloudy day, they saw a ship's anchor fastened in a heap of stones, with its cable reaching up from it to the clouds. Presently they saw the cable strained, as if the crew were trying to haul it up, but it still stuck fast. Voices were then heard above the clouds, apparently in clamorous debate, and a sailor came sliding down the cable. As soon as he touched the ground the crowd gathered round him, and he died, like a man drowned at sea, suffocated by our damp thick atmosphere. An hour afterwards his ship-mates cut their cable and sailed away; and the anchor they had left behind was made into fastenings and ornaments for the church door, in memory of the wondrous event. The same author tells another tale to the like effect. A native of Bristol

* D. M. 604.

† In his Otia Imperialia, composed about A.D. 1211.

sailed from that port for Ireland, leaving his wife and family at home. His ship was driven far out of its course to the remote parts of the ocean, and there it chanced that his knife fell overboard, as he was cleaning it one day after dinner. At that very moment his wife was seated at table with her children in their house at Bristol, and behold! the knife fell through an open skylight, and stuck in the table before her. She recognised it immediately; and when her husband came home long afterwards they compared notes, and found that the time when the knife had fallen from his hand corresponded exactly with that in which it had been so strangely recovered. "Who, then," exclaims Gervase, "after such evidence as this, will doubt the existence of a sea above this earth of ours, situated in the air or over it?" Such a sea is still known to Celtic tradition. "If our fathers have not lied," say the peasants of La Vendée, "there are birds that know the way of the upper sea, and may no doubt carry a message to the blessed in Paradise."*

The elemental nature of the early Aryan gods, however obscured in the monstrous growths of the later Hindu theology, is most transparent in the Rig Veda, the oldest collection of writings extant in

* Huber, "Skizzen aus der Vendee." Berlin, 1853. p. 65.

any Indo-European tongue. It was put together somewhere about the year 1400 B.C., and consists of the hymns chanted by the southern branch of the Aryans, after they had passed the Indian Caucasus, and descended into the plain of the Seven Rivers (the Indus, the Punjaub or Five Rivers, and the Sarasvati), thence to overrun all India. The Sanscrit tongue in which the Vedas are written is the sacred language of India: that is to say, the oldest language, the one which was spoken, as the Hindus believe, by the gods themselves, when gods and men were in frequent fellowship with each other, from the time when Yama descended from heaven to become the first of mortals. This ancient tongue may not be the very one which was spoken by the common ancestors of Hindus and Europeans, but at least it is its nearest and purest derivative, nor is there any reason to believe that it is removed from it by more than a few degrees. Hence the supreme importance of the Sanscrit vocabulary and literature as a key to the languages and the supernatural lore of ancient and modern Europe.

"The divinities worshipped [in the Rig Veda] are not unknown to later [Hindu] systems; but they there perform very subordinate parts; whilst those deities who are the great gods—the dii majores—of the subsequent period, are either wholly unnamed in the Veda or are noticed in a different and inferior capacity. . . . The far larger number of hymns in the first book are dedicated to Agni and Indra, the deities or personifications of Fire and Firmament."* Indra has for friends and followers the Maruts, or spirits of the winds, whose host consists, at least in part, of the souls of the pious dead; and the Ribhus, who are of similar origin, but whose element is rather that of the sunbeams or the lightning, though they too rule the winds, and sing like the Maruts the loud song of the storm. Their name means the "artificers," and not even the divine workman of Olympus was more skilled than they in all kinds of handicraft. The armour and weapons of the gods, the chariot of the Asvins (deities of the dawn), the thunderbolt and the lightning steed of Indra, were of their workmanship. They made their old decrepid parents young and supple-jointed again. But the feat for which they are most renowned is the revival of the slaughtered cow on which the gods had feasted. Out of the hide alone these wonder-working Ribhus reproduced the perfect living animal; and this they did not once, but again and again. In other words, out of a small portion of the

* Wilson, Translation of Rig Veda.

imperishable cloud that had melted away in rain and seemed destroyed, they reproduced its whole form and substance. Similar feats were ascribed to the Northern thunder-god Thor, whose practice it was to kill the two buck goats that drew his car, cook them for supper, and bring them to life again in the morning by touching them with his hammer.

In the gloomy season of the winter solstice the Ribhus sleep for twelve days in the house of the sun-god Savitar; then they wake up, and prepare the earth to clothe itself anew with vegetation, and the frozen waters to flow again. It appears certain, from some passages in the Vedas, that twelve nights about the winter solstice were regarded as prefiguring the character of the weather for the whole year. A Sanscrit text is noticed by Weber, which says expressly, "The Twelve Nights are an image of the year."* The very same belief exists at this day in Northern Germany. The peasants say that the calendar for the whole year is made in the twelve days between Christmas and Epiphany, and that as the weather is on each of those days so will it be on the corresponding month of the ensuing year. They believe also that whatever one dreams on any

* Mannhardt, p. 50.

of the twelve nights will come to pass within the next year.*

Before the dispersion of the Aryan race the Ribhus were also called Arbhus, and this form of the word is strictly identical with the Greek name, Orpheus.† Of this, as of most other Greek mythical names, the Greek language affords no explanation, but Sanscrit reveals its origin and gives a new interest to its story. We see how the cruder idea of the Ribhus, sweeping trees and rocks in wild dance before them by the force of their stormy song, grew under the beautifying touch of the Hellenic imagination into the legend of that master of the lyre whose magic tones made torrents pause and listen, rocks and trees descend with delight from their mountain beds, and moved even Pluto's unrelenting heart to pity. In Northern Europe, the word Arbhus became changed, in conformity with the laws of the Germanic languages, into Albs, Alb, or Alp; plural Elbe, Elfen; English Elf, Elves. The Maruts also survived under the name of Mârt, or Mahr. The English Nightmare, French Cauchemar, is one of them, and the whole family formed the retinue of Odin, when he rode abroad as the Wild Huntsman.

* Kuhn, Ndd. p. 411; Kuhn, Westf. ii. 115.

† Max Müller, "Oxford Essays," 1856.

Odin's prototypes are Indra and Rudra, the storm-god and dragon-slayer. The latter is called the father of the Maruts, or Winds, and they are as often in attendance on him as on Indra. The stormy Apollo of the older Greek legends is also a close copy of Rudra. The latter "is evidently a form of Agni, or Indra."*

Agni, the god of fire (Latin, ignis), has for retainers the Bhrigus and the Angirases. They are his priests on earth whilst they dwell there in mortal form; and after death they are his friends and companions in heaven. They are also the companions of the clouds and the storms. The Angirases tend the heavenly cows (the clouds), and the Maruts (the storms) milk them. On the whole, it is manifest that all these divine tribes, Maruts, Ribhus, Bhrigus, and Angirases, are beings identical in nature, distinguished from each other only by their elemental functions, and not essentially different from the Pitris, or fathers. The latter are simply the souls of the pious dead. High above the clouds and the blue firmament there is a shining realm, whence the sun, the moon, and the stars receive their light, and whence also is drawn the fire of the lightning, which again is the origin of the earthly fire. Here the

* Wilson, Rig Veda, Introd.

Pitris dwell in everlasting bliss with their great progenitor, the god Yama. The myths relating to the origin of mankind are many and various, but they all agree in this, that the soul of the first man came down to earth as a particle of living fire in the lightning. So it is in the Greek legend of Prometheus: he brought down fire from heaven and created the first men. In the Vedas, Yama is the first lightning-born mortal, the first, too, who trod the path of death, and therefore he became king of the departed fathers. His brother, Manu, (i.e., *man*,) is the chief of the living. It is manifest that Yama and Manu were originally one, but were subsequently divided, Manu becoming the supreme representative of human life on earth, and Yama that of its continuance after death.

Manu is the *thinking* being* (from the root *man*, whence also the Greek, Latin, and English words, ménos, mens, mind). The Minos and Minyas of the Greeks, and the Mannus of the Germans are identical with Manu. Minos is judge of the dead; Yama, who is only another form of Manu, is their king.

The Pitris, or fathers, led no inactive lives in their blissful abode. They were elementary powers, and

* Max Müller, "Lectures on Language."

it was their office to distribute the light that filled that lustrous region, and to adorn the firmament with stars. They themselves too shone as stars to mortal eyes. This most ancient belief is not yet extinct in England and Germany. It has come down to our own day through the fairy mythology of the north, and has become blended with popular conceptions of the nature of the angels. The author of the prose Edda says that, "at the southern end of heaven stands the palace of Gimli, the most beautiful of all, and more brilliant than the sun. It will continue to stand when heaven and earth pass away, and all good and upright men of all times will dwell therein. It is said, that above and southward of yonder heaven, there is another called Andlângr, and also a third above these two, which is called Vîdblâinn; and in this heaven, as we believe, is that palace situated, and only inhabited now by the bright elves (liosâlfar)." These bright elves are in all respects identical with the Pitris. "The idea," says Sommer, "that men, at their birth, come out from the community of the elves, and return to it after death, is deeply-rooted in our (German) paganism." In most English villages children are taught that it is very wrong to point at the stars, but they are not often told why it is wrong.

Their parents have probably forgotten the reason, for that is a common occurrence in matters of superstition. The rule remains in force long after its principle has faded from popular recollection. But in Germany the same precept is inculcated, and the reason is always given for it: "the stars are the angels' eyes."*

The cloud-maidens, of whom we have already spoken, are known in the Vedas as Âpas, (waters), and are styled brides of the gods (Dêvapatnis) and Nâvyah, i.e., navigators of the celestial sea. Nearly related to them, but less divine, are the Apsarases, damsels whose habitat is between the earth and the sun. They are the houris of the Vedic paradise, destined to delight the souls of heroes. Their name means either "the formless" or "the water going," and they appear to have been personifications of the manifold but ill-defined forms of the mists; but other natural phenomena may also have been represented under their image. The Apsarases are fond of transforming themselves into water fowl, especially swans; they are the originals of the swan-maidens of Germanic story, and are closely related to the Elves, Mahrs, and Valkyries.

The Apsarases had shirts of swan plumage, and it

* Wolf, Beitr., ii. 291.

was by putting on these garments that they transformed themselves into swans. The Persian peris, and the German swan-maidens changed their forms in the same way and by the same means. The German and Norse swan-maidens were in the habit of taking off their swan shirts, and leaving them on the margin of a lake, while they bathed there in human form; but it often happened that the shirt was stolen by some mortal who had watched the proceeding, and who thereby became possessed of the person of the swan-maiden. He made her his wife, and they lived long and happily together; but the end of the story always was, that she found the shirt at last, or wheedled him out of it, and then flew away from him for ever. Odin's Valkyries had also their swan-shirts, and the Norse goddess Freyja had her falcon-shirt, which she lent to Loki, when he went in quest of Thor's stolen hammer, and to rescue Idunn, the goddess of youth, from captivity among the frost giants. Thiassi, who kept her in custody, had an eagle-shirt, and his fellow giant, Suttungr, had another, in which he pursued Odin.

Opposed to the beneficent genii of the elements, are troops of dark demons, from whom proceed all the hurtful influences of nature. They hide the heavenly luminaries from mortal eyes, and prevent the fertilizing waters from descending upon the earth. It is they who produce the burning heat of midsummer, and wither the green herbage with scorching sunbeams. They are called by many different names, accordingly as they are engaged in one or other of their works of mischief. Vritra is the demon who steals the heavenly cows, (*i.e.*, the light rain clouds), the Âpas, and the golden treasure of the sun, and shuts them up in his dark cavern. There the captive Âpas, the brides of the gods (Dêvapatnis), are forced to become brides of the fiends (Dâsapatnis) until they are rescued by Indra and the other luminous gods. The dark cavern in which they are imprisoned is the black storm-cloud, that hangs long in the sky without unloading itself. Vritra means the concealer, him who covers up; from his work in the dog-days, the same demon receives the names of Sushna, or the parcher, and Ahi (Greek, échis), the serpent or dragon. Sushna steals the golden wheel of heaven (the sun), and would burn up the earth with it but for Indra, who strikes Sushna dead with his thunderbolt, extinguishes the wheel in the sky sea, and lights it up again with a milder radiance. The annually recurring battle between the god and the demon is described with great animation in the Vedas, and we shall see by-

and-by how it was dramatically represented every year in one of the popular customs of modern Europe. It was, in fact, the model of all the victorious dragon fights that have been subsequently fought, whether by pagan or christian champions, from Apollo, Hercules, and Siegfried, down to St. George, and to that modern worthy, More of More-hall,

"Who slew the dragon of Wantley."

Of Indra's weapon, the thunderbolt, we shall speak at some length in another chapter. Here we will only mention, that every time it was hurled by the god it returned of itself to his hand. So also did Odin's spear, and the same extremely convenient property was manifested on all ordinary occasions by Thor's lightning club or hammer. It was only in the last storms of autumn that the latter remained buried in the earth, and was lost to the god until the following spring. In consequence of this peculiarity of the hammer, or thunderbolt, it was necessary to take precautions, not only against its direct blow, but also against its back-stroke when it was returning to its master's hand. For this reason it continues to be the custom in many places in Bavaria, as Mannhardt relates, to throw open all the windows as wide as possible during a thunderstorm, so that if the lightning should enter the house it may have free vent to get out again. I can also testify from personal knowledge, that the same practice, with the addition of opening all the doors as well as the windows, is carefully observed in some places in Hertfordshire and Essex.

In the elevated and inland region of Arya, winter was a rigorous season of seven months' duration. Its cold and its gloom were believed, like the burning heat of the dog-days, to be the work of a demon, who weakened the light of the sun in the dwindling days before the winter solstice, locked up the waters of the sky, and bound those of the earth in icy fetters. Or, as the Aryans expressed the fact, he built himself seven wintry castles (i.e., the clouds piled up by the wintry winds), in which he confined the women, the cows, and the gold of the sun. Such cloud-built towers and their architects occur frequently in the Grecian and German mythologies. An offer was made to the gods, by one of the Norse giants, to build them a strong castle in a year and a half, if they would give him the sun and moon, and the great goddess, Freyja. After consulting together upon the proposal, the gods resolved to accept it, on these conditions: the giant was to complete the building in *one winter,* and to do it all alone without any man's help; if any part of it were unfinished by the first day of summer, he was to forfeit all claim to remuneration. The giant, aided by his strong horse, Svadilfari, nearly completed the building, though hindered by Loki (for the gods had repented of their bargain), and at last he was killed by the lightning god, Thor.

This myth, says Grimm, after passing through those curious fluctuations which are often observable in genuine popular traditions, survives in a new form, in other times, and on other ground. A German popular tale puts the devil in place of the giant, and there is a whole string of legends, in which the devil erects buildings and flings stones, just like the giants of yore. The devil contracts to build a house for a peasant, and to have his soul for the job; but he must complete it before the cock crows, otherwise, the peasant goes scot-free. The work is all but finished, there only remains one tile to be put upon the roof, when the peasant imitates the crowing of a cock, all the cocks in the neighbourhood fall a-crowing, and the fiend is foiled of his bargain. A Norwegian legend of a more archaic kind, tells that King Olaf, of Norway, was wending his way, in deep thought, over hill and dale; he had it in his mind to build a church, the like of which should nowhere be found, but he saw that he could not complete the building without greatly burthening his kingdom. In his perplexity, he was met by a man of strange appearance, who asked him why he was so thoughtful. Olaf told him what he was meditating, and the giant, or troll, offered to complete the building singlehanded, by a certain time, stipulating that he should have for payment the sun and moon, or St. Olaf himself. The bargain was struck, but Olaf laid down such a plan for the church, as he thought could not possibly be fulfilled; the church was to be so big that seven priests could preach in it at once, without disturbing each other; the pillars, and the architectural ornaments, without and within, were to be carved out of hard flint, &c. All this was soon done, and nothing remained wanting, but the roof and the spire. Again disturbed in mind at the bargain he had made, Olaf wandered over hill and dale. All at once he heard a child crying within a hill, and a giantess soothing it with these words: "Hush! Hush! To-morrow WIND AND WEATHER, your father, will come home, and bring with him the sun and the moon or St. Olaf himself." Delighted with this discovery (for with the name of the evil spirit one can destroy his power), Olaf turned and went home. The work was finished, even to the point of the spire. Then said Olaf, "Wind and Weather! you have set the spire awry." At the word, down fell the giant with a horrible crash from the roof-ridge of the church, and broke into a great many pieces, and every piece a flint stone.*

In the middle ages, the devil, who is proverbially busy in a gale of wind, was in very extensive practice as an architect, but his buildings were always left unfinished, or were ruined, as those of the Aryan demon were by the thunderbolts of Indra.

To come back to the southern Aryans, their Râkshasas, a very numerous tribe of demons, are also called Atrin, or devourers, and are palpably the earliest originals of the giants and ogres of our nursery tales. They can take any form at will, but their natural one is that of a huge mis-shapen giant, "like a cloud," with hair and beard of the colour of the red lightning. They go about open-mouthed, gnashing their monstrous teeth and snuffing after human flesh. Their strength waxes most terrible in twilight, and they know how to increase its effect by all sorts of magic. They carry off their human prey through the air, tear open the living bodies, and with their faces plunged among the entrails they suck up

* D.M. p. 514.

the warm blood as it gushes from the heart. After they have gorged themselves they dance merrily. Sometimes it happens that a giantess, smitten with love for the imperilled man, rescues him from the Râkshasa, and changes her shape for his sake into that of a beautiful maiden. Besides the demon giants there are demon dwarfs also, called Panis.

The collective appellation of the Vedic gods is Dêvas, and this name has passed into most of the Indo-European languages; for corresponding to the Sanscrit dêva is the Latin deus, Greek theós, Lithuanian déwas, Lettish dews, Old Prussian deiws, Irish dia, Welch duw, Cornish duy. Among the German races the word dêva survives only in the Norse plural tìvar, gods; and among those of the Slave stock, the Servians alone preserve a trace of it in the word diw, giant. The daêvas of the Medes and Persians were in early times degraded from the rank of gods to that of demons by a religious revolution, just as the heathen gods of the Germans were declared by the Christian missionaries to be devils; and the modern Persian div, and Armenian dev, mean an evil spirit. Dêvá is derived from div, heaven (properly "the shining"), and means the heavenly being.

Hence it appears that certain gods were common

to all the Indo-Europeans before their dispersion, and the greatest of those "heavenly" beings must have been he who was heaven itself—Div (nom. Dyâus, gen. Divás). He is addressed in the Vedic hymns as Dyaush pitâ, *i.e.*, Heaven Father, and his wife is Mâtâ Prithivi, Mother Earth. He is the Zeus Pater of the Greeks, the Jupiter of the Romans,* the German Tius, Norse Tyr. Dyaush pitâ was the god of the blue firmament, but even in the Vedic times his grandeur was already on the wane. Indra, the new lord of the firmament, had left him little more than a titular sovereignty in his own domain, whilst Varuna, another heavenly monarch, who was still in the plenitude of his power, commanded more respect than the *roi fainéant*, his neighbour. The all-covering Varuna,* the Uranos of the Greeks, was lord of the celestial sea and of the realm of light above it, that highest heaven in which the Fathers dwelt with their king Yama. After the southern branch of the Aryans had entered India, Varuna was brought down from the upper regions, to be thenceforth the god of the earthly sea, which had

* Zeús (gen. Diòs) = Deús, = Dyâus; Jupiter (Diupiter) = Div-pater; or Diespiter = Dyaus-pater.

† Varuna and the demon Vritri both derive their names from var, vri, to cover, enfold.

then for the first time become known to his votaries.

Whilst the sun was still a wheel, a store of gold, a swan or a flamingo, an eagle, falcon, horse, and many other things, it was also the eye of Varuna; just as among the Anglo-Saxons and other Germans it was held to be the eye of Woden. Varuna and Mithra (the friend), the god of daylight, used to sit together at morning on a golden throne, and journey at evening in a brazen car. At the same time there was a special god of the sun, Savitar or Sûrya, who also had his beaming chariot, drawn by two, seven, or ten red or golden coloured mares, called Haritas, a name in which Professor Max Müller has recognised the original of the Greek Charites.* The ideas of the horse-sun and the wheel-sun had naturally coalesced to form the chariot, and then the divine charioteer followed as a matter of course. The utter inconsistency of all these various representations of the same visible object did not give the Vedic hymnists the least concern. They took their materials as they found them in the floating speech and unmethodised conceptions of their people, and used them with the freedom of an imagination which had never been taught to run in critical

* "Oxford Essays," 1856, p. 81.

harness. It is difficult at this day for men whose hereditary ideas of nature and its phenomena are such as the long growth of science has made them—it is difficult for minds thus trained and furnished to go back to the point of view from which the primitive Aryans looked upon a world wherein they had everything to learn for themselves. To them it was by no means self-evident that the sun which shone upon them to-day was the same they had seen yesterday or the day before; on the contrary it seemed to them quite as reasonable to suppose that every new day had its new sun. The Greek mythology shows us a whole people of suns* in the Cyclops, giants with one eye, round as a wheel, in their foreheads. They were akin to the heavenly giants and dwelt with the Phæacians, the navigators of the cloud-sea, in the broad Hypereia,† the upper-land, i. e., heaven, until the legend transplanted them both to the western horizon.

The morning twilight is represented in the Vedas by twin gods, and the ruddy dawn by the goddess Ushas, who is one in name and fact with the Greek Eôs. Her light was conceived to be a herd of red cows, and she herself figures in some hymns as a

* W. Grimm, "Die Sage von Polyphem." p. 27 ff.
† Homer, Od. vii. 58, 206.

quail. Vartikâ, the Sanscrit name of the bird, corresponds etymologically with ortyx, its Greek name; and in the myths of Greece and Asia Minor the quail is a symbol of light or heat. Instead of one Ushas, a plurality is sometimes mentioned, and indeed there was no end of them, since every new dawn appeared to be a new goddess.

The twin brothers who chase away the demons of the night and bring on the morning, are the Asvins, or Riders. There are points of resemblance between them and the twin sons of Leda which may be more than casual. They are extolled for having rescued many men from danger, and particularly for the aid they frequently afforded to storm-beaten sailors, whom they carried safely to shore in their chariot, or on the backs of their horses. They were bounteous givers, too, of wealth, food, and divine remedies for the ills that flesh is heir to. The wife of Cyavana, the son of Bhrigu, with whom they were in love, induced them by stratagem to renew her husband's youth, and this they effected by bathing him in a lake, from which the bather emerges with whatever age he pleases. Here we have for the first time that "fountain of youth" which reappears, after so long a period of apparent oblivion, in the poems of the middle ages. The renovating lake is the cloud water which contains the drink of immortality, the amrita of the Vedas, the ambrosia of the Greeks.

This heavenly beverage was brought down to earth and bestowed on mortals by the god Soma, the personification of the soma plant, which the Hindus now identify with the Asclepias acida, or Sarcostemma viminale. This is a plant containing a milky juice of a sweetish subacid flavour, which, being mixed with honey and other ingredients, yielded to the enraptured Aryans the first fermented liquor their race had ever known. The poetic fire with which Burns sings the praises of John Barleycorn may help us, but only in a faint degree, to comprehend the tumult of delight and wonder, the devout ecstasy, with which the first draught of the miraculous soma possessed the souls of a simple race of water-drinking nomades. What a Vedic hymn would Burns have raised had he been one of them! But there was not wanting many a sacred poet to commemorate the glorious event, nor did it fail to be hallowed in the traditions of succeeding generations from the Ganges to the Atlantic. Among all the Indo-Europeans it gave rise to a multitude of myths and legends, having for their subject the simultaneous descent of fire, of the soul of man, and of the drink of the gods. One of the synonymes of soma is madhu, which means a mixed drink ; and this word is the methu of the Greeks, and the mead of our own Saxon, Norse, and Celto-British ancestors.

The Gandharves, a tribe of demigods, are represented in some of the Vedic legends as custodians of the amrita, or soma, and as keeping such close watch over it that only by force and cunning can the thirsty gods obtain a supply of the immortal beverage. The horses of these Gandharves are highly renowned, and they themselves often assume the form of their favourite animals. Among Dr. Kuhn's many interesting discoveries, not the least curious is that of the identity of these Gandharves, in name and in nature, with the half-human, half-equine Kentaurs, or Centaurs, of Grecian fable. The parallel between the Aryan and the Greek semihorses holds good even as to the fight with the gods for the divine drink, which the former refused to share with the latter. The Kentaurs had a butt, or tun, of precious wine, which was given to them by Dionysos, or Bacchus. Pholos, one of their number, allowed Hercules to drink of this wine, and that was the cause of the war between the son of Jove and the Kentaurs. The divine perfume of the wine was wafted to the nostrils of its absent owners, and rushing to the spot they assailed their kinsman's guest with stones and other missiles. This scene of turbulence, though described as having occurred on earth, must be understood as a piece of cloud-history. The Kentaurs, like the Gandharves, were undoubtedly cloud-demons, or demigods, and the wine butt of the former corresponds to the vessel in which the latter kept their amrita, or soma, and which is called in Sanscrit *kabandha*, a word that signifies both butt and cloud.

According to Nonnus, the Kentaurs were sons of the Hyades, the rainy constellation, who are also spoken of as the nurses of Dionysos. Asklepiades states that the most distinguished amongst these starry nymphs was named Ambrosia. Euripides speaks of the fountains of ambrosia, the drink of immortality, as situated at the verge of the ocean, the region where heaven and earth meet together, and the clouds rise and fall.

CHAPTER II.

THE DESCENT OF FIRE—PROMETHEUS—NEEDFIRES—DRAGONS—WHEEL BURNING—FRODI'S MILL.

THE gods Agni and Soma are described in the Vedas as descending to earth to strengthen the dominion of their own race, the Devas, who are at war with their rivals, the Asuras, and to exalt men to the gods. The story of this great event is variously told. One of its many versions as relates to Agni, the god of fire, is that he had hid himself in a cavern in heaven, and that Mâtarisvan, a god, or demi-god, brought him out from it and delivered him to Manu, the first man, or to Bhrigu, the father of the mythical family of that name. Mâtarisvan is thus a prototype of Prometheus, and the analogy between them will appear still closer when we come to see in what way both were originally believed to have kindled the heavenly fire which they brought down to earth. The process was the same as that by which Indra kindles the lightning, and which is daily imitated in the Hindu temples in the production of sacred fire. It is so like churning, that both operations are designated by the same word.

"In churning in India, the stick is moved by a rope passed round the handle of it, and round a post planted in the ground as a pivot; the ends of the rope being drawn backwards and forwards by the hands of the churner, gives the stick a rotatory motion amidst the milk, and this produces the separation of its component parts."—*Wilson, Rig Veda, I.* 28, 4 *n.*

"The process by which fire is obtained from wood is called churning, as it resembles that by which butter in India is separated from milk. The New Hollanders obtain fire by a similar process. It consists in drilling one piece of arani wood into another by pulling a string, tied to it, with a jerk with one hand, while the other is slackened, and so alternately till the wood takes fire. The fire is received on cotton or flax held in the hand of an assistant Brahman."—*Stevenson, Sâma Veda, Pref. VII.*

Besides the churn, there is another well-known domestic machine to which the "chark," or fire generator of India, is nearly related. This is the mangle or instrument for smoothing linen by means of rollers. *Mangle* is a corruption of *mandel* (from the root *mand,* or *manth,* which implies rotatory motion), and as a verb it means properly to roll, in which sense it is still used in provincial German. In North Germany the peasants say, when they hear the low rumbling of distant thunder, *Use Herr Gött mangelt*, "The Lord is mangling," or rolling—rolling the thunder. The same verb in Sanscrit is *manthami*, which is always used to denote the process of churning, whether the product sought be butter, or fire, or a mixture of the ingredients for making soma-mead. The drilling, or churning, stick is called mantha, manthara, or, with a prefix, pramantha. The Hindu epics tell how that once upon a time the Devas, or gods, and their opponents, the Asuras, made a truce, and joined together in churning the ocean to procure amrita, the drink of immortality (p. 34). They took Mount Mandara for a churning stick, and wrapping the great serpent Sesha round it for a rope, they made the mountain spin round to and fro, the Devas pulling at the serpent's tail, and the Asuras at its head. Mount Mandara was more anciently written Manthara, and manthara is the Sanscrit name of the churning stick which is used in every dairy in India.

The invention of the chark was an event of immeasurable importance in the history of Aryan civilisation. Scattered through the traditions of the race there are glimpses of a time when the progenitors of those who were to "carry to their fullest growth all the elements of active life with which our nature is endowed," had not yet acquired the art of kindling fire at will. From that most abject condition of savage life they were partially raised by the discovery that two dry sticks could be set on fire by long rubbing together. But the work of kindling two sticks by parallel friction, effected by the hand alone, was slow and laborious, and at best of but uncertain efficacy. A little mechanical contrivance, of the simplest and rudest kind, completely changed the character of the operation. The chark was invented, and from that moment the destiny of the Aryan race was secured. Never again could the extinction of a solitary fire become an appalling calamity under which a whole tribe might have to sit down helpless, naked, and famishing, until relief was brought them by the eruption of a volcano or the spontaneous combustion of a forest. The most terrible of elements, and yet the kindliest and most genial, had become the submissive servant of man, punctual at his call, and ready to do whatever work he required of it. Abroad it helped him to subdue the earth and have dominion over it; at home it was the minister to his household wants, the centre and the guardian genius of his domestic affections.

Always prompt to explain the ways of nature by their own ways and those of the creatures about them, the Aryans saw in the fire-churn, or chark, a working model of the apparatus by which the fires of heaven were kindled. The lightning was churned out of the sun or the clouds; the sun wheel that had been extinguished at night, was rekindled in the morning with the pramantha of the Asvins. The fire-churn was regarded as a sacred thing by all branches of Indo-Europeans. It is still in daily use in the temples of the Hindus, and among others of the race here and there recourse is had to it on solemn occasions to this day. In Greece it gave birth to the sublime legend of Prometheus. Greek tragedy had its rise in the recital of rude verses in a cart by uncouth actors daubed with lees of wine. The noblest production of the Greek tragic stage was but a transcendant version of the story of a stick twirling in a hole in a block of wood.

To rub fire out of a chark is to get something that does not come to hand of its own accord, and to get it by brisk, if not violent action. Hence we find, along with pramantha, the fire-churning stick, another word of the same stock, *pramatha*, signifying theft;

for manthami had come by a very natural transition to be used in the secondary sense of snatching away, appropriating, stealing. In one of these senses it passed into the Greek language, and became the verb *manthanô*, to learn, that is to say, to appropriate knowledge, whence *prometheia*, foreknowledge, forethought. In like manner the French *apprendre*, to learn, means originally to lay hold on, to acquire. Derivatives of pramantha and pramatha are also found in Greek. A Zeus Promantheus is mentioned by Lycophron as having been worshipped by the Thurians, and Prometheus is the glorious Titan who stole fire from heaven. This is the explicit meaning of the name; but, furthermore, it has implicitly the signification of fire-kindler. Prometheus appears distinctly in the latter character when he splits the head of Zeus, and Athene springs forth from it all armed; for this myth undoubtedly imports the birth of the lightning goddess from the cloud. In other versions of the story, Hephaistos takes the place of Prometheus, but this only shows that the latter was, in like manner as the former, a god of fire. At all events in this myth of the birth of Athene, Prometheus figures solely as a fire-kindler, and not at all as a fire-stealer; and since in all the older myths, names were not mere names and nothing more, but had a meaning which served as groundwork for the story, it follows that in this instance the name must have had reference to the Sanscrit *pramantha.* This conclusion is strong enough to stand alone, but it seems also to be corroborated by a name belonging to the later epic times of the Hindus. In the Mahâbhârata and some other works, Siva, who has taken the place of the older fire gods, Agni and Rudra, has a troop of fire-kindling attendants called Pramathas, or Pramâthas.

Prometheus is then essentially the same as the Vedic Mâtarisvan. He is the pramantha personified; but his name, like its kindred verb, soon acquired a more abstract and spiritual meaning on Grecian ground. The memory of its old etymon died out, and thenceforth it signified the Prescient, the Foreseeing. Given such a Prometheus, it followed almost as a matter of course that the Greek story-tellers should provide him with a brother, Epimetheus, his mental opposite, one who was wise after the event, and always too late.

With the fire he brought down from heaven, Prometheus gave life to the human bodies which he had formed of clay at Panopeus, in Phocis. Here again his legend is in close coincidence with that of Mâtarisvan, for Panopeus was the seat of the

Phlegyans, a mythical race, whose name has the same root as that of the Bhrigus,* and the same meaning also—fulgent burning. Both races incurred the displeasure of the gods for their presumption and insolence. Phlegyas and others of his blood were condemned to the torments of Tartarus. Bhrigu is of course let off more easily in the Brahmanic legend which tells of his offences, for the Brahmans numbered him among their pious ancestors; but his father, Varuna, sends him on a penitential tour to several hells, that he may see how the wicked are punished, and be warned by their fate.

After what has gone before, the reader will perhaps be prepared to discover a new meaning in the words of Diodorus (v. 67), a meaning not fully comprehended by that writer himself, when he says of Prometheus, that according to the mythographers he stole fire from the gods, but that in reality he was the inventor of the fire-making instrument.

The Aryan method of kindling sacred fire was practised by the Greeks and Romans down to a late period of their respective histories. The Greeks

* From the same root as Bhrigu come the German word *blitz*, Old German, *blik*, lightning; Anglo-Saxon, *blican*, and with the nasal, German, *blinken*, English, *blink*, to twinkle, shine, glitter, and also to wink, as the result of a sudden glitter.—See Wedgwood, Dict. Engl. Etymology.

called the instrument used for the purpose *pyreia,* and the drilling stick *trupanon.* The kinds of wood which were fittest to form one or other of the two parts of which the instrument consisted are specified by Theophrastus and Pliny, both of whom agree that the laurel (daphne) made the best trupanon, and next to it thorn and some other kinds of hard wood; whilst ivy, athragene, and Vitis sylvestris, were to be preferred for the lower part of the pyreia. Festus states that when the vestal fire at Rome happened to go out, it was to be rekindled with fire obtained by drilling a flat piece of auspicious wood (tabulam felicis materiæ). We gather from Theophrastus and Pliny whence it was that the chosen wood derived its "auspicious" character, for they both lay particular stress upon the fact, that the three kinds recommended by them were parasites, or—what amounted to the same thing in their eyes—climbers, that attached themselves to trees. The Veda prescribes for the same purpose the wood of an asvattha (religious fig), growing upon a sami (Acacia suma).* The idea of a marriage, suggested by such a union of the two trees, is also developed in the Veda with great amplitude and minuteness of detail, and is a

* The sami sprang from heavenly fire sent down to earth, and the asvattha from the vessel which contained it.

very prominent element in the whole cycle of myths connected with the chark.

Among the Germans, as Grimm remarks, fire that had long been in human use, and had been propagated from brand to brand, was deemed unfit for holy purposes. As holy water needed to be drawn fresh from the well, in like manner fire which had become common and profane was to be replaced by a new and pure flame, which was called "wild-fire," in contrast with the tame domesticated element. "Fire from the flint was no doubt fairly entitled to be called new and fresh, but either this method of procuring it was thought too common, or its production from wood was regarded as more ancient and hallowed." *

The holy fires of the Germanic races are of two classes. To the first class belong those which the Church, finding herself unable to suppress them, took under her own protection, and associated with the memory of Christian saints, or of the Redeemer. These are the Easter fires, and those of St. John's day, Michaelmas, Martinmas, and Christmas. The second class consists of the "needfires," which have retained their heathen character unaltered to the present day. With occasional exceptions in the case

* D.M. 569.

of the St. John's day fires, those of the first class are never lighted by friction, yet the Church has not quite succeeded in effacing the vestiges of their heathen origin. This is especially evident in the usages of many districts where the purity of the Easter fire (an idea borrowed from pagan tradition) is secured by deriving the kindling flame either from the consecrated Easter candles, or from the new-born and perfectly pure element produced by the priest with flint and steel. Montanus states, but without citing authorities, that in very early times the perpetual lamps in the churches were lighted with fire produced by the friction of dry wood. Formerly, "throughout England the [house] fires were allowed to go out on Easter Sunday, after which the chimney and fireplace were completely cleaned, and the fire once more lighted." How it was lighted may be inferred from the corresponding usages in Germany and among the Slavonians. In Carinthia, on Easter Sunday, the fires are extinguished in every house, and fresh ones are kindled from that which the priest has blessed, having lighted it with flint and steel in the churchyard. In the district of Lechrain, in Bavaria, the Easter Saturday fire is lighted in the churchyard with flint and steel, and never with sulphur matches. Every household brings to it a walnut branch, which, after being partially burned, is carried home to be laid on the hearth fire during tempests, as a protection against lightning. Wolf says* that the Church began by striking new fire every day; afterwards this was done at least every Saturday, and in the eleventh century the custom was confined to the Saturday before Easter, on which day fire from the flint is still produced, and blessed throughout the whole Catholic Church. With this new and consecrated fire, says Le Long, a Flemish writer of the sixteenth century, "every man lighted a good turf fire in his house, and had thereby holy fire in his house throughout the whole year."

It is otherwise with the needfires, which are for the most part not confined to any particular day. They used to be lighted on the occasion of epidemics occurring among cattle, and the custom is still observed here and there to this day. Wherever it can be traced among people of German or Scandinavian descent, the fire is always kindled by the friction of a wooden axle in the nave of a waggon wheel, or in holes bored in one or two posts. In either case the axle or roller is worked with a rope, which is wound round it, and pulled to and fro

* Beiträge, ii. 389.

with the greatest possible speed by two opposite groups of able-bodied men. The wheel was, beyond all doubt, an emblem of the sun. In a few instances of late date it is stated that an old wagon-wheel was used, but this was doubtless a departure from orthodox custom, for it was contrary to the very essence of the ceremony. In Marburger official documents of the year 1605 express mention is made of new wheels, new axles, and new ropes; and these we may be assured were universally deemed requisite in earlier times. It was also necessary to the success of the operation that all the fires should be extinguished in the adjacent houses, and not a spark remain in any one of them when the work began. The wood used was generally that of the oak, a tree sacred to the lightning god Thor because of the red colour of its fresh-cut bark. Sometimes, especially in Sweden, nine kinds of wood were used, but their names are nowhere specified. The fuel for the fire was straw, heath, and brushwood, of which each household contributed its portion, and it was laid down over some length of the narrow lane which was usually chosen as the most convenient place for the work. When the fire had burned down sufficiently, the cattle were forcibly driven through it two or three times, in a certain order, beginning with the swine and ending with the horses, or *vice versâ*. In several places in Lower Saxony, according to recent accounts, it is usual for the geese to bring up the rear. When all the cattle have passed through the fire, each householder takes home an extinguished brand, which in some places is laid in the manger. The ashes are scattered to the winds, apparently that their wholesome influence may be spread far abroad, or they are strewed over the fields (as in Appenzell, for instance) that they may preserve the crops from caterpillars and other vermin. In Sweden the smoke of the needfires was believed to have much virtue; it made fruit-trees productive, and nets that had been hung in it were sure to catch much fish.

The earliest account of the needfire in England is that quoted by Kemble* from the Chronicle of Lanercost for the year 1268. The writer relates with pious horror how "certain bestial persons, monks in garb but not in mind, taught the country people to extract fire from wood by friction, and to set up a "simulacrum Priapi," as a means of preserving their cattle from an epidemic pneumonia. This "simulacrum Priapi" was unquestionably an image of the sungod Fro or Fricco, whom Latin writers of the

* "The Saxons in England."

middle ages commonly designated by the name of the Roman god, and for a manifest reason.*

The following account of a Celtic needfire, lighted in the Scottish island of Mull in the year 1767, is cited by Grimm: "In consequence of a disease among the black cattle the people agreed to perform an incantation, though they esteemed it a wicked thing. They carried to the top of Carnmoor a wheel and nine spindles of oakwood. They extinguished every fire in every house within sight of the hill; the wheel was then turned from east to west over the nine spindles long enough to produce fire by friction. If the fire were not produced before noon, the incantation lost its effect. They failed for several days running. They attributed this failure to the obstinacy of one householder, who would not let his fires be put out for what he considered so wrong a purpose. However, by bribing his servants,

* Wolf (Beitr. i. 107) has shown that the worship of Fro in the likeness of Priapus continued down to a late period in Belgium, and quotes, among other pertinent passages, the following from Adam of Bremen: "Tertius est Fricco pacem voluptatemque largitus mortalibus, cujus etiam simulachrum fingunt ingenti priapo; si nuptiæ celebrandæ sunt, sacrificia offerunt Fricconi." Wolf mentions several images of this kind now or till recently extant in Belgium. They are certainly not Roman. The queer little statue which is held in such high honour in Brussels is, according to Wolf, a modernised edition of an image of Fro.

they contrived to have them extinguished, and on that morning raised their fire. They then sacrificed a heifer, cutting in pieces and burning, while yet alive, the diseased part. They then lighted their own hearths from the pile, and ended by feasting on the remains. Words of incantation were repeated by an old man from Morven who came over as a master of the ceremonies, and who continued speaking all the time the fire was being raised. This man was living a beggar at Bellochroy. Asked to repeat the spell, he said, the sin of repeating it once had brought him to beggary, and that he dared not say those words again. The whole country believed him accursed."

In the Scottish highlands, especially in Caithness, recourse is still had to the needfire, chiefly for the purpose of counteracting disorders in cattle caused by witchcraft. "To defeat the sorceries, certain persons who have the power to do so are sent for to raise the needfire. Upon any small river, lake, or island, a circular booth of stone or turf is erected, on which a couple or rafter of a birch tree is placed, and the roof covered over. In the centre is set a perpendicular post, fixed by a wooden pin to the couple, the lower end being placed in an oblong groove on the floor; and another pole is placed horizontally, between the upright post and the leg of the couple, into both which the ends, being tapered, are inserted. This horizontal timber is called the auger, being provided with four short arms, or spokes, by which it can be turned round. As many men as can be collected are then set to work, having first divested themselves of all kinds of metal, and two at a time continue to turn the pole by means of the levers, while others keep driving wedges under the upright post so as to press it against the auger; which by the friction soon becomes ignited. From this the needfire is instantly procured, and all other fires being immediately quenched, those that are rekindled in dwelling-houses and offices are accounted sacred and the cattle are successively made to smell them."*

The needfire is described under another name by General Stewart, a recent writer on Scottish superstitions, who says that "the cure for witchcraft, called *Tein Econuch* (or Forlorn Fire), is wrought in the following manner:—

"Notice is previously communicated to all those householders who reside within the nearest of two running streams to extinguish their lights and fires

* Logan, "The Scottish Gael," ii. 64.

on some appointed morning. On its being ascertained that this notice has been duly observed, a spinning-wheel, or some other convenient instrument calculated to produce fire by friction, is set to work with the most furious earnestness by the unfortunate sufferer and all who wish well to his cause. Relieving each other by turns, they drive on with such persevering diligence that at length the spindle of the wheel, ignited by excessive friction, emits forlorn fire in abundance, which by the application of tow, or some other combustible material, is widely extended over the whole neighbourhood. Communicating the fire to the tow, the tow communicates it to a candle, the candle to a fir torch, the torch to a cartful of peats, which the master of the ceremonies, with pious ejaculations for the success of the experiment, distributes to messengers, who will proceed with portions of it to the different houses within the said two running streams to kindle the different fires. By the influence of this operation the machinations and spells of witchcraft are rendered null and void."*

It appears from the preceding accounts that, both by Celts and Germans, a wheel was often used for kindling the needfire. Jacob Grimm was the first

* Stewart, "Pop. Superstitions," &c. Lond. 1851.

to make it evident that, for the Germans at least, the wheel was an emblem of the sun, and numerous facts which have come to light since he wrote, abundantly verify his conclusion. He mentions, among other evidence, that in the Edda the sun is called *fagrahvel,* "fair or bright wheel," and that the same sign ⊙, which in the calendar represents the sun, stands also for the Gothic double consonant HW, the initial of the Gothic word *hvil,* Anglo-Saxon *hveol,* English *wheel.* In the needfire on the island of Mull the wheel was turned, according to Celtic usage, from east to west, like the sun. Grimm has also noticed the use of the wheel in other German usages as well as in the needfire, and he is of opinion that in heathen times it constantly formed the nucleus and centre of the sacred and purifying sacrificial flame. In confirmation of this opinion he mentions the following remarkable custom which was observed on the day when those who held under the lord of a manor came to pay him their yearly dues. A wagon-wheel which had lain in water, or in the pool of a dung-yard, for six weeks and three days, was placed in a fire kindled before the company, and they were entertained with the best of good cheer until the nave, which was neither to be turned nor poked, was consumed to ashes, and then they were to go away. "I hold this," says Grimm, "to have been a relic of a heathen sacrificial repast, and I look upon the wheel as what had served to light the fire, about which indeed nothing further is stated. At all events the fact proves the employment of the wagon-wheel as fuel on occasions of solemnity."*

There was a twofold reason for this use of the emblem of the sun; for that body was regarded not only as a mass of heavenly fire, but also as the immediate source of the lightning. When black clouds concealed the sun, the early Aryans believed that its light was actually extinguished and needed to be rekindled. Then the pramantha was worked by some god in the cold wheel until it glowed again; but before this was finally accomplished, the pramantha often shot out as a thunderbolt from the wheel, or was carried off by some fire-robber. The word thunderbolt itself, like its German equivalents, expresses the cylindrical or conical form of the pramantha.† When the bolts had ceased to fly from the nave, and the wheel was once more ablaze, the storm was over. Vishnu undoubtedly figures in the Vedas as a god of the sun, and the great epic of the Hindus relates that when he was armed for the

* D.M. 578.

† Compare cross-bow bolt.

fight, Agni gave him a wheel with "a thunderbolt nave." This can only mean a wheel that shoots out thunderbolts from its nave when it is turned. Mithra, the sun-god of the Aryans of Iran, is also armed with a thunderbolt; and the names of Astrape and Bronte, two of the horses of Helios, show plainly that, for the early Greeks also, sun and lightning were associated ideas.*

The Midsummer or St. John's-day fires, which were kindled at the season of the summer solstice, have been commonly spoken of as if they were of one kind only, whereas they were of three kinds, as specified by a medieval writer quoted by Kemble. There were, first, bonfires; secondly, processions with burning brands round the fields; thirdly, wheels blazing and set rolling. The bonfires, he says, were lighted for the purpose of scaring away the dragons that poisoned the waters with the slime that fell from them at that hot season, and therefore bones and all sorts of filth were thrown into the fire, that the smoke might be the fouler and more offensive to the dragons. (Here we have again the primitive Aryan dragon Ahi, at his old work in the sultry midsummer weather.) As for the wheel, the same writer says, "it is rolled to signify that

* Kuhn, Herabk., p. 66.

the sun ascends at that time to the summit of his circle, and immediately begins to descend again."*

Writers of the twelfth and thirteenth centuries speak of this practice as common in France. It has been found in the Tyrol and in Carinthia; and many North German examples of it are on record. We will quote two of the latter, the first being that which took place at Conz, on the Moselle, in the year 1823, as described by Grimm:†

* The original was found by Kemble in a Harleian MS., and is as follows:—"Ejus venerandam nativitatem cum gaudio celebrabitis; dico ejus nativitatem cum gaudio; non illo cum gaudio, quo stulti, vani et prophani, amatores mundi huius, accensis ignibus, per plateas, turpibus et illicitis ludibus, comessationibus et ebrietatibus, cubilibus et impudicitiis intendentes illam celebrare solent. . . . Dicamus de tripudiis, quæ in vigilia Sancti Johannis fieri solent, quorum tria genera. In vigilia enim Beati Johannis colligunt pueri in quibusdam regionibus ossa et quædam immunda, et insimul cremant, et exinde producitur fumus in aëre. Faciunt etiam brandas, et circuunt arva cum brandis. Tertium de rota, quam faciunt volvi: quod, cum immunda cremant, hoc habent ex gentilibus. Antiquitus enim dracones in hoc tempore excitabantur ad libidinem propter calorem, et volando per aëra frequenter spermatizabantur aquæ, et tunc erat letalis, quia quicunque inde bibebant, aut moriebantur aut grave morbum paciebantur. Quod attendentes philosophi, jusserunt ignem fieri frequentur et sparsim circa puteos et fontes, et immundum ibi cremari, et quæcumque immundum reddiderunt fumum; nam per talem fumum sciebant fugari dracones. . . . Rota involvitur ad significandum, quod sol tunc ascendit ad alciora sui circuli, et statim regreditur; inde venit quod volvitur rota."

† D.M. 586.

"Every house delivers a sheaf of straw on the top of the Stromberg, where the men and lads assemble towards evening, whilst the women and girls gather about the Burbacher fountain. A huge wheel is now bound round with straw in such a manner that not a particle of the wood remains visible; a stout pole is passed through the middle of the wheel, and the persons who are to guide it lay hold on the ends of the pole, which project three feet on either side. The rest of the straw is made up into a great number of small torches. At a signal from the mayor of Sierk (who according to ancient custom receives a basket of cherries on the occasion) the wheel is kindled with a torch and set rapidly in motion. Everybody cheers and swings torches in the air. Some of the men remain above, others follow the burning wheel down hill in its descent to the Moselle. It is often extinguished before it reaches the river, but if it burns at the moment it touches the water, that is held to be prophetic of a good vintage, and the people of Conz have a right to levy a *fuder* of white wine upon the surrounding vineyards. Whilst the wheel is passing before the female spectators they break out into cries of joy, the men on the hill-top reply, and the people from the neighbouring villages, who have assembled on the banks of the river, mingle their voices in the general jubilee."

Our next example is also from the neighbourhood of the Moselle, and is reported by Hocker.* At first sight it may appear inapposite, because the ceremony did not take place on St. John's-day, but in .Passion week. The difference, however, is not important, because, as Kuhn has shown, the St. John's-day customs were not always observed on the day to which they properly belonged, but were often transferred to St. Vitus's, St. Peter and St. Paul's, Easter or Lent, according to local circumstances.

"It was the custom of the butchers and weavers of Treves, on the Thursday in Passion week, to plant an oak near the cross on the Marxberg (Mons Martis, Donnersberg, Dummersberg), and to fit a wheel to the oak. This having been done, the peculiar and ancient popular sport took place on Invocavit Sunday. Two guilds, the butchers on horseback, the weavers on foot, well mounted, well armed, and handsomely dressed, appeared in orderly array in the corn-market. The bells of the cathedral now began to peal, and were followed by those of all the other steeples. The people poured into the

* "Geschichten, Sagen und Legenden der Mosellandes," p. 415.

market-place, and thronged around the armed squadrons to the bridge over the Moselle, where the weavers remained behind as a garrison, whilst the butchers rode to the Marxberg to protect the work of the people. The latter began forthwith to cut down the oak, kindle the wheel, and roll both into the valley of the Moselle. The horsemen fired on the blazing wheel, and if it rolled into the Moselle, they received a *fuder* of wine from the Archbishop of Treves. After this the butchers, surrounded by the exulting people, rode back to the bridge, the bells still pealing, and went with the weavers to the abbeys and to the rich, who gave each man a cup of wine. The solemnity was closed by marching three times through Weaver's Street and the Back Lane, stopping each time before the Crown-well, which was adorned with lemon-trees hung with ribbons and garlands. There the captain of the horsemen spoke some rhymes, quaffed a silver cup of white wine, and every horsemen fired off his piece. Then the weavers gave the butchers a repast with wine, and the rest of the day was spent in jubilant carousing.—The first mention of this ceremony occurs in the year 1550, the last in 1779."

It has been clearly demonstrated by Dr. Kuhn

that all the foregoing details respecting the St. John's fires are in striking accordance with the Vedic legend of Indra's fight with the midsummer demons. The passage quoted from Kemble, besides stating expressly that the course of the blazing wheel was meant to represent the descent of the sun from its solstitial height, brings the St. John's fires in immediate connection with the dragons that poison the waters, just as did the demon Vritra, otherwise called Ahi, the dragon. He possessed himself of the sun-wheel and the treasures of heaven, seized the (white) women, kept them prisoners in his cavern, and "laid a curse" on the waters, until Indra released the captives and took off the curse. The same conception is repeated in countless legends of mountains that open on St. John's-day, when the imprisoned white women come forth, and the hour approaches in which the spell laid upon them and upon the buried treasures will be broken.

The points of most significance in the two extracts from Grimm and Hocker are these: the rolling of the wheel down the hill-side; its plunge into the water; the prediction of a good vintage connected therewith; and, in the last custom described, the gun-shots fired at the wheel by its pursuers. The whole meaning of the ceremony lies in these details, and the key to it is found in the following passage from a Vedic hymn :—

"With thee conjoined, O Indu (Soma) did Indra straightway pull down with force the wheel of the sun that stood upon the mighty mountain top, and the source of all life was hidden from the great scather."

Here we see at once that the German custom was nothing else than a dramatic representation of the great elemental battle portrayed in the sacred books of the Southern Aryans. In the one the blazing wheel stands on the top of the hill, in the other the sun stands on the summit of the cloud mountain. Both descend from their heights, and both are extinguished, the sun in the cloud sea, behind the cloud mountain, the wheel in the river at the foot of the hill. Here Indra, Soma, and the army of the Maruts hurl their deadly weapons and charge the demon host; there the triumphant combatants fire upon the foe or brandish their mimic lightning—straw torches—and pursue him to the water's edge. It is worthy of note that the women do not, as on other occasions, take any active part in the German ceremony; their doing so would be inconsistent with its character as an act of mimic warfare. They assemble only as spectators to watch the fortunes of the fight, and to exult in the victory of their own party. One of the many names given in the Vedas to the commander who is opposed to Indra in this great battle, is Kuyava, which means the harvest-spoiler or the spoiled harvest; hence the extinction of his blighting instrument in the river was regarded in the vine-growing districts of Germany as portending a good wine year. In Poitou an obscure reminiscence of the same principle seems to have been preserved in the custom of kindling a wheel wrapped in straw, and running it through the corn-fields to make them fruitful.

Dr. Kuhn has anticipated and refuted an objection that might be raised against the latter part of this explanation. The Aryans, before their dispersion, were but very little acquainted with regular agriculture, and therefore it might be supposed that the Indian conception of a harvest-spoiling demon could hardly have been ancient enough to be common to the Hindus and to another branch of the parent stock. But the second part of the name Ku-yava must have meant originally grass in general (as appears from its derivative yavasa, *i. e.*, pasture ground, meadow), and perhaps it signified in a more special sense the grasses which produced seed fit for human food—the cereal grasses.* Thus the word *corn* is known as a generic term wherever the Gothic languages are spoken, but popularly it is used to signify that particular grain which is most important in the rural economy of each country. In England wheat is generally called corn. In most parts of Germany this name is given to rye; in the Scandinavian kingdom to barley; and in North America to maize or Indian corn.† Now if yava meant both

* This seems to Dr. Kuhn to be the more probable because no one name of a cereal is found so extensively as yava among different Indo-European nations. The word yava is common both to Sanscrit and Zend; it is the Greek zea, zeiá, and the Lithuanian javai. Hence there are philological grounds for supposing that the oldest bread-stuff was a grain called by that name, and we have even the direct testimony of ancient tradition to that same effect, for, according to Eleusinian legends, barley (zeá) was the first corn that was harvested (Preller, Dem. u. Pers. 293). The same belief prevailed in Crete, insomuch that the name of Demeter was there explained as meaning barley-mother, as if the *de* were a contraction of dêa = zeiá (Preller Griech. Myth. 474). But since zeá stood not only for barley but also for dinkel and spelt, all this agrees very well with Pliny's statement (Hist. Nat. 18, 8) that *far* was the oldest corn in all Latium, and also with the statement in the Alvísmâl, that corn was by the gods called barr (radical bar), an expression which means nothing more than that this was its most ancient name. Now bar-r is the Latin far, Gothic bares, Anglo-Saxon bere, English bere, barley; and it is also found in the word barn, Anglo-Saxon berern, bærn, from bere and ern, a place. The compound word barley, according to Wedgwood (Dict. Eng. Etym.), "seems derived from Welsh barllys, which might be explained bread-plant, from *bara*, bread, and *llys*, a plant."

† Marsh, "Lectures on the English Language," p. 246.

grass and corn, the name Kuyava, as that of the demon who spoiled the growth of both, might very naturally have been current from the earliest times among a pastoral people. "But I go still further," says Kuhn, "and I believe that Kuyava was also regarded as the spoiler of vegetation in general, who parched up the plants used in making the fermented liquor, soma, and among these plants the Hindus included yava—which in this case meant barley or rice. It will be seen in the sequel that the demon possesses himself also of the heavenly soma (the moisture of the clouds), that he is robbed of it by Indra, and that the like conception is found also among the Greeks and the Germans. This then sufficiently explains the hope of a good wine year which was associated with the victory in the above described German customs."

In the few examples we have given of the need-fire, as used in Christian times, it appears only as a superstitious practice, occasionally resorted to for the cure of epidemics among cattle; but this was not its original character. It was an ancient and solemn religious rite, accompanied with sacrifice, and we have direct testimony to the fact that it was observed on stated anniversaries, when men and cattle passed through the flames to preserve them from future maladies. Delrio, who wrote in the sixteenth century, states that the cattle which were first driven through the fire were sacrificed to the *saints*,* and Nicolaus Gryse is quoted by Grimm as giving this account of the St. John's fires in 1593:—"Towards evening, people warmed themselves at St. John's flame and needfire, which they sawed out of wood; such fire they kindled not in God's but in St. John's name, leaped and ran through the fire, drove the cattle through it, and were full of joy when they had passed the night in great sins, scandals, and wickednesses." †

The needfire was kindled by the Celts in their great popular assemblies on the occasion of their annual festivals at the beginning of May and November. Their Mayday, which was generally the first of the month, but sometimes the second or third, is called in the Irish and Gaelic tongues, *la bealtine, beiltine,* or *beltein. Lá* is day; *teine,* fire; and *beal* or *beil* is understood to be the name of a god, which is not immediately one with that of the Asiatic Belus, but designates an exalted luminous deity peculiar to the Celts.‡ The celebra-

* Wolf, Beiträge, i. 220.

† D. M. 578.

‡ Ibid. 579.

tion of bealtine, as at present practised in Scotland, is thus described by Armstrong:—

"In some parts of the Highlands the young folks of a hamlet meet in the moors on the first of May. They cut a table in the green sod of a round figure, by cutting a trench in the ground of such circumference as to hold the whole company. They then kindle a fire and dress a repast of eggs and milk in the consistence of a custard. They knead a cake of oatmeal, which is toasted in the embers against a stone. After the custard is eaten up, they divide the cake in so many portions, as similar as possible to one another in size and shape, as there are persons in the company. They daub one of these portions with charcoal until it is perfectly black. They then put all the bits of the cake into a bonnet, and every one, blindfold, draws out a portion. The bonnet-holder is entitled to the last bit. Whoever draws the black bit is the devoted person who is to be sacrificed to Baal, whose favour they mean to implore in rendering the year productive. The devoted person is compelled to leap three times over the flames."

Here, says Grimm, there is no mistaking the features of a religious rite. The leaping three times over the flames shows that the main business had been the sacrifice of a man for the purpose of appeasing the god and making him gracious, but that subsequently brute victims were offered in place of human, and that at last the actual sacrifice was transmuted both for man and beast into a mere jumping over the fire. The kindling of the fire by friction is not mentioned in this passage from Armstrong, but as that method was deemed requisite in the case of needfires for the cure of epidemics in cattle, much more must it originally have been practised on the occasion of the great annual festival.*

The first known mention of *beiltine* is that made by Cormac, Archbishop of Cashel, who died in the year 908. Two fires were made near each other, and it was wholesome for men and cattle to pass between them uninjured; hence the proverbial expression, *ittir dha theinne beil,* "between two fires," to signify a great danger. Usher (Trias thaumat. p. 125) states expressly that priests strictly superintended the sacrifice, and quotes Evinus as saying that "it was provided by a rigorous law that all fires should be extinguished in every district on that night, and that no one should be at liberty to rekindle fire before the pile of sacrifice had been

* D. M. p. 580.

raised by the magi at Temoria (the Tighmora of Ossian), and whoever transgressed this law in any respect was visited for the offence with nothing less than capital punishment." *

A heifer was sacrificed in the needfire in Mull (p. 52), and Grimm cites an example of the same practice in Northamptonshire in the present century:—"Miss C. and her cousin, walking, saw a fire in a field, and a crowd round it. They said, 'What is the matter?' 'Killing a calf.' 'What for?' 'To stop the murrain.' They went away as quickly as possible. On speaking to the clergyman, he made inquiries. The people did not like to talk of the affair, but it appeared that when there is a disease among the cows, or the calves are born sickly, they sacrifice (*i. e.*, kill and burn) one 'for good luck.'"

Those who have read Mr. Dasent's "Popular Tales from the Norse" are aware that to this day the peasants of Norway still tell of the wondrous mill that ground whatever was demanded of it. The tradition is of great antiquity, but the earliest known version of it is that which Mr. Dasent has repeated as follows, after the author of the Prose Edda.

"Of all beliefs, that in which man has, at all times

* D. M. 580.

of his history, been most prone to set faith, is that of a golden age of peace and plenty, which had passed away, but which might be expected to return. . . Such a period of peace and plenty, such a golden time, the Norseman could tell of in his mythic Frodi's reign, when gold, or *Frodi's meal,* as it was called, was so plentiful that golden armlets lay untouched from year's end to year's end on the king's highway, and the fields bore crops unsown. . . . In Frodi's house were two maidens of that old giant race, Fenja and Menja. These daughters of the giant he had bought as slaves, and he made them grind his quern or handmill, Grotti, out of which he used to grind peace and gold. Even in that golden age one sees there were slaves, and Frodi, however bountiful to his thanes and people, was a hard task-master to his giant handmaidens. He kept them to the mill, nor gave them longer rest than the cuckoo's note lasted, or they could sing a song. But that quern was such that it ground anything that the grinder chose, though until then it had ground nothing but gold and peace. So the maidens ground and ground, and one sang their piteous tale in a strain worthy of Æschylus as the other rested—they prayed for rest and pity, but Frodi was deaf. Then they turned in giant mood, and ground no longer peace and plenty, but fire and war. Then the quern went fast and furious, and that very night came Mysing the sea-rover, and slew Frodi and all his men, and carried off the quern; and so Frodi's peace ended. The maidens the sea-rover took with him, and when he got on the high seas he bade them grind salt. So they ground; and at midnight they asked if he had not salt enough, but he bade them still grind on. So they ground till the ship was full and sank, Mysing, maids, and mill, and all, and that's why the sea is salt."

This wonder-working mill stood once in heaven, for Frodi, its owner, was no other than the sun-god Freyr* (Swedish Frö, German Fro), whom Snorri Sturlason and Saxo Grammaticus converted into an earthly monarch, or found already brought down to that condition, just as the great god Odin figures in Snorri's Edda as a mortal king of Sweden.† The flat circular stone of Frodi's quern is the disk of the sun, and its handle, or *möndull*,‡ is the pramantha with

* Mannhardt, 243.

† Ibid. 45.

‡ *Möndull* is an Icelandic word, from the same root as *manthami* (p. 39), and is defined by Egilsson, in his "Lex. Poët. Antiquæ Ling. Septentrionalis," as "lignum teres, quo mola trusatilis manu circumagitur, mobile, molucrum."

which Indra or the Asvins used to kindle the extinguished luminary. An ancient popular ditty, which still survives in Germany, tells of a mill that grinds gold, silver, and love. The peasants in various parts of Germany call the Milkyway the Mealway, or the Millway, and say that it turns with the sun, for it first becomes visible at the point where the sun has set. It leads therefore to the heavenly mill, and its colour is that of the meal with which it is strewed.*

* Kuhn, Westf. ii. 86.

CHAPTER III.

FIRE AND SOUL BRINGING BIRDS AND INSECTS—BABIES FOUND IN FOUNTAINS, TREES, ROCKS, PARSLEY BEDS, ETC. — THE SOULS OF THE DEAD AS BIRDS.

THE approach of windy weather is often indicated by a peculiar form of light streaming clouds, which in England are very aptly named grey mares' tails. In Northern Germany a modification of the same appearance is called a weather or wind tree (wetter-baum)—a name wherein we may read the original conception out of which grew the Aryan prototype of the Norseman's heavenly ash, Yggdrasil. Among the many curious notions that met together in the primitive Aryan cosmogony, was that of a prodigious tree overspreading the whole world. The clouds were its foliage; sun, moon, and stars were its fruit; lightning lurked in its branches and mingled with their sap. Hence arose a whole order of myths, which accounted accordingly for the descent to earth of fire, soma, and the soul of man, but which were often blended with those that were based upon the process of extracting fire from wood with the pramantha. Birds that nestled in the fire-bearing tree came down to earth, either as incorporations of the lightning, or bringing with them a branch charged with latent or visible fire. Agni, the god of fire, sometimes appears in the Vedas as a bird—falcon or eagle—engaged in an errand of this kind. Such a bird was Jove's eagle, and such another was its rival the little wren, which is mentioned by both Aristotle and Pliny as disputing with the eagle the sovereignty of the feathered creation.* The pretensions of the wren are not unknown to German tradition, but Celtic memory has best preserved the exalted mythic character of the smallest of European birds. In the legends of Bretagne and Normandy he is spoken of expressly as a fire-bringer. "A messenger was wanted to fetch fire from heaven, and the wren, weak and delicate as it is, undertook the perilous task. It nearly cost the bold bird its life, for its plumage was burned off even to the down. The other birds with one accord gave each of them one of their feathers to the little king, to cover his naked and shivering skin. The owl alone stood aloof, but the other birds were so indignant

* Τρόχιλος ἀέτῳ πολέμιος. Aristotle. Dissident aquila et trochilus, si credimus, quoniam rex appellatur avium. Plin. Hist. Nat. x. 74.

at his unfeeling conduct that they would never more admit him into their society." *

General Vallancey, who in this instance may be quoted with safety, says of the wren: "The Druids represented this as the king of all birds. The superstitious respect shown to this little bird gave offence to our first Christian missionaries, and by their commands he is still hunted and killed on Christmas-day; and on the following (St. Stephen's-day) he is carried about, hung by the leg in the centre of two hoops crossing each other at right angles, and a procession is made in every village, of men, women, and children, singing an Irish catch importing him to be the king of all birds." †

Sonnini says: "While I was at La Ciotat (near Marseilles) the particulars of a singular ceremony were related to me, which takes place every year at the beginning of Nivôse (end of December). A numerous body of men, armed with swords and pistols, set off in search of a very small bird which the ancients called Troglodytes. When they have found it (a thing not difficult, because they always take care to have one ready) it is suspended on the middle of a pole, which two men carry on their

* Amélie Bosquet, p. 220.

† Collectanea de rebus Hibernicis, xiii. p. 97.

shoulders, as if it were a heavy burthen. This whimsical procession parades round the town; the bird is weighed in a great pair of scales, and the company then sit down to table and make merry."* At Carcassonne the wren was carried about upon a staff adorned with a garland of olive, oak, and mistletoe.

In the Isle of Man the wren is believed to be a transformed fairy. "The ceremony of hunting the wren is founded on this ancient tradition. A fairy of uncommon beauty once exerted such undue influence over the male population, that she seduced numbers at various times to follow her footsteps, till by degrees she led them into the sea, where they perished. This barbarous exercise of power had continued so long that it was feared the island would be exhausted of its defenders. A knight errant sprang up, who discovered some means of countervailing the charms used by the siren, and even laid a plot for her destruction, which she only escaped at the moment of extreme hazard by assuming the form of a wren. But though she evaded punishment at that time, a spell was cast upon her by which she was condemned to reanimate the same form on every succeeding New Year's-day, until she should

* "Travels in Upper and Lower Egypt." Lond., 1800, pp. 11, 12.

perish by a human hand. In consequence of this legend, every man and boy in the island devotes the hours from the rising to the setting of the sun, on each returning anniversary, to the hope of extirpating the fairy. Woe to the wrens which show themselves on that fatal day; they are pursued, pelted, fired at, and destroyed without mercy. Their feathers are preserved with religious care; for it is believed that every one of the relics gathered in the pursuit is an effectual preservative from shipwreck for the ensuing year, and the fisherman who should venture on his occupation without such a safeguard would by many of the natives be considered extremely foolhardy." *

A simpler, and perhaps more genuine, version of this rather artificially coloured narrative were desirable, but even in its present form it shows sufficiently that the Celts of Man looked upon the wren as a divine being transformed, and that they hunted the bird for the sake of its talismanic feathers.

The story of the contest for the crown, in which the wren outwitted the eagle, is traditional in Ireland, and the country people tell it to this effect: —"The birds all met together one day, and settled

* Brand, "Pop. Antiquities," iii. 198.

among themselves that whichever of them could fly highest was to be the king of them all. Well, just as they were on the hinges of being off, what does the little rogue of a wren do but hop up, and perch himself unbeknownst on the eagle's tail. So they flew and flew ever so high, till the eagle was miles above all the rest, and could not fly another stroke, he was so tired. 'Then,' says he, 'I'm the king of the birds,' says he, 'hurroo!' 'You lie,' says the wren, darting up a perch and a half above the big fellow. Well, the eagle was so mad to think how he was done, that when the wren was coming down he gave him a stroke of his wing; and from that day to this the wren was never able to fly higher than a hawthorn bush."

The same story, but with a different ending, is told in Germany, where the wren is called "hedge-king" (Zaunkönig). According to the German version, the tricky wren was imprisoned in a mouse-hole, and the owl was set to watch before it, whilst the other birds were deliberating upon the punishment to be inflicted on the offender. But the owl fell asleep, and the prisoner escaped. The owl has never since ventured to show himself by daylight.* The mention of the owl in this story, and

* Wolf, Beiträge, ii. 438.

in the preceding French one (p. 75), is worthy of note. In both he is represented as behaving in an unfriendly manner to the wren, possibly from a feeling of jealousy, because the owl himself had claims to be considered as a highly distinguished fire-bird. Was he not the favourite of the lightning goddess Athene,* and was she not even called after him Glaucopis, "owl-eyed," because her eyes, like his, were two orbs of lightning? And, not to speak at present of other matters which may be more conveniently dealt with hereafter, was it not a moot point among the Iranians whether he or the eagle sat in the place of honour on the "inviolable tree"?†

In France, besides its ordinary name, *roitelet,* "little king," the wren is also called *poulette au bon Dieu,* "God's little hen." In the Pays de Caux it is still a sacred bird. To kill it or rob its nest is deemed an atrocity which will *bring down the lightning* on the culprit's dwelling. Such an act is also regarded with horror in Scotland,‡ and

* Φωσφόρος δὲ ἡ Ἀθηνᾶ. Eustathius.

† Kuhn, Herab. p. 126.

‡ "What, for instance, could be more poetical than the puerile malediction upon those who rob the nest of the wren?

'Malisons, malisons, mair than ten,
That harry the Ladye of Heaven's hen!'"

Robert Chambers, Pop. Rhymes.

not less so in the most purely Saxon parts of England—Hertfordshire for instance—for

> Robin Redbreast and Jenny Wren
> Are God Almighty's cock and hen.

The reverence paid to the robin is not peculiar to England. Grimm testifies that the feeling has prevailed among the whole German race from unknown antiquity, and he refers to the bird's colour and its name as evidences that it was sacred to Thor, the god of the lightning. Robin is Robert, in Anglo-Saxon Hrodhbeorht or Hrodhbriht, *i.e.*, fame-bright, and this name belonged to Thor. There is no legend extant, of Germanic origin, which directly connects the robin with the descent of fire, but there is one in Wales, as reported by a correspondent of "Notes and Queries,"* which manifestly points that way. His old nurse, he says, a Carmarthenshire woman, used to tell the children that, "Far, far, far away, is a land of woe, darkness, spirits of evil, and *fire*. Day by day does the little bird bear in his bill a drop of water to quench the flame. So near to the burning stream does he fly that his dear little feathers are scorched; and hence he is named Bron-rhuddyn (*i.e.*, breast-

* Choice Notes, p. 185.

burned or breast-scorched). To serve little children the robin dares approach the infernal pit. No good child will hurt the devoted benefactor of man. The robin returns from the land of fire, and therefore he feels the cold of winter far more than his brother birds. He shivers in the brumal blast; hungry he chirps before your door. Oh! my child, then in gratitude throw a few crumbs to poor redbreast."

Here we have evidently an ancient pagan tradition altered and adjusted to popular notions of Christianity; but its original features may easily be detected under their modern disguise. The bird that goes to the land of fire and has its breast scorched, is plainly a double of the Celto-Norman wren (p. 75) that brought down fire from heaven, but had all its plumage burnt off.

It is a popular belief in Germany as well as in England that when the robin finds the corpse of a human being in the woods, he covers the face at least, if not the whole body, with flowers, leaves, and moss, as he did by the babes in the wood, in the old English ballad of the Babes in the Wood.

The woodpecker is a bird of great mythic celebrity. The Romans called it Picus, and surnamed it Martius from the god Mars, and Feronius from the Sabine goddess Feronia, who was very potent in fire, and whose name also indicates that she, and consequently her bird, were fire-bringers. The name Feronia is related in the closest manner to that of Phoroneus, of whom a Peloponnesian legend asserted that he it was, and not Prometheus, who first bestowed fire on man; and both names are identical with *bhuranyu*,* a frequent epithet of Agni, signifying one who pounces down, or bears down rapidly.

Picus is then the fire-bringing bird, but also, quite in accordance with that character, he is the son of Saturn and first king of Latium. This is only another way of saying that he too (like Manu, Minyas, Minos, Phoroneus, and other fire-bringers) is the first man; and therefore it is that, under the name of Picumnus, he continued in later times to be the guardian genius of children along with his brother Pilumnus.

Grimm has pointed out a remarkable coincidence between the story of the first king of Latium and the Anglo-Saxon pedigree of Odin, which makes Beav or Beovolf one of the god's ancestors. Beovolf means beewolf (*i.e.*, bee-eater), and that is a German appellation of the woodpecker.†

* From the root bhar, φέρω, fero. Kuhn, Herab. p. 26.

† D.M. p. 342.

A Roman legend, which throws much light on the mythic character of Picus, relates that Numa, being desirous of knowing by what rites the lightning might be deprecated, took, by the advice of Egeria, the following means to obtain the desired information. There was in the Aventine grove a fountain, whither Picus and his son Faunus often came to rest in the cool shade and quench their thirst, which was great. Here Numa set huge goblets of mead and wine, and placed twelve young men in ambush, each with a fetter in his hand. The tempting bait was swallowed without delay or stint, the pair dropped with heavy heads upon the spot, and were fast bound as they lay asleep. When they awoke and found escape impossible, they readily disclosed the secret by which Jupiter Elicius might be brought down and constrained to specify the requisite propitiation. This Jupiter Elicius (called also "hospitalis," as Agni was called "atithi," the guest) was the lightning which could be drawn down by certain sacrifices and ceremonies. It is plain from the legend, first, that Picus was believed to be particularly fond of mead and wine (=soma), for otherwise Numa would not have thought of entrapping him with them; and secondly, that a very close connection with the heavenly fire was imputed to him. Either it was thought that he could give the best intelligence concerning its nature, or perhaps the original intention of his capture was that he might be forced to bring it down innocuously. This latter supposition appears the more probable, because the *springwort* (a vegetable embodiment of the lightning, of which more hereafter) was known to the Romans as well as to the Germans, and was believed by both to be at the command of the picus or woodpecker.

It was the custom at Rome, as soon as a child was born, to strew a couch for Pilumnus and Picumnus, who were supposed to remain in the house until it was ascertained that the babe, for whom they had brought the fire of life, was likely to live. Pilumnus, the brother of Picus, who seems to be only his double, had his name from *pîlum*, which means both javelin and pestle, and is in either case equivalent to the thunderbolt. Pilum in the sense of pestle, and the sound made by the bill of the picus rapping at the trees, combined to make Pilumnus the god of the bakers; for in old times the baker and the miller or corn-brayer were one, and *pistor*, the Latin for baker, means also the person who plies the pîlum or pis-lum.* In

* "There were no bakers in Rome down to the time of the Persian

Norway the black red-crested woodpecker is called Gertrude's bird, and a Norse tale, in which the names alone are Christian and all the rest purely heathen, makes the bird a transformed baker.

"In those days when our Lord and St. Peter wandered upon earth, they came once to an old wife's house who sat baking. Her name was Gertrude, and she had a red mutch on her head. They had walked a long way and were both hungry, and our Lord begged hard for a bannock to stay their hunger. Yes, they should have it. So she took a little tiny piece of dough and rolled it out, but as she rolled it, it grew till it covered the whole griddle.

"Nay, that was too big; they couldn't have that. So she took a tinier bit still; but when that was rolled out, it covered the whole griddle just the same, and that bannock was too big, she said; they couldn't have that either.

"The third time she took a still tinier bit—so tiny you could scarce see it; but it was the same story over again—the bannock was too big.

war, more than 580 years after the foundation of the city. The citizens made their own bread, and that was the work of the women, as it is still among most nations." Plin. Hist. Nat. xviii. 11, 28. In the Western Islands of Scotland to this day each household prepares its own barley meal by pounding the corn in a large stone mortar.

"'Well,' said Gertrude, 'I can't give you anything; you must just go without, for all these bannocks are too big.'

"Then our Lord waxed wroth and said, 'Since you loved me so little as to grudge me a morsel of food, you shall have this punishment,—you shall become a bird, and seek your food between bark and bole, and never get a drop to drink save when it rains.'

"He had scarce said the last word before she was turned into a great black woodpecker, or Gertrude's bird, and flew from her kneading-trough right up the chimney; and till this very day you may see her flying about, with her red mutch on her head, and her body all black, because of the soot in the chimney; and so she hacks and taps away at the trees for her food, and whistles when rain is coming, for she is ever athirst, and then she looks for a drop to cool her tongue." *

The curse pronounced upon the woodpecker in this story, that it shall "never get a drop to drink save when it rains," accords with the supposed intimate connection between the bird and the clouds, and points, perhaps, to the reason which first suggested that mythic relation. The green

* Dasent, "Popular Tales from the Norse," p. 230.

woodpecker is the best known of its genus in England, and is widely spread on the continent of Europe. Its loud cry, when frequently uttered, is commonly supposed to foretell the approach of rainy weather. Hence one of its English provincial names is Rainbird.

Tales like that of Gertrude's bird are told of the cuckoo, and "They say the owl was a baker's daughter."* The cuckoo was a baker's or miller's man, and that is why his feathers are dusted with meal. He robbed poor people of their dough in hard times, and when the dough swelled by God's blessing in the oven, he drew it out and nipped off a portion of it, crying out each time, "gukuk" (look! look!). To punish him, God turned him into a bird of prey that is everlastingly repeating the same cry.† According to another legend, our Lord passed by a baker's shop, from which there came a pleasant smell of fresh bread, and sent his disciples in to beg for a loaf. The baker refused it, but his wife, who was looking on from a distance with her six daughters, gave it in secret. For this she and her daughters were placed in heaven as the Seven Stars (the Pleiades; English, hen with her chickens), but the baker was turned into a

* Hamlet, iv. 5.

† D. M. 641.

cuckoo; and so long as his cry is heard in the spring, from St. Tiburt's to St. John's day, the Seven Stars are visible in the heavens.* The cuckoo's connection with storms and tempests is not clearly determined, but the owl's is indisputable. Its cry is believed in England to foretell rain and hail, the latter of which is usually accompanied with lightning, and the practice of nailing it to the barn door, to avert the lightning, is common throughout Europe, and is mentioned by Palladius in his treatise on Agriculture.†

The stork, which in Holland, Denmark, and North Germany is everywhere a welcome guest, is known there universally as a fire-fowl and baby-bringer. There are obvious reasons why these offices should have been assigned to him. He is a bird of passage coming with the storms, departing with them; he is the attendant and messenger of the goddess, with whom he arrives in spring after her winter enchantment or banishment, and his red legs mark him also as a servant of the fire-god. In Hesse a wagon-wheel (emblem of the sun) is laid upon the roof for the stork to build his nest on. The house on which he builds is safe from fire, even though the neighbourhood be burned down. He must not

* D.M. 691.

† De re rusticâ, I. 35.

be killed, for he is a sacred bird; nor must his nest be disturbed, lest the house be struck with lightning. At Rothenburg an incensed stork, whose young had been flung out of the nest, fetched a firebrand in his bill, threw it into the empty nest, and set the house on fire.* When the storks are seen fluttering round the steeple, a fire may be expected to break out somewhere; then they come with water in their bills, and let it fall from the air into the flames.†

Our English nursery fable of the Parsley-bed in which little strangers are found, is doubtless a remnant of a fuller tradition, like that of the woodpecker among the Romans and that of the stork among our continental kinsmen. Adebar or Odebaro, an ancient German name of the stork, means literally child or soul bringer;‡ and it is not unknown to Hans Andersen's readers that Danish ladies are often obliged to keep their beds, because the stork, which has brought another little brother or sister to the house, has bitten mamma in the leg. There is hardly a German village that has not its *kinderbrunnen* (child fountain), where the stork takes up the little ones and brings them home.§

* Wolf, Beiträge, ii. 435.

† Mannhardt, 193.

‡ D.M. 638. Kuhn, Herabk. p. 106.

§ The Sanscrit word *utsa*, fountain, is a frequent Vedic appellation of the clouds.

The fountain is an image of the fire and light bearing cloud, and is named in many places after Frau Holda, or Lady Gracious, the goddess who sits in her radiant hall beneath the waters, and cherishes the unborn babes on her motherly bosom. Other accounts tell of a beautiful sunny garden, in the very heart of a hill or mountain (another image of the clouds), where the little ones play about under the eye of the divine protectress, and sip honey from the blossoms. A woman, whose child had disappeared, made her way into such a subterraneous garden, which she found thronged with babies. In the midst of them sat a lady of noble presence, clad in white, nursing the lost child on her lap. Instead of the heathen goddess, the Mother of God is commonly spoken of in modern times as the Lady of the Fountain. She has her nursery, for instance, in the Cunibert's Fountain in Cologne; and the Queckbrunnen * in Dresden, out of which "the clapperstork fetches the Dresden children," is sacred to her. Its waters, through our Lady's grace, make childless women fruitful, and a chapel was built over them in 1514, repaired in 1745, and enlarged in 1783. In place of a weather vane the chapel is surmounted by the figure of a stork, holding a

* That is, quick or 'live fountain.

babe in swaddling clothes in its beak, and two others in its claws.*

Instead of the usual fountain, a hollow tree overhanging a pool is known in many places, both in North and South Germany, as the first abode of unborn infants. In this form of the common tradition we have both the cloud sea and the tree growing beside it, whence the spark of life is immediately derived; and here, too, we discover a relic of the old belief, common to the Greeks and the Germans, that the progenitors of mankind were *born* of trees. "Frau Holda's tree" is a common name in Germany for old decayed boles; and she herself, the cloud-goddess, is described in a Hessian legend as having, in front, the form of a beautiful woman, and behind, that of a hollow tree with a rugged bark.† It is not unimportant, with reference to the parsley-bed theory, that the baby's tree is sometimes spoken of as growing in a kitchen-garden (krautgarten); that in Saterland they say "infants are fetched out of the cabbage," and that in the Walloon part of Belgium they are said to be found in the parson's garden. Parsley, cabbage, and other vegetables may stand for the wholesome and

* Mannhardt, 280—3.

† Ibid. 284.

precious plants that clustered round the foot of the heavenly tree (p. 74).

But trees, plants, fountains, and hills are not the only cloud-forms that present themselves in this legendary cycle. "Northward of the island of Gristow, about halfway between Cammin and Zünz, there is a huge block of granite in the Diwenow, not far from its bank. Many a grey year ago that rock was a fine castle, in which dwelt a greedy robber. Maidens above all were his prey; but one of them to whom he offered violence, happening to be skilled in magic, shrunk the whole castle together into a big block of stone, and shut the wicked robber up in it for ever. They tell the children in Cammin that the stork brings them to their parents from the big stone."*

The legend is transparent in all its details. It is a meteoric drama, with its action and scenery transplanted from sky to earth. The robber and ravisher is the storm-god who issues from his cloud-castle, and chases the white-cloud maidens; but his force is spent, his cloud-castle collapses, and he is banned by the power of nature's magic.

The stork must needs be a supernatural being, like the Manx wren and the picus or woodpecker.

* Kuhn u. Schwartz, Ndd. p. 14.

He too is both bird and man, as we learn from Gervase of Tilbury.* The transformation of storks into men, and *vice versâ*, is an article of popular belief in Friesland,† and in Prussia, where it is forbidden to hurt a stork, "for he is elsewhere a man."‡ A Flemish legend recounts that a citizen of Bruges met a man near Mount Sinai, who told him they were neighbours in Bruges, for the nest of the one was next door to the house of the other. In confirmation of this statement the stork-man showed a ring he had stolen from the Fleming once upon a time, and gave it back to him on condition that he would not for the future allow his herdsman to molest his feathered neighbour.§

The goddess Holda is only another form of Freyja or Fria, the wife of Odin and sister of Freyr or Fro, the god of the sun and of love, in whose attributes she participates. The Ladybird has many names, all of them mythic,‖ and it is sacred to both goddesses. Its home is in heaven or in the sun,¶ and

* P. 35.

† D.M. 638.

‡ Tettau und Temme, 285.

§ Liebrecht, G. T. 157.

‖ In England, Lady bird, lady fly, lady cow—names pointing originally to Freyja, but subsequently to the Virgin; in Holland, our Dear Lady's little beast; in Germany, sun calf, moon calf, sun chick, God's calf—little bird, Mary bird—chafer—calf, Lady hen, Lady cow, &c.; in Bretagne, la petite vache du bon dieu; in Bohemia, the same (Bozj krawicku).

¶ D.M. 658.

German children tell it in rhyme to fly up thither, mount the chair (Freyja's throne) and bring back sunshine and fine weather. They believe that, were they to kill the insect, the sun would not shine the next day.* The English rhyme—

> Ladybird, ladybird, fly away home,
> Your house is on fire, your children will burn—

seems to have some reference to the insect's ministrations with fire, the more so as the ladybird is very commonly addressed in Germany to the same purpose, and the children in Westphalia have a rhyme which plainly implies that the burning house is in heaven, for it states that the *angels* are crying about it.† Lastly, this important little creature is appealed to in the same country as a child-bringer, and asked to fly up to heaven and bring down a golden dish and in it a golden baintling.‡

There is a German tradition of a little girl, the daughter of poor parents, who was fond of playing with ladybirds in the wood. One day when she was thus engaged, a carriage drawn by ladybirds drove up; she stepped into it, and was carried through the air to Lady Holda, who was sitting

* Wolf, ii. 449. † Kuhn, Westf. ii. 78.
‡ Mannhardt, 283.

at her spinning-wheel in front of a cottage. The lady had sent for the child because a frightful war was raging on the earth, and during the five years of its continuance the child remained safe with the kind goddess. At the end of that time she was sent home with a fine bridal outfit of linen.*

The majority of the fire-bringers, if not all of them, are more or less prophetic, like Agni himself. Prometheus foretold the defeat of the Titans by Jupiter, and prevented the latter from ruining himself by marrying Thetis, who was destined to bear a son who would eclipse his father. Picus delivered oracles to the Sabines from the top of a wooden pillar in the grove at Matiena. Omens are drawn from the stork in North Germany. The first time in the year a girl hears the bird, if it clatter with its bill, she will break something; if it be flying, she will be a bride before the year is out; if it be standing, she will be asked to stand god-mother. If a flight of storks pass over a group of men standing in a circle, one of the group will die soon. The ladybird, which is so intimate with the goddess of love and with Frau Holda, must know a great many things. Its services in affairs of love were known to Gay—

* Mannhardt, p. 287.

This ladyfly I take from off the grass,
Whose spotted back might scarlet red surpass.
Fly, ladybird, north, south, or east, or west,
Fly where the man is found that I love best.

Little girls in Westphalia set the ladybird on the point of their forefinger and invoke it in rhyme to say when they will be married: in one year? two years? three years? &c.; and they grow very impatient if the insect lets them count too high before it flies away. Sometimes it is asked, as it sits on the finger, how the questioner will fare in the next world. If it fly upwards, the questioner will go to heaven; if downwards, to the opposite place; if horizontally, to purgatory. In Sweden, if the black spots on the wing-covers of the ladybird exceed seven, the usual number, it is thought to be a sign that corn will be dear; if they are fewer, a plentiful harvest is expected.

To no bird has the gift of augury been more generally attributed than to the cuckoo.* Mannhardt states positively that this herald of the spring is one of the lightning-bearers,† and Kuhn inclines to the same opinion, but abstains, with characteristic caution, from asserting as proved a fact which as yet appears to him to be no more than highly probable. The cuckoo is, at all events, intimately connected with the lightning gods—with Zeus and with Thor. It

* D. M. 640. † P. 194.

was in the form of a cuckoo that Zeus first flew to the bosom of coy Hera and made her his bride.* A seated image of the goddess shows a cuckoo upon her wand; in a bas-relief representing the marriage procession of Zeus and Hera, a cuckoo sits upon the god's sceptre; and the mountain which was the scene of their union had its name changed from Thronax, or Thornax, to Oros Kokkugion, *i. e.*, Cuckoo mountain.† According to Mannhardt the cuckoo is the messenger of Thor, the god in whose gift were health and strength, length of days and marriage blessings, and therefore it is that people call upon the bird to tell how long they have to live, how soon they will be married, and how many children they shall have; and that in Schaumburg the person who acts at a wedding as master of the ceremonies carries a cuckoo on his staff.‡ At the first call of the cuckoo a German peasant does the same thing as when he hears thunder for the first time in the year: he rolls himself two or three times on the grass, thinking himself thereby insured against pains in the back throughout the rest of the year, and all the more so if the bird continues its cry whilst he is on the ground.§

Cæsarius (A.D. 1222) tells of a convertite who was

* Pausanias II., 17, 4; 36, 2.

† D. M. 644. ‡ Mannhardt, 198. § Ibid., 200.

about to become a monk, but changed his mind on hearing the cuckoo's call, and counting twenty-two repetitions of it. "Come," said he, "I have certainly twenty-two years still to live, and why should I mortify myself during all that time? I will go back to the world, enjoy its delights for twenty years, and devote the remaining two to penitence." In the English invocation,

> Cuckoo, cherry-tree,
> Good bird tell me—
> How many years have I to live?

is the cherry-tree lugged in only to make rhyme, or is there any allusion in it to the three full meals of cherries which, it is said, the bird must eat before it leaves off crying? In Sweden, girls bid the cuckoo sit on the bough and tell them for certain how many years they are to remain unmarried. If the bird cries more than ten times, they say it sits upon a foolish or bewitched bough, and they pay no heed to its augury. In that country it is also of much importance from what quarter of the heavens the cuckoo's voice is first heard in spring. Heard from the north, the unlucky side, it portends a year of sorrow to the hearer; from the east and west it betokens luck, and from the south it gives promise of a good butter year.*

* D. M. 641.

The cuckoo's oracles were believed by the Poles to be actually given by the great god Zywie, the life-giver, who transformed himself into the bird on purpose to utter them.*

If the first note of the cuckoo comes upon you when you have no money in your pocket, that is held, both in Germany and England, to portend want of money throughout the year. On the contrary, he that has coin in his pocket at that critical moment, and does not forget to turn it, will have plenty. It strikes me that this superstition tends not a little to confirm the hypothesis of the cuckoo's being one of the lightning-bearers; for, as we shall find when we come to speak of the divining-rod, it is a first principle of Indo-European mythology that the heavenly fire is the main source of all wealth and prosperity.

The form of the cuckoo remotely resembles that of some of the falcon tribe. May we hazard a conjecture that hence, in Germanic tradition, that bird in some degree represents the fire-bringing falcon of the Aryans? It is a popular belief in Germany, as we learn from Grimm, that after St. John's day, about which time the cuckoo becomes mute, it *changes into a hawk.*†

* D. M. 643.

† D. M. 1222—See note, p. 105.

Gay has these lines in his "Shepherd's Week":

> When first the year, I heard the cuckoo sing,
> And call with welcome note the budding spring,
> I straightway set a-running with such haste,
> Deb'rah that won the smock scarce ran so fast;
> Till spent for lack of breath, quite weary grown,
> Upon a rising bank I sat adown,
> And doff'd my shoe, and by my troth I swear,
> Therein I spied this yellow frizzled hair—
> As like to Lubberkin's in curl and hue,
> As if upon his comely pate it grew.

The delightful inference was, that Lubberkin was destined to be her own. The same thing is mentioned in the "Connoisseur," No. 58: "I got up last May morning, and went into the fields to hear the cuckoo, and when I pulled off my left shoe, I found a hair in it exactly the same colour with his."

Golden hair, or fiery red, like Thor's beard, is a very common symbol of the sunbeams or the lightning; and Schwartz has noticed,* as a casualty which frequently befalls the stormgods and demigods, the loss of their thick clustering locks in the elemental strife. It would be quite in accordance with all that is known to us of the natural history of myths, should it appear that some of this fallen hair was the very same that Lubberkin's sweetheart found in her shoe, when prompted to look for it by a lightning-bird.

* Ursprung, pp. 143—145.

The same omen is given in Westphalia by another herald of the spring. When a man sees the first swallow, he should look if there be a hair under his foot. If he find one, his future wife's hair will be of the same colour.* The swallow is everywhere a sacred bird, and in some places, like the stork, it preserves the house on which it builds its nest from fire and lightning. On the other hand, if the swallows do not return to their old nest, somebody will die in the house, or it will be burned down.†

In Swabia, the man who kills a swallow will have his cows give red milk, or his house will be struck with lightning,‡ and some believe that such a sacrilegious act will be followed by rain of four weeks' duration.§ In Perigord, the swallow is "the messenger of life." The people call it la Poule de Dieu (just like the wren), and this bird and the cricket are regarded as members of the family.‖ In Normandy, it is the subject of a tradition analogous to that concerning the woodpecker and the springwort, as will be seen hereafter. Its chestnut-red head and throat are probably not without significance; and it may be that, as in the case of the robin (p. 81), some old wife's tale, snatched from the oblivion to which

* Kuhn, Westf. ii., 71. † Ibid., pp. 70—72.
‡ Meier, 221. § D. M. 633. ‖ De Nore, 162.

it is now hastening, will eventually complete the evidence upon which we shall be justified in assigning to this guest of summer no uncertain place among the fire-bringing birds.

That the soul quits the dead body in the form of a bird is a wide-spread belief, and in Kuhn's opinion it is intimately connected with the tradition of birds as soul-bringers. The soul and the bird that brought it down to earth may have been supposed to become one, and to enter and quit the body together. Stories of disembodied souls appearing as doves are numerous, but lend only an ambiguous support to Kuhn's conjecture, since we cannot tell whether or not their origin is due, in part or wholly, to biblical and ecclesiastical ideas. We are on surer ground when we have to deal with such heathen, or at least non-Christian, instances as the following:—

In the Sæmundr Edda it is said that souls in the form of singed birds flit about the nether world like swarms of flies. According to the heathen Bohemians, the soul flew out of the mouth of the dying as a bird, and flitted from tree to tree until the body was burned, after which it had rest. The Finns, and also the Lithuanians, the latter an Indo-European people, call the Milky Way the

Birds' Way, *i. e.*, the way of souls. In Poland it is said that every member of the Herburt family is turned into an eagle after death; and that the eldest daughters of the Pileck line are transformed into doves if they die unmarried, into owls if they die married, and that they give previous notice of their death to every member of their race by pecking a finger of each.* The people in North Germany believe that the soul of one who has died on shipboard passes into a bird,† and when it shows itself it is to foretell the death of another person. It is a local Irish tradition that the first father and mother of mankind exist as eagles in the island of Innis Bofin, at the mouth of Killery Bay, in Galway.‡

"Look, my dear," said S. S.'s wife to him one morning as he lay in bed. "Look at that kite flying round the room." He saw nothing, but heard a noise like a large bird flapping its wings. A few minutes afterwards a sparrow came, dashed its bill against the window, and flew away again. "Oh," said Mrs. S., "something is the matter with poor Edward" (her brother). She had hardly said the word when a man on horseback rode up and said,

* D.M. 788.

† Kuhn und Schwartz, Ndd. p. 436.

‡ Liebrecht, Gerv. Tilb. p. 115.

when S. opened the door to him, "Don't frighten poor Mary; but master has just expired." The messenger had only ridden from Somers Town to Compton Street, Soho. I had this story from S. himself, who was possessed with a notion that the sparrow that tapped at his window was the soul of his brother-in-law.

Supplementary Note.

This sheet was already in type and just going to press when I found, in the *Times* of September 3, 1863, the following corroboration of the conjecture offered in the last paragraph of page 100. At the meeting of the British Association at Newcastle-on-Tyne on the preceding day, the Rev. H. B. Tristram said:—

"The gentlemen of Durham and Northumberland believed that the hedgehog ate the partridge eggs; and so great was the ignorance of natural history that, a short time ago, when he remonstrated with a man for shooting a cuckoo, the defence was that it was well known that *sparrowhawks turned into cuckoos* in the summer."

CHAPTER IV.

THE DEAD—THEIR WORLD AND THE WAY TO IT—PSYCHOPOMP DOGS AND COWS—DEATH OMENS GIVEN BY DOGS AND COWS—THE DEAD-SHOE—THE BRIG O' DREAD—SHIPS AND BOATS—THE FERRYMAN'S FEE—ENGLAND THE LAND OF THE DEAD—BERTHA—TEARS FOR THE DEAD—SOULS OF UNCHRISTENED BABES—ZWERGS CROSSING THE FERRY.

It was the belief of the Aryans that the soul—that spark of heavenly fire—passed upwards after death, to mingle with the spirits of the winds, the clouds, the lightning, the sunbeams, and the stars, and to find its everlasting abode in the highest heaven. On its way thither it had to cross a vast river—the cloud-water—which flows between the world of men and the bright realm of Yama and the Pitris, or fathers. But it was not left to make the dread journey alone or unprotected; for, as the Vedas tell, it was taken up by a cow (*i.e.*, a cloud) from the divine world, which conveyed it across the heavenly waters and over the Milky Way to Yama's dwelling. For this reason it was made a religious ordinance of the Hindus that the dying person should lay hold of the tail of a cow in his last moments. Cows drew the corpse to the funeral pile, and a black cow was led after it to the same spot, slaughtered and flayed there. The flesh of the animal was heaped upon the corpse as it lay on the pile, and its hide was spread over all. Fire was then applied, and when the flames rose high a hymn was sung, in which the cow was invoked to ascend with the deceased to the land of the departed fathers.*

Other Vedic accounts state that the wind, under the form of a dog (p. 7), sent by Yama, accompanies and protects the soul on its journey; and again, it is said, that two four-eyed dogs, acquainted with men, watch the path that leads to Yama's abode. In accordance with the conception of the dog as the soul's escort to heaven, it is the custom of the Parsees of Bombay to place a dog before the dying, so that their eyes may rest upon the animal at the last moment; and two dogs are set before a woman dying in pregnancy, one for each departing soul. After death, according to Parsee belief, the soul arrives at the bridge Tchinavat, where the gods and the unclean spirits fight for possession of it. If it be one of the righteous, it is defended by

* Mannhardt, p. 51.

the other pure souls and by the dogs that guard the bridge.*

The reader will probably be surprised to learn how many of these particulars have been preserved in the mythologies and popular traditions of Europe. It was an ancient belief of the whole German race that the Milky Way is the way of souls, and in Friesland it is even called the Cow-path (kaupat). It was also believed that whoever had given a cow to the poor on earth would not stumble or be dizzy when he had to cross the fearful Gjallar bridge—the bridge Tchinavat of the Persian Aryans—for there, as in the Vedic times, he would find a cow that would carry his soul safely over. "Hence it was of yore a funeral custom in Sweden, Denmark, England, Upper and Lower Germany, that a cow should follow the coffin to the churchyard. This custom was partially continued [on the Continent] until recent times, being accounted for on the ground that the cow was a gift to the clergy for saying masses for the dead man's soul or preaching his funeral sermon."† In England, when heathen sacrifices had been abolished, the animal was likewise devoted to pious uses, in the way of what our Saxon ancestors called *saul sceat*, *i.e.*, soul-shot,

* Mannhardt, p. 51.

† Ibid., p. 320.

or mortuary payment. "It was considered as a gift left by a man at his death by way of recompense for all failures in the payment of tithes and oblations, and called a corse present. It is mentioned in the national council of Ensham about the year 1006."*

In the office assigned to the dog of the Aryans, as a messenger from the world of the dead, we see the origin of that very wide-spread superstition which recognizes a death-omen in the howling of a dog. An intelligent Londoner tells me he has often seen the omen given, and verified its fulfilment. The dog's mode of proceeding on such occasions, he says, is this: The animal tries to get under the doomed person's window; but if the house stands within an inclosure, and it cannot get in, it runs round the premises very uneasily, or paces up and down before them like a sentry. If the dog succeeds in making an entry, it stops under the window, howls horribly, finishes with three tremendous barks, and hurries away. The same superstition prevails in France and in Germany. In the latter country, a dog howling before a house portends either a death or a fire. If it howls along the highway, that is held in West-

* Brand, ii. 248.

phalia to be a sure token that a funeral will soon pass that way. In the German, as in the Aryan mythology, the dog is an embodiment of the wind, and also an attendant on the dead. It appears in both characters in Odin's wild hunt. Dogs see ghosts,* and when Hel, the goddess of death, goes about, invisible to human eyes, she is seen by the dogs.†

Yama's canine messengers were called Sârameyas; and that very name, put into a Greek form, was borne, as Dr. Kuhn has demonstrated,‡ by Hermeias or Hermes, the messenger of the Grecian gods, who led the shades to Hades.

The fatal significance of the howling dog is notorious, but it is not so generally known that the other Aryan psychopomp, the cow, is sometimes a foretokener of death. A correspondent of "Notes and Queries" gives the following record as written down by him about the time to which it relates:—

"A bad omen seems to be drawn from an ox or a cow breaking into a garden. Though I laugh at the superstition, the omen was painfully fulfilled in my case. About the middle of March, 1843, some cattle were driven close to my house, and, the back door

* D.M. 632. † Ibid.

‡ Zeitschr. f. v. Sprachf.

being open, three got into our little bit of garden and trampled it. When our school-drudge came in the afternoon and asked the cause of the confusion, she expressed great sorrow and apprehension on being told—said it was a bad sign—that we should hear of three deaths within the next six months. Alas! in April we heard of dear J——'s murder; a fortnight after A—— died; and to-morrow, August 10, I attend the funeral of my excellent son-in-law. I have just heard of the same omen from another quarter.

"This was added the next day:—

"But what is still more remarkable is, that when I went down to Mr. M——'s burial, and was mentioning the superstition, they told me that while he was lying ill, a cow got into the front garden, and was driven out with great difficulty." *

"What does the 'black cow' signify," asks Grimm,† "in such [German] phrases as 'the black cow is pressing him'; 'the black cow has trodden upon him'?" It is a common saying in Scotland, when a man is ill and not likely to recover, or when he has lost one of his family or kindred by death, "the black ox has tramped upon him." King Oluf Digrbeen was forewarned of a great mortality, in a dream, by a black

* "Choice Notes," p. 20. † D. M. 631, n.

ox that came from the eastward, and went about from house to house, in each of which the majority of the inmates were laid low at the sound of its bellowing.*

The heaven of the Aryans belonged alike to the gods and to the souls of the dead; but gradually, as men came to have a higher sense of the might and majesty of the gods, it seemed fit to separate the realm of shades from the bright abode of the divine rulers of the world. The former was therefore brought down below and placed, sometimes in islands of the far West, sometimes beneath the surface of the earth; but, wherever it was supposed to be, its scenery, bright or sombre, was that which had belonged to it in the sky, and its rulers were gods who had descended with it from the upper regions.†

Niflheimr, the world of mists, beneath one of the roots of the world-tree Yggdrasil, was the dismal realm of Hel or Hela, the Norse and German goddess of death.‡ Cold and gloomy it was, like herself, but

* Liebrecht, G. T. p. 92. † Schwartz, p. 271.

‡ Whom Christianity transformed from a person into a place, in like manner as it transformed the goddess Ostara into a season—Easter. "The Christian notion of Hell," says Mr. Dasent, "is that of a place of heat; for in the East, whence Christianity came, heat is often an intolerable torment, and cold, on the other hand, everything that is pleasant and delightful. But to the dweller in the North heat

of old it was never spoken of as a place of punishment and torment. Those who went to it were not the bad alone, but all who died, even the noblest and the best,—Brynhild for instance, and Baldr. The only apparent exceptions were the heroes who had fallen in battle, and whom Odin gathered to himself in Valhalla.* But the idea of retribution after death for crimes done in the body was not unknown to German paganism. It was a part of the Aryan creed, and the Vedas speak of the goddess Nirriti, and her dreadful world Naraka, the destined abode of all guilty souls. It is not conceivable that such a tradition could have died out, even for a time, among any of the pagan Indo-Europeans, and we know that, according to Anglo-Saxon belief, "for the perjurer and the secret murderer Nástrond existed, a place of torment and punishment—the strand of the dead—filled with foulness, peopled with poisonous serpents, dark,

brings with it sensations of joy and comfort, and life without fire has a dreary outlook; so their Hel ruled in a cold region over those who were cowards by implication, while the mead-cup went round, and huge logs blazed and crackled in Valhalla for the brave and beautiful who had dared to die on the field of battle. But under Christianity the extremes of heat and cold have met, and Hel, the cold uncomfortable goddess, is now our Hell, where flames and fires abound, and where the devils abide in everlasting flame."—Popular Tales from the Norse, Introd.

* D.M. p. 764.

cold, and gloomy: the kingdom of Hel was *Hades*, the invisible, the world of shadows; Nástrond was what we call Hell."* Dr. Roth, one of the most distinguished Vedic scholars, is of opinion that the souls of the wicked swelled the host of the Râkshasas (p. 28) as those of the good became members of the community of Ribhus and Maruts. The heaven of the Pitris (p. 18) is often called "the world of good deed, the world of the righteous," and they themselves were spirits of light and ministers of good to men. Hence there is strong reason for inferring, although the fact is nowhere expressly stated, that the inhabitants of the opposite world became spirits of darkness, and confederates of all the evil powers. If this conjecture prove to be well founded, it will have brought to light another remarkable instance of the continuity of Aryan tradition.

Long and dreary was the road to Hel's dark dominion; the descent to it from heaven was a journey of nine days and nine nights for the gods themselves. The greater part of the way lay through morasses and vast moors overgrown with furze and thorns; and that the dead might not pass over them barefoot, a pair of shoes was laid

* Kemble, "Saxons in England," ii. 393.

with them in the grave. Hence a funeral is still called "dead-shoe" (todtenschuh) in the Henneberg district and perhaps in some others, and in Scandinavia the shoe itself is called "hel-shoe" (helskô).* In a MS. of the Cotton Library, containing an account of Cleveland in Yorkshire, in the reign of Queen Elizabeth, there is a passage which illustrates this custom. It has been quoted by Sir Walter Scott in the notes to the "Minstrelsy of the Scottish Border," and runs thus: "When any dieth, certaine women sing a song to the dead bodie, reciting the journey that the partye deceased must goe, and they are of beliefe (such is their fondnesse) that once in their lives it is good to give a pair of new shoes to a poor man, for as much as after this life they are to pass barefoote through a great launde, full of thorns and furzen, except by the meryte of the almes aforesaid they have redemed the forfeyte; for at the edge of the launde an oulde man shall meet them with the same shoes that were given by the partie when he was lyving, and after he hath shodde them, dismisseth them to go through thick and thin without scratch or scalle." The dirge in question continued to be sung in Yorkshire until the year 1624, and is as follows: †

* Mannhardt, p. 320. D.M. 795.

† Brand, ii. 274.

This ean* night, this ean night,
  Every night and awle,
Fire and fleet† and candle light,
  And Christ receive thy sawle.

When thou from hence away dost pass,
  Every night and awle,
To Whinny‡ Moor thou comest at last,
  And Christ receive thy sawle.

If ever thou gave either hosen or shoon,
  Every night and awle,
Sit thee down and put them on,
  And Christ receive thy sawle.

But if hosen nor shoon thou never gave naen,
  Every night and awle,
The whinnes shall prick thee to the bare beane,
  And Christ receive thy sawle.

From Whinny Moor that thou mayst pass,
  Every night and awle,
To Brig§ o' Dread thou comest at last,
  And Christ receive thy sawle.

From Brig o' Dread, na brader than a thread,‖
  Every night and awle,
To Purgatory fire thou comest at last,
  And Christ receive thy sawle.

If ever thou gave either milke or drink,
  Every night and awle,
The fire shall never make thee shrink,
  And Christ receive thy sawle.

* Ean = one. † Fleet = water.
‡ From whin = furze. § Brig = bridge.
‖ Like Al Sirat, the Mahomedan bridge of souls.

But if milk nor drink thou never gave naen,
Every night and awle,
The fire shall burn thee to the bare beane,
And Christ receive thy sawle.

The water that lies between the world of the living and that of the dead is found, in one shape or other, in all the Indo-European mythologies. In that of the Greeks it was the river Styx, Acheron, or Cocytus, over which Charon ferried the shades in his small two-oared boat; or it was the Western Ocean in which lay the Islands of the Blest. Charon's boat is one of those cloud-ships which were often seen by the Aryans floating upon the upper sea; and he himself, the "glittering eyed"* mariner, used to ply of old across those dark and stormy waters. He was one of the primitive storm-gods, and in modern Greece he is still to be seen marching in clouds and darkness over the mountains with his ghostly train.†

The Northern nations also believed that their dead crossed the water in boats and ships, and so far were they from expecting the passage to be always effected over a bridge, that in Scandinavia

* This is the meaning of his name. *Charon* and *charopos* are epithets applied to the eyes of the lion, the serpent, and the lightning goddess Athene.

† Firmenich, Τραγουδια Ρωμαικα, p. 61; Schwartz, p. 126.

bodies were *buried* in ships.* This was manifestly done with the intention that the dead should have means at hand to carry them over whatever water they might come to on their journey. The Norse story of the death of Baldr tells how the Æsir raised his funeral pile on board a ship, laid his body upon it, and committed the blazing vessel to the waves. The corpse of the deified hero Scild was placed in a ship which "was wafted away by the sea, no one knows whither." Sigmundr carried the body of his beloved son Sinfiötli to the sea-shore, where a man with a small boat offered it a passage. Sigmundr laid the body in the boat, which had then its full lading; the unknown boatman pushed off from the shore, and floated away with the corpse. Frotho's law specified how many bodies of warriors—from one to ten according to the rank of the deceased—should be burned in one ship. A Swedish popular legend tells of a golden ship lying underground in Runemad, on board of which Odin conveyed the slain in Brâvalla to Valhalla. In the old French romance of Lancelot du Lac the demoiselle d'Escalot (Tennyson's Lady

* D.M. 790, n. Among the Garrows of Bengal "The dead are kept for four days; burnt on a pile of wood in a dingy or small boat, placed on the top of the pile," &c.—Coleman, p. 319.

of Shalott) gives these directions for the disposal of her body after death: "*le pria que son corps fût mis en une nef, richement equippée, que l'on laisseroit aller au gré du vent sans conduite.*" Did the belief prevail, says Grimm, that the body, abandoned to the sacred sea and to the winds, would arrive by itself at the land of death to which no human hand could guide it? *

There is a legend of a Herr von Falkenberg who is condemned to beat about the ocean until the day of judgment, on board a ship without helm or steersman, playing at dice for his soul with the devil.† "Seamen traversing the German Ocean often meet with the infernal vessel." It was probably no uncommon occurrence in early times for seafarers to fall in with ships abandoned to the winds and waves, with corpses on board, and out of such encounters may have grown this legend of Falkenberg, that of the Flying Dutchman, and others of the same kind.

Whilst the preceding instances relate to the shipment of dead or living bodies, that of disembodied souls is the subject of other legends. A drowsy boatman is roused up one stormy night by

* D.M. 790.

† Wolf, Niederländische Sagen. No. 130.

the figure of a monk who puts a fare into his hand and asks to be ferried over the river. At first six monks step into the boat, but no sooner is it afloat than a crowd of others, black and white, suddenly fill it, and scarcely leave any room for the boatman. He rows across with difficulty, the passengers step ashore, and the boat is driven back by a stiff gale to its berth on the other side, where more passengers are waiting for it. As they enter, the foremost of them puts the fare into the ferryman's hand with his ice-cold fingers. The return trip is made in the same boisterous manner. A similar story is told, but with less detail, of monks crossing the Rhine by night at Spires.* It appears that in former times the Rhine, the political boundary of Germany, was also regarded as the boundary between the upper and the lower world, and that "to go to the Rhine" and "to die" were mutually equivalent expressions.†

The Greeks used to put a small piece of money, an obolus, into the mouth of the dead, wherewith the ghost might pay its fare to the Stygian ferryman. The very same practice prevailed generally in Germany, and is still continued in Altmark and Havelland. The pretext now assigned for it is

* D.M. 791.

† Kuhn, Westf. i. 129.

that it may prevent the corpse from returning as a *Nachzehrer*—a kind of vampire peculiar to Germany. But this, says Grimm, is a spurious motive devised in later times. The coin placed under the dead man's tongue was originally nothing else than the *naulus*, or ferryman's fee.*

The historian of the Gothic war † relates a legend of the island of Brittia, the substance of which is given as follows by Sir Walter Scott in his "Count Robert of Paris" (I. 5):—"I have read," says Agelastes, "in that brilliant mirror which reflects the times of our fathers, the volumes of the learned Procopius, that beyond Gaul, and nearly opposite to it, but separated by an arm of the sea, lies a ghastly region, on which clouds and tempests for ever rest, and which is known to its continental neighbours as the abode to which departed spirits are sent after this life. On one side of the strait dwell a few fishermen, men possessed of a strange character, and enjoying singular privileges in consideration of their being the living ferrymen who, performing the office of the heathen Charon, carry the spirits of the departed to the island which is their residence after death. At the dead of the night these fishermen

* D.M. 791 ; Schwartz, p. 273.

† Procopius, De Bello Goth. iv. 20.

are, in rotation, summoned to perform the duty by which they seem to hold permission to reside on this strange coast. A knock is heard at the door of his cottage who holds the turn of this singular office, sounded by no mortal hand; a whispering, as of a decaying breeze, summons the ferryman to his duty. He hastens to his bark on the sea-shore, and has no sooner launched it than he perceives its hull sink sensibly in the water, so as to express the weight of the dead with whom it is filled. No form is seen; and though voices are heard, yet the accents are undistinguishable, as of one who speaks in his sleep."

Brittia, according to Procopius, lay not further than 200 stadia from the coast, between Britannia and Thule (the Scandinavian peninsula), opposite the mouth of the Rhine, and was inhabited by the Angili, the Frissones, and the Brittones. By Britannia he means the western portion of Gaul, one end of which is now called Bretagne, but which extended in the sixth century over what was afterwards Normandy and Frisian Flanders to the mouths of the Scheldt and the Rhine. His Brittia is generally believed to have been Great Britain, but this has been made matter of controversy. It is enough for our purpose that popular opinion in Germany and in Bretagne has settled the question affirmatively. In the former country it was of old an established belief that Britain was the island of souls, and such to this day it is still held to be under its new name of England. "How the bells are ringing in England!" "How my children are crying in England!" "I hear my mother in England calling the pigs!" are exclamations usually uttered by the amorous nightmare, a being of the under world, when she wants an excuse for hastily quitting her German lover.*

According to Villemarqué,† the place from which the boat used to depart with its ghostly freight was near Raz, at the furthest point of the Armorican coast, where there is a bay called the Bay of Souls (baie des ames, boé ann anavo). It is said to be customary to this day in the parish of Plouguel, on the river Treguier in Bretagne, for corpses to be conveyed to the churchyard by boat, over a narrow arm of the sea, called *passage de l'enfer*, instead of taking them by the shorter land route. Moreover, it is a popular belief throughout all Armorica, that the dead betake themselves at the moment of their departure to the parish priest of Braspar, whose dog escorts them to Great Britain. The wheels of the cart, which is overloaded with souls, are heard

* Kuhn, Westf. i. 54. † Barzas Briez. i. 136.

creaking in the air; it is covered with a white cloth, and is called *carr an ancou, carrikel an ancou, i.e.*, soul car. These, says Grimm, are merely popular variations of the old legend. The Christian inhabitants of Bretagne were no longer allowed to ship the bodies of their dead over to the island, so they conveyed them by water at least to the churchyard; and now their tradition runs that, instead of on shipboard, the passage is made in a cart through the air, as in the case of the mesnie furieuse, or wild host.

The priest of Braspar's dog, that accompanies them on their journey, manifestly belongs to the breed of the Sârameyas (p. 110).

Niflheimr (p. 105) is a creation of the Norse mythology, and Hel or Hela, its mistress, is less generally known in Germany as the goddess of death than is Holda or Bertha, with whom we are already acquainted as the goddess of birth. In the district of Linz, in Austria, a belated labourer or workman is often met at the junction of cross-roads by Bertha, who offers him a black cloth. If he takes it he dies within the same year; but if he cries out

> Dame Berth, dame Berth,
> Throw the cloth upon the earth,

the goddess will send him luck and plenty. The

black cloth is the black cloud which portends death to somebody within the house over which it passes.* When the goddess throws it down—that is to say, when she lets it fall as rain upon the earth—it becomes changed from a fatal presage into a source of fruitfulness and prosperity.

The primeval belief that the soul returns after death to the community of the elves out of which it came, is expressed in the clearest manner in other legends of Bertha. She has a very numerous retinue, consisting of the souls of still-born children, or, as Christian tradition expresses the same belief, of children that died unbaptized. They act in her service as elementary spirits, watering the fields whilst she herself tills them with her plough which she works underground.†

A young mother, whose only child had died, wept beyond measure over her loss, and would not be comforted. Every night she went to the little grave, and cried and sobbed over it, till on the night

* Mannhardt, p. 290.

† D.M. p. 253. Bertha's elves are called Heimchen, a name which in Grimm's opinion they can hardly have received on account of any resemblance they bear to chirping crickets, which are also called heimchen; nor can it be derived from *heim* (home), for these elves are not household spirits. He thinks that the proper orthography is *heinchen*, and that the name is related to that of Friend *Hein*, *i. e.*, death, and the Lower Saxon word *heinen*kleed, *i. e.*, death-cloth, shroud.

before Epiphany she saw Bertha pass not far from her, followed by her troop of children. The last of all these was one whose little shroud was all wet, and who seemed exhausted by the weight of a pitcher of water it carried. It tried in vain to cross a fence over which Bertha and the rest had passed; but the mother, instantly recognizing her child, rushed to it and lifted it over. "O how warm are mother's arms," said the little one; "but don't cry so much, mother, for I must gather up every tear in my pitcher. You have made it too full and heavy already. See how it has run over and wet all my shift." The mother cried her fill once more, and then dried her tears.*

It is a very ancient maxim that it is not good to weep for the dead. According to the belief of the Zend branch of the Aryans, all the tears that were shed for the departed flowed into the great river which the soul had to cross before it could reach the Tchinevar Gate (= Tchinevat bridge). The following passage is found in a Hindu dirge: "The souls of the dead do not like to taste the tears let fall by their kindred; weep not therefore."† Every tear,

* Mannhardt, p. 290.

† Schlosser, Universal Hist. Uebersicht der Gesch. d. alt. Welt, I., 45.

according to the Edda, falls as blood upon the ice-cold bosom of the dead. About the year 1154, as we learn from the contemporary writer, Helmold, the banished Bishop Vicelin appeared in a dream to a maiden, and said, "Tell our brother Eppo, who has wept many days for me, that he must cease to weep; for see, I carry his tears in my clothes." And he showed her his garment, which was all wet with tears. A lover's ghost says to his mistress in an old Swedish ballad,

För hvar och en tår som du fäller på jord
Min kista hon blifver så full utaf blod.*

Every time thou weepest, for each tear in that flood
The coffin I am laid in is filled with so much blood.

Sir Walter Scott says in a note to "Redgauntlet," letter xi., "The belief was general throughout Scotland, that the excessive lamentation over the loss of friends disturbed the repose of the dead, and broke even the rest of the grave." It exists also in Ireland.†

In a Servian popular song‡ it is said that a sister wept incessantly over her brother's grave, but her

* *Sorgens magt* (Geijer et Afzelius, I., 31).
† Croker's "Fairy Legends of the South of Ireland."
‡ Talvj i., 274, 1st edit.

tears at last became intolerable to the deceased because he was detained on earth by her excessive grief, and suffered great torment. He cursed her, therefore, and in consequence of his malediction she was changed into a cuckoo, so that she might always lament for herself.

Holda and Bertha, or Perchta as she is called in Southern Germany, are identical with Freyja; and in Aargau another, but nameless, representative of the same supreme goddess is known as a kind and bounteous lady with golden hair, who has her dwelling in the interior of the Schlossberg. A vaulted passage, through whose roof the stars are seen, leads into a hall of apparently boundless extent, glittering with thousands of lights, where many old men sit fast asleep before an iron trough. Before an oaken trough, in another vault well lighted with candles, sit thousands of sleeping youths and maidens. And in a third hall, filled with a milky, palpable light, there is an oaken trough containing a countless multitude of sleeping children. These are the unborn. The white lady of the mansion feeds them with anemones and snowdrops, flowers of wondrous virtue, the stalks of which placed in the mouth, supply for many a day the place of every other kind of food. If there are parents that want a child, the white lady opens the trough with a golden key, takes out a babe and gives it to the midwife. Should it die unbaptised, it comes back to the mountain, and is replaced in the same trough. But if several weeks elapse before its death, or if the white lady takes it back because mankind have not been worthy of it, then it is placed in another trough nearer the heart of the mountain, and fed there with honey, which the bees of the village deposit every time they swarm in the oaks of the Schlossberg.

In Lower Saxony another form of Freyja is called Waldminchen, *i. e.*, Woodnymph. Two hares hold up the train of her robe, and two others carry lights before her. Within her grotto there is a meadow on which infant souls disport themselves, pluck flowers, and weave garlands; and beyond it there is a mill, in which old men and women are ground young, and naughty children are ground into good ones. In England we have often heard of such a mill, but no one seems to know where it is to be found. It is only another form of Frodi's mill (p. 71).

Christian and pagan traditions are curiously mingled in the account which the Tyrolese give of Perchta. They say that she is Claudia Procula, the wife of Pontius Pilate, who sent this message to her husband, "Have nothing to do with that just man." She was the first heathen who became a Christian after the Saviour's death, and therefore she was chosen to be the guardian angel of the souls of children that die unbaptised.*

A Tyrolese peasant, who was returning home at a late hour on one of the "twelve nights," saw Perchta pass by with her unchristened babes. All the little ones had short white smocks, but that of the last one was too long, and the child was continually treading upon it and tripping. "Come here, Draggle-tail," said the peasant, "and I'll tie up your little skirt." The child came to him, and the man having taken off his garter and done as he had promised, "Oh, thank you," said the wee thing; "now I have got a name;" and it vanished, no doubt believing itself as good as baptised.†

A similar story of the ghost of an "unchristened wean," the scene of which is laid at Whittinghame, in Scotland, is recorded by Mr. Robert Chambers. "An unnatural mother having murdered her child at a large tree not far from the village, the ghost of the deceased was afterwards seen, on dark nights, running in a distracted manner between the said tree and the churchyard, and was occasionally heard crying. The villagers believed that it was obliged

* Mannhardt, p. 291. † Ibid.

thus to take the air, and bewail itself, on account of wanting a name—no anonymous person, it seems, being able to got a proper footing in the other world. Nobody durst speak to the unhappy little spirit, from a superstitious dread of dying immediately after; and to all appearance the village of Whittinghame was destined to be haunted till the end of time for want of an exorcist. At length it fortunately happened that a drunkard, one night on reeling home, encountered the spirit, and being fearless in the strength of John Barleycorn, did not hesitate to address it in the same familiar style as if it had been one of his own flesh-and-blood fellow-topers. 'How's a' wi' ye this morning, Short-Hoggers?' cried the courageous villager; when the ghost immediately ran away, joyfully exclaiming—

> Oh, weel's me noo, I've gotten a name;
> They ca' me Short-Hoggers o' Whittinghame!

And since that time it has never been either seen or heard of. The name that the drunkard applied to it denotes that the ghost wore *short stockings without feet*—a probable supposition, considering the long series of years during which it had walked." *

* Robert Chambers, "Pop. Rhymes," p. 115. "My informant," says Mr. Chambers, "received this story, with the rhyme, from the lips of an old woman of Whittinghame, who had *seen* the ghost."

The passage of souls across the sky-water is localised in sundry popular myths concerning Perchta and her little ones. The goddess dwelt of old in the valley of the Saal, but the people of the place and she fell out, and she resolved to quit the neighbourhood. On Perchta's eve the services of the ferryman of Altar were bespoken for that night, and when he came to the water-side he saw there a great stately lady and a throng of weeping children ready to be ferried over. The lady stepped on board, and the children dragged a plough and lots of other implements into the boat, loudly bewailing their departure from that pleasant land. When Perchta landed upon the opposite bank of the river she ordered the ferryman to go back for the rest of her party, and the man could not help obeying, little as he liked the job. When he returned, Perchta pointed to some chips she had cut from the plough, and told him to take them for his pains. He put three of them sulkily in his pocket, threw them on the window-sill when he got home, and went to bed in no very good humour. In the morning his eyes were gladdened with the sight of three bright gold pieces that lay where he had thrown the chips.*

* D. M. p. 253.

Many similar tales are told of the German Zwergs or dwarfs, who are the same race of little people as the elves and fairies that live in the hearts of green hills and mounds in Great Britain and Ireland. Often does it happen that a whole colony of these Zwergs effects an exodus from a German district, because the people have given them some offence, or "have become too knowing for them;" and on these occasions there is always a river to be crossed.

"Many years ago a little underground man came to the ferryman at Gross-Wieden on the Weser, and asked him if he would ply all night long for good pay. Of course the ferryman did not say no; so the little man came again at dusk, stepped on board, and bade him push off. The ferryman did so, and was greatly astonished at seeing that the boat lay as deep in the water as if it had a full freight. Still more astonished was he, after they had reached the other side, when the little man, still remaining in the boat, told him to row back again; and so they plied backwards and forwards continually until morning. At last the passenger stepped ashore, and said to the ferryman, 'You would like to know now who it is you carried over.' The ferryman said he would. 'Then look over my right shoulder,' said the other. The man did so, and beheld thousands upon thousands of underground people, all of whom he had ferried over in the course of the night. The little man then went away, after telling him that the passage-money lay ready for him in the boat; but when the ferryman went to take up his hard-earned money, what did he find lying there but a great heap of horse-dung! 'Ugh!' said he; 'fine pay, truly;' and catching up his baling-pan he pitched it all into the Weser; only a lump of it fell into his boot. After that, when he went home, 'Well,' said his wife, 'you have earned something tidy, I suppose; why, you have been at work the whole night.' He was so cross that he hardly answered her; but when he drew off his big boot, chink! chink! it went all at once, and out tumbled the good solid pistoles one after the other. Away he ran to the Weser to pick up the rest of the dung, but dung it remained just as it was before. However, he had got enough already, even as it was, and he became a rich man, as his descendants are to this day."*

Sometimes the migrating Zwergs cross the river by bridge instead of boat. When they took their departure from the Harz it was agreed upon beforehand that they should go over a narrow bridge at

* Kuhn u. Schwartz, Ndd. p. 242.

Neuhof, where each of them was to drop his toll into a vessel placed for that purpose, but no human inhabitant of the land was to be present. Some inquisitive persons, however, stationed themselves under the bridge, and heard the light tramp of their feet for hours, as if a flock of sheep were passing over.* Grimm has compared this with the words of the keeper of the Gjallar bridge to Hermôdr, when he went down to Niflheimr to see if he could bring back Baldr from the dead: "My bridge sounds more under you alone than under five troops of dead men that rode over it yesterday." In the passage over the river by bridge or ferry Grimm sees a very clear proof of the relationship between this class of elves and the souls of men. Other facts confirm the same view. Some of the many names by which the Zwergs are known in North Germany mean the "ancients" or the "ancestors,"† and mark the analogy between the beings so designated and the Hindu Pitris or Fathers (p. 19); whilst other names—Holden (*i. e.*, good, kind) in Germany; good people, good neighbours, in Ireland and Scotland—

* D. M. p. 794.

† Uellerken, ülleken, ölken, aulken, alken, ôlken. Kuhn und Schwartz, Ndd. p. 485. In East Friesland and Westphalia, countries in which these names are current, old burial mounds are called Aulken-gräben, and the urns found in them are called ôlken-pött.

connect the same elves with the Manes of the Romans.*

We shall meet again with the spirits of the dead when we come to speak of the Wild Hunt and the Furious Host.

* Kuhn, Ndd. p. 485. The meaning of the obsolete adjective *manis* (of which manes is the plural, as holden is of *hold*) is seen in its opposite *immanis*.

CHAPTER V.

THE DRINK OF THE GODS—THE UNIVERSE A TREE—THE ASH—THE BIRTH OF MAN FROM TREES—CREEPING THROUGH HOLES IN TREES, ROCKS, &C.

THE primeval drink of immortality is called soma by the Hindus and haoma by the Zend branch of the Aryans. These names are identical; the plants which yield the juices so called are different, but resemble each other in both having knotty stems. The haoma plant grows like the vine, but its leaves are like those of the jessamine; the Indian soma is now extracted from the *Asclepias acida.* The Iranians, or West Aryans, describe two kinds of haoma, the white and the yellow. The former is a fabulous plant, believed to be the same as the gaokerena of the Zendavesta; the latter, which is used in religious rites, and is extolled for its yellow colour, as soma is in India, grows on mountains, and was known to Plutarch. The Parsees of India send one of their priests from time to time to Kirmân to procure supplies of the plant for sacred uses. The fabulous white haoma, or gaokerena, grows in heaven, near another tree called the "impassive" or "inviolable," which bears the seeds of every kind of vegetable life. Both grow in the Vouru Kasha lake, in which ten fish keep incessant watch upon a lizard,* sent by the evil power Agramainyus (Ahriman) for the destruction of the haoma. The "inviolable" tree is called also the eagle's, or, according to some, the owl's tree. A bird of one kind or the other, but most probably an eagle, sits on its top. When he rises from it, a thousand branches shoot forth; when he perches again, he breaks a thousand branches and makes their seed fall. Another bird, that is constantly beside him, picks them up, and carries them to where Tistar draws water, which he then rains down upon the earth with the seeds it contains. The two trees—the eagle's and the white haoma—appear to have been originally one. The hostile lizard is the serpent or dragon of India, already known to us as the ravisher of the Âpas, and the harvest-spoiler.

Besides the earthly soma the Hindus recognise a heavenly soma or amrita (ambrosia) that drops from

* Lest the reader should think disparagingly of the powers of Ahriman's lizard, we may remind him that "alligator" is a corruption of the Spanish *el lagarto*, the lizard.

the imperishable asvattha or peepul (*Ficus religiosa*), out of which the immortals shaped the heavens and the earth (p. 74). Beneath this mighty tree, which spreads its branches over the third heaven, dwell Yama and the Pitris, and quaff the drink of immortality with the gods. At its foot grow plants of all healing virtue, incorporations of the soma. Two birds sit on its top, one of them eating figs, whilst the other looks on without eating, and others again press out the soma juice from its branches. These details are from the Vedas; later writings have preserved the ancient tradition that the soma-dropping tree bears fruit and seed of every kind in the world. They call the tree Ilpa, and say it grows in Brahma's world, surrounded by lake Âra, beyond the ageless stream, which renews the youth of those who but behold it, or at least of those who bathe in it (p. 33).

The parallelism between the Indian and the Iranian world-tree on the one hand, and the Ash Yggdrasil on the other, is very striking. The latter extends its branches over the whole world, and they reach higher than heaven; beneath them the gods have their chief and holiest abode. The tree has three roots, one striking upwards to heaven, one towards the home of the frost giants, and one towards the under-world. From beneath each root springs a sacred fountain, the Urdhrbrunnr, the Mimirbrunnr, and the Hvergelmir. The first has its name from Urdhr, the Norn or Fate, and beside it the gods and the Norns had their judgment-seat. Every morning the Norns draw water from their fountain and pour it on the branches of the ash; it falls from them into the valleys as honey-dew, and the bees feed upon it. The precious water in the second fountain—Mimir's—is so charged with wisdom and understanding, that only for one draught of it Odin pledged his eye, and laid it as a pawn in the well. An eagle sits on the tree, and a hawk between the eagle's eyes. Four stags roam about the forest-like ash. Through the branches and the roots creep many serpents, chief among which is Nidhöggr. That deadly serpent or dragon lies in Hvergelmir, the infernal fountain, and gnaws at the roots; whilst the squirrel Ratatöskr runs up and down, and tries to stir up strife between Nidhöggr and the eagle. The water of Mimir's well is mead; that of the Urdhrbrunnr falls as honey-dew from the ash; honey is the chief ingredient in mead, and a main one in soma. Soma, mead, and honey are mythically one; and each and all of them are identical with the precious rain that drops from the cloud-tree, and fills the fountains or lakes* in which its roots are dipped.

Yggdrasil, this cloud-tree of the Norseman, was an ash (Norse, *askr*), the tree out of which the gods formed the first man,† who was thence called Askr. The ash was also among the Greeks an image of the clouds, and the mother of men.

Phoroneus (p. 83), in whom in the Peloponnesian legend recognised the fire-bringer and the first man, was the son of the river-god Inachos and the nymph Melia, *i. e.*, the ash. There were many Grecian nymphs of this name, and all of them were daughters either of Oceanos or of Poseidon, sea-gods whose domain was originally the cloud-sea, and whose daughters, one and all, were originally cloud-goddesses. One of these Melian nymphs was carried off by the summer-god Apollo, who killed her brother Kaanthos with his arrows, when the latter, failing to recover his sister, set fire to the sacred grove of the ravisher. The tomb of Kaanthos was to be seen near the fountain of Ismenios, sacred to Ares, who placed a dragon there to keep guard over it. Now,

* The fountain of the Norns is called a lake in the Völuspa; on the other hand, the water in which the white haoma grows is sometimes called the well Ardvisura.

† D. M. p. 527.

Kaanthos, or, with the digamma restored, Kavanthos, answers exactly to the Sanscrit Kavandha or Kabandha, which means a big-bellied cask, a cloud of that form, or a demon dwelling in such a cloud (p. 36). In the Greek legend this demon flings fire (lightning) at his sister's ravisher, who kills him as Indra killed Kabandha. The fountain sacred to Ares, a god of winter and the under-world, and the dragon that guards it, are Hvergelmir, the infernal fountain at the foot of Yggdrasil, with its inmate, the dragon Nidhöggr ; and, to complete the parallel, we have but to replace the Ismenian fountain at the foot of the ash (Melia), where doubtless it lay originally, before the myth had been localised as a legendary tale. A third Melia is the mother of Amykos by Poseidon Genethlios, whose surname marks him emphatically as the god at whose disposal is the moisture that is the cause of all fruitfulness and nourishment. His connection therefore with Melia distinctly represents the Aryan tree, in which are comprised the seeds of all vegetation. A fourth Melia is the daughter of Poseidon and wife of Danaos, a husband and a father that show what was her own nature, for the watering of the arid Argos was ascribed, as a most remarkable feat, to Danaos and his daughters. Lastly, there is a Melia who bears to Silenos a son Pholos, who is one of the Centaurs, a race of cloud-demons (p. 35).

Another indication of the original cloud-nature of these Melian or ash nymphs is seen in the fact that the Dodonæan legends put in place of them, as nurses of Zeus, the Hyades, the nymphs of the constellation that rises at the rainy and stormy season of the year. Furthermore, there is a fragment of the poetess Moiro, preserved by Athenæus, which describes the infant Zeus as being fed in Crete with nectar brought by the eagle; so that whilst the Meliai or nymphs of the ash appear as personifications of an older Grecian world-tree, this story of the eagle shows that the birds also that lodged in the tree were once known to the Greeks.

Phoroneus was not the only man known in Greek story who was born of the ash. According to Hesiod, Jove made the third or brazen race out of ash-trees;* but the same idea must have been entertained in a still more comprehensive form, for another authority † states that the *first* race of men sprang from the Melian nymphs; and Hesychius says in direct terms, "The fruit of the ash: the race of men."

We have not yet exhausted the list of analogies

* "Works and Days," 144. † Schol. on Hesiod Theog. 187.

between Yggdrasil and the Grecian ash, for the latter was, like the former, a honey-dropping tree. Its name implies no less, for *melia*, ash, and *meli*, *melit*, honey, have the same root, *mel*, which is found in many other words with the sense of sweet, pleasing, delightful. There was a positive, as well as a mythic, reason why the Greeks should give the ash a name signifying sweetness, because the *Fraxinus ornus*, a species of ash indigenous in the south of Europe, yields manna from its slit bark. They may also have conceived that honey dropped upon the earth as dew from the heavenly ash, for Theophrastus mentions a kind of honey which fell in that form from the air, and which was therefore called *aeromeli*. We now perceive the reason why the honey-giving nymphs of the ash and the honey-giving bees (melissai) were so assimilated in the minds of the Greeks, that the nurses of the infant Zeus (Meliai) were called by them indifferently Meliai and Melissai. The goat Amaltheia gave him her milk, and the nymphs, his nurses, fed him with their golden produce. Among the ancient Germans that sacred food was the first that was put to the lips of the newborn babe.* So it was also among the Hindus, as appears from a passage in one of their sacred

* D. M. 659.

books:—"The father puts his mouth to the right ear of the newborn babe, and murmurs three times, 'Speech! speech!' Then he gives it a name, 'Thou art Veda;' that is its secret name. Then he mixes clotted milk, honey, and butter, and feeds the babe with it out of pure gold." * The superstitious reverence in which bees are everywhere held makes it probable that a similar practice prevailed among all Indo-European races. It is found in a very surprising shape among one Celtic people:—

"Lightfoot says that in the Highlands of Scotland, at the birth of an infant, the nurse takes a green stick of ash, one end of which she puts into the fire, and while it is burning, receives in a spoon the sap that oozes from the other, which she administers to the child as its first food." †

Amazing toughness of popular tradition! Some thousands of years ago the ancestors of this Highland nurse had known the *Fraxinus ornus* in Arya, or on their long journey thence through Persia, Asia Minor, and the South of Europe, and they had given its honey-like juice, as divine food, to their children; and now their descendant, imitating their practice in

* Çatap. brâhm. Weber, 1108, quoted by Kuhn.

† "Sylvan Sketches," by the author of "The Flora Domestica." London: 1825. p. 24.

the cold North, but totally ignorant of its true meaning, puts the nauseous sap of her native ash into the mouth of her hapless charge, because her mother and her grandmother, and her grandmother's grandmother had done the same thing before her.

"The reason," we are told by a modern native authority, "for giving ash-sap to newborn children in the Highlands of Scotland, is, first, because it acts as a powerful astringent; * and, secondly, because the ash, in common with the rowan, is supposed to possess the property of resisting the attacks of witches, fairies, and other imps of darkness. Without some precaution of this kind they would change the child, or possibly steal it away altogether. The herd boys in the district of Buchan, in Aberdeenshire, always prefer a herding stick of ash to any other wood, as in throwing at their cattle it is *sure* not to strike on a vital part, and so kill or injure the animal as a stick of any other kind of wood might do:

Rowan, ash, and red thread
Keep the devils frae their speed.

"It is a common practice with the housewives in the same district to tie a piece of red worsted thread

* This is evidently not the reason why the practice was first adopted, but an excuse, and a very bad one, for its continuance.

round their cows' tails previous to turning them out to grass for the first time in the spring. It secures their cattle, they say, from an evil eye, from being elfshot by fairies," &c.*

The sap of the ash, tapped on certain days in spring, is drunk in Germany as a remedy for the bites of serpents; and the Czecks in Bohemia eat honey (of which ash-sap is the equivalent) fasting, on Holy Thursday, thinking that it will protect them throughout the year against the usual effects of such accidents, as well as against poisons in general. They also give their cattle pieces of bread and honey for the same purpose, and throw some before sunrise into the wells and fountains, in order that the water may remain pure and clear, and free from frogs and other vermin.† In Cornwall, venomous reptiles are never known to rest under the shadow of an ash, and a single blow from an ash stick is instant death to an adder. Struck by a bough of any other tree, the reptile is said to retain marks of life until the sun goes down.‡

According to Pliny, a serpent will rather leap into fire than into the shadow of an ash-tree. When it is

* "Choice Notes," p. 24. Red thread is typical of lightning.

† Reinsberg-Düringsfeld, p. 120.

‡ "Choice Notes," p. 88.

touched with an ash rod, it lies as if dead; and out of a circle drawn round it while it sleeps, with such an instrument, the creature cannot escape.* This inherent virtue of the ash was known also to the Greeks, as appears from a fragment of Nicander. A contributor to Wolf's Journal states that the wood of the tree, cut at certain holy seasons, is reputed to be incorruptible and to heal wounds—a property due, no doubt, to the amrita with which it is impregnated. Its character as an embodiment of fire, of which we have already had so many evidences, is manifested in a remarkable Swedish legend, quoted by Grimm,† which tells that some seafaring people received an ash-tree from a blind giant, with instructions to set it upon the altar of a church he wished to destroy. Instead of doing as he bade them, they placed the ash on the mound over a grave, which instantly burst into bright flames. The grave, it may be presumed, was that of an unholy being of the old pagan times. Plot says in his History of Staffordshire, "The common people believe, that 'tis very dangerous to break a bough from the ash, to this very day." The sacredness of the tree is further

* So says likewise a piece of Devonshire folklore. "Quarterly Rev." July, 1863, p. 226.

† D. M. 907.

shown by the fact, recently discovered, that courts were held under it at Froidnow in Schweiz, and Buochs in Unterwalden. Grimm has expressed his surprise at nowhere finding any traces of a practice which seemed likely to have been universal among the Germans, since the gods sat in judgment under the ash Yggdrasil. The supposition that the hazel, which stands in close mythical relationship to the ash, almost entirely supplanted the latter in judicial usages, affords a probable explanation of the anomaly.

There are facts tending strongly to the conclusion, though they may not suffice to place it beyond all question, that a world-wide tree, with its appurtenances was a conception known to the Romans in early times. All the qualities belonging to a bird connected with such a tree are exhibited, explicitly or by implication, in the history of their Picus; and the descent of men from trees appears to have been a popular belief in Italy as well as in Greece.

> Hæc nemora indigenæ Fauni Nymphæque tenebant
> Gensque virum truncis et duro robore nata.
>
> Æn. viii., 314.

> These woods were first the seat of sylvan powers,
> Of nymphs and fauns, and savage men, who took
> Their birth from trunks of trees and stubborn oak.
>
> Dryden.

Quippe aliter tunc orbe novo cœloque recenti
Vivebant homines, qui rupto robore nati,
Compositive luto, nullos habuere parentes.

Juvenal, Sat. vi., 11.

For when the world was new, the race that broke,
Unfathered, from the soil or opening oak,
Lived most unlike the men of later times.

Gifford.

In another passage Virgil speaks of a sacred tree, the æsculus, in a manner which Grimm has noticed as strikingly suggestive of Yggdrasil :—

Æsculus in primis, quæ quantum vortice ad auras
Ætherias, tantum radice in tartara tendit.

Georg. ii., 291.

Jove's own tree,
High as his topmost boughs to heaven ascend,
So low his roots to hell's dominions tend.

Dryden.

Evidently these lines have a mythical import. The æsculus was a species of oak sacred to Jove; and in Greece the oak, as well as the ash, was accounted a tree from which men had sprung. The disguised hero of the Odyssey is asked to state his pedigree, since he must needs have one, "for," says the interrogator, "belike you are not come of the oak told of in old times, nor of the rock." The "ruminal fig-tree" seems to play a part in the legend of the foundation of Rome like that attributed to the oak by the Greeks and to the ash by the Germans. Picus also has his share in the legend, for he helped the she-wolf to nourish the twins; and though Ovid does not tell us what kind of aliment he gave them, we may venture to surmise that he fed them with the mead which he himself loved so well, in like manner as the eagle in Crete fed the infant Jove with nectar, the equivalent of mead.

The mythic characteristics of the ash help to explain some English superstitions, the true meaning of which appears to have been generally misunderstood. White says in his "Natural History of Selborne," "At the south corner of the area near the church there stood about twenty years ago a very old grotesque hollow pollard ash, which for ages had been looked on with no small veneration as a shrew-ash. Now a shrew-ash is an ash whose twigs or branches, when gently applied to the limbs of cattle, will immediately relieve the pains which a beast suffers from the running of a shrew-mouse over the part affected. For it is supposed that a shrew-mouse is of so baneful and deleterious a nature, that wherever it creeps over a beast, be it horse, cow, or sheep, the suffering animal is afflicted with cruel anguish, and threatened with the loss of the use of the limb. Against this accident, to which they were continually liable, our provident forefathers always kept a shrew-ash at hand, which, when once medicated, would maintain its virtue for ever. A shrew-ash was made thus: Into the body a deep hole was bored with an auger, and a poor devoted shrew-mouse was thrust in alive, and plugged in, no doubt with several quaint incantations long since forgotten. As the ceremonies necessary for such a consecration are no longer understood, all succession is at an end, and no such tree is known to subsist in the manor or hundred. As to that on the area, 'the late vicar stubbed and burned it,' when he was waywarden, regardless of the remonstrances of the bystanders, who interceded in vain for its preservation."

It is manifest that this practice was founded principally upon the supposed virtue inherent in the ash of neutralising every kind of venom. It is a tree that will tolerate nothing poisonous within its shadow, and wounds are cured with its sap. As to the insertion of the shrew-mouse within it, this may very probably have been done in accordance with a medical doctrine of great antiquity—the doctrine of sympathy. The spear of Achilles healed with one end of its ashen shaft the wound it had made with the other; it was a common practice, so common as to have given rise to a well-known proverb, to mix some hairs of a dog with the salve laid on the part he had bitten; and there have been famous leeches who cured sword wounds by applying their remedies, not to the patient, but to the weapon. "Fairies," says Grose, "sometimes shoot at cattle with arrows headed with flint stones; these are often found and are called elfshots. In order to effect the cure of an animal so injured, it is to be touched with one of those elfshots, or to be made drink the water in which one has been dipped." The venom of the shrew-mouse, neutralised by the sap of the ash, would co-operate with it in curing the injured limb to which the twigs were applied. A correspondent sent the following scrap from a newspaper to Notes and Queries, vol. v., p. 581:—"At Oldham, last week, a woman summoned the owner of a dog that had bitten her. She said she should not have adopted this course had the owner of the animal given her some of its hair, to ensure her against any evil consequences from the bite."

There stood in the village of Selborne in Gilbert White's time "a row of pollard ashes, which," he says, "by the seams and long circatrices down their sides, manifestly show that in former times they have been cleft asunder. These trees, when young and flexible, were severed and held open by wedges, while ruptured children, stripped naked, were pushed through the apertures, under a persuasion that by such a process the poor babies would be cured of their infirmity. As soon as the operation was over, the tree, in the suffering part, was plastered with loam and carefully swathed up. If the part coalesced and soldered together, as usually fell out where the feat was performed with any adroitness at all, the party was cured; but where the cleft continued to gape, the operation, it was supposed, would prove ineffectual. We have several persons now living in the village, who in their childhood were supposed to be healed by this superstitious ceremony, derived down perhaps from our Saxon ancestors, who practised it before their conversion to Christianity."

This mode of cure has not yet gone quite out of use in England, so far as the ash is concerned,* and it is still a practice much in vogue in the southern counties, when children are suffering from hooping-cough and some other complaints, to make them pass through the loop formed by a bramble which has taken root at both ends. This custom, and that of passing children and cattle through perforated

* Children are still passed through a split ash for the cure of hernia, in Cornwall. "Choice Notes," p. 88.

earth or rocks, or through natural or artificial openings in trees, especially the ash and the oak, is common to most European countries. In our own it appears to have been no unusual thing in Saxon times for women who were troubled with crying brats to dig a hole in the ground and make a tunnel through which they dragged the poor little squallers. There was a bushy oak near Wittstock in Altmark, the branches of which had grown together again at some distance from the stem, leaving open spaces between them. Whoever crept through these spaces was freed from his malady whatever it might be, and many crutches lay about, which had been thrown away by visitors to the tree who no longer needed them.* Close to the road passing through the forest of Süllingswald, there was an aged oak with a hole shaped like the eye of a needle in its huge stem. This gave the foresters and charcoal burners a welcome opportunity for "hanselling" strangers who passed that way, that is to say, forcing them to pay a small sum if they did not wish to be dragged through the needle's eye. This custom of hanselling travellers kept its ground after the belief in the healing virtue of the tree had died out.

"This creeping through oak-cleft, earth or stone,"

* D. M. 1119.

says Grimm, "seems a transference of the malady or the bewitchment to the genius of the tree or the earth." But this is not a satisfactory explanation; for though such a mode of shifting off bodily disorders from men to trees is well known, nothing of the kind appears to have been intended in the case in question. For the cure of hernia, for instance, it was thought essential that the cleft tree should become whole again. Moreover, Grimm's theory is manifestly untenable with reference to a cure-working hole in a church wall, such as that of Stappenbeck, to which "there was formerly a great resort of sick people, for whenever one of them crept through it he was instantly cured. But it lost its virtue at last when sick animals were made to pass through it, and then it was stopped up."* The best explanation which has been given of this superstition is that proposed by Liebrecht,† who thinks that the whole proceeding was originally designed to symbolise the new birth of the patient, who, coming naked again into the world, left all his former maladies behind him. It appears indeed to be a close copy of a Hindu religious usage, and probably had its origin, like the latter, in times previous to the dispersion of the Aryans.

* Kuhn u. Schwartz, Ndd. p. 129. † Ger. Tilb. p. 170.

"For the purpose of regeneration," says Coleman, "it is directed to make an image of pure gold, of the female power of nature, in the shape either of a woman or of a cow. In this statue the person to be regenerated is enclosed and dragged through the usual channel. As a statue of pure gold and proper dimensions would be too expensive, it is sufficient to to make an image of the sacred yoni, through which the person to be regenerated is to pass. . . . . . Perforated rocks are considered as emblems of the yoni, through which pilgrims and others pass for the purpose of being regenerated. The utmost faith is placed in this sin-expelling transit." *

The Hindu custom symbolises the new birth of the soul, the European that of the body. The cloud, the matrix of the vital spark, is represented in the one by the figure of the woman or the cow, in the other by the tree, and in both by the rock.

* Coleman, "Hindu Mythology," 151, 175.

CHAPTER VI.

THE ROWAN OR MOUNTAIN ASH—THE DIVINING ROD—THE MANDRAKE—THE SPRINGWORT—FORGET-ME-NOT—HAZEL—THORN—MISTLETOE.

Of the many ways in which the Vedas recount the descent of the heavenly soma to earth, one is to the following effect. When gods and men were pining for the precious beverage, the falcon undertook to steal it from the demons who kept it shut up in the rock (cloud). The attempt was successful, but as the falcon was flying off with its prize, it was grazed by an arrow shot after it by one of the demons, and lost a claw and a feather. They fell to the earth and struck root there, the claw becoming a species of thorn, and the feather a palasa tree, otherwise called parna, which has a red sap and scarlet blossoms. Trees owning such an origin could not fail to possess many supernatural properties, the more so as the bird from which the claw and the feather had dropped was a transformed god—some hymnists say Indra, others say Agni. Sprung from a god of the lightning, the trees were themselves divine, and they were incorporations not only of the heavenly fire, but also of the soma with which the claw and the feather were impregnated. The virtues which distinguish them exist in no less degree in many of their European representatives, such as the black and white thorn, rowan or mountain ash, hasel, fern, &c.

The palasa was much employed by the Hindus in religious ceremonies, and particularly in one which has descended to the dairy farms of Germany and Sweden, where it is retained to this day with surprisingly little change.

The milk used in the sacrifice which it was customary to offer in the new moon (the season of increase) on behalf of the Hindu master of a herd, was only to be taken from cows that were still suckling their calves. That there might be enough of it, therefore, it was necessary that the calves should be separated from their dams and driven to pasture. To this end the officiating priest chose on the night of the new moon, or on that preceding it, a palasa or sami rod which grew on the north-east, north, or east side of the tree, and he cut it off saying, "For strength cut I thee." Then having stripped off its leaves with the words, "For sap (strip I) thee," and having placed together at least six calves with their dams, he struck each of the calves with the rod and drove them out saying, "Ye are winds." This done, he touched the cows, one for all, with the rod, and blessed them, bidding them be good milkers, good breeders, safe from sickness and robbers, and abidingly numerous in the possession of the master for whom the sacrifice was offered. Lastly, he stuck up the rod in front or eastward of one of the two places of the holy fire (the sacrificial and the domestic), and bade it protect the cattle of the same person. A Sanscrit commentator on this rite says that the calf is struck with the parna-rod in order that the soma contained in the latter may pass into the former and enrich its udder. Another states that the calves which have been commended to the protection of the rod will, in consequence thereof, be sure to come safely home from their pasture in the evening—a plain proof that the rod was regarded not as a thing but as a person; it was the incorporation of a god who was able from a distance to protect the young cattle from robbers and wild beasts.

Kuhn has compared with this ancient Hindu ceremony the custom of "quickening" the calves, as it is observed in the county of Mark in Westphalia.

On the first of May the herdsman gets out of bed

before dawn, and goes to that part of the hill on which the sun first shines. There he chooses that sapling quicken tree (rowan, mountain ash) on which the first rays fall, and fells it. This must be done at one stroke, otherwise it is a bad sign. He takes the sapling to the farm-yard, where the people of the house and the neighbours assemble, and the yearling heifer which is to be quickened is led on to the mixen. There the herdsman strikes it with a branch of the quicken tree, first on the loins, then on the haunches, repeating at each stroke a verse, in which he prays that, as sap comes into the birch and beech, and the leaf comes upon the oak, so may milk fill the young cow's udder. Lastly, he strikes the heifer on the udder and gives her a name. After this, having been regaled with eggs, he adorns the sapling with the shells, buttercups, &c., and plants it in front of the cow-house or over the door.*

Throughout Dalsland, in Sweden, the first "mid-day driving" of the year is celebrated as follows, a day or two before or after Ascension Day, or Holy Thursday, formerly the high festival of Thor. When the cattle have been driven out to grass, a garland of flowers is set upon one of the posts of the nearest gate through which they will have to return home.

* Woeste, Volksüberlieferungen der grafschaft Mark, p. 25.

Meanwhile the herdsman trims their horns and tricks them out as gaily as he can with flowers. At noon, when he returns with the herd, that they may be milked for the first time in the year at that hour, he takes the garland off the gate post, and setting it on the top of a rowan sapling, which he carries erect in both hands, he marches before the herd to the homestead, and plants the rowan on the haystack, where *it remains during the whole grazing season.* The bells are then hung for the first time on the cows, and if there be any among them that have not yet got a name, the herdsman gives them one as he strikes them three times on the back with a rowan branch. The cows are fed at noon with the choicest fodder, and the people of the house take their dinner at the entrance of the cattle-yard.

In this ceremony, says Kuhn, the festive adornment of the cattle, the choice fodder set before them, the assemblage of the whole household, and their meal taken near the kine, are evidently relics of an old sacrificial feast in which the guardian god had his share, along with his votaries, in the fresh-drawn milk. The holding of the feast on the day on which the thrice-a-day milking began, shows how important an event that was for an ancient pastoral people. That it occurred of old in May is plain from the Anglo-Saxon name of the month. May was called Thrimilci, says Bede, because in that month the cows were milked thrice a day.

These German and Swedish customs reveal the cause of that reputation for magical powers which the rowan tree or mountain ash has enjoyed from time immemorial in all parts of our own country as well as on the continent. Like its congener the ash, and the palasa and sami of India, it is an embodiment of soma and lightning. It is observed to be frequent in the neighbourhood of what are commonly called druidical circles. A rowan stood in every churchyard in Wales, as the yew did in England; and on a certain day of the year every person wore a cross of the wood. It averted fascination and evil spirits.* For that reason "many," says Plot, "are very careful to have a walking staff of it, and will stick the boughs of it about their beds."† In Cornwall, where it is called "care," it "has still great repute among our countryfolk in the curing of ills arising from supernatural as well as ordinary causes. It is dreaded by evil spirits; it renders null the spells of the witch, and has many other wonderful properties. The countryman will

* Evelyn, "Silva," ch. xvi.

† "Nat. Hist. of Staffordshire," ch. vi., § 52.

carry for years a piece of the wood in his pocket as a charm against *ill wish,* or as a remedy for his rheumatism. If his cow is out of health, and he suspects her to be 'overlooked'—i.e., smitten by an 'evil eye'—away he runs to the nearest wood, and brings home bunches of care, which he suspends over her stall, and wreathes round her horns; after which he considers her safe."* In Scotland "the dairymaid will not forget to drive the cattle to the shealing or summer pastures with a rod of the rowan tree, which she carefully lays up over the door of the sheal-boothy or summer house, and drives them home again with the same."†

"At Modrufell, on the north coast of Iceland, is, or was, a large rowan, always on Christmas-eve stuck full of torches, which no wind could possibly extinguish; and one of the Orkneys possessed a still more mysterious tree, with which the fate of the islands was bound up, since if a leaf was carried away they would pass to some foreign lord."‡

Among the many English names of the mountain ash, are witchen tree, witch elm, witch hazel, witch wood; quicken tree, quick beam (*quick*=alive, *beam*

* "Choice Notes," p. 88.

† Dr. George Johnston, "Flora of Berwick-upon-Tweed," p. 110.

‡ "Quart. Rev.," July, 1863, p. 243.

=German *baum*, tree); roan tree, roun tree, rowan. These last three synonymes are from the Norse tongues, and denote, as Grimm conjectures, the runic or mysterious and magic character of the tree.

The red berries of the mountain ash correspond in colour with the blossoms and the sap of the Indian palasa, and they also mark the European tree as appropriate to Thor, the German fire god. It was called Thor's refuge in the North, because he was said to have clung to it when swept away by the river Vimur. Kuhn shows it to be probable that under the figure of the river we are to understand the clouds, and that the legend originally represented Thor as taking refuge, not upon the tree, but actually within it, like Agni when he hid himself in the heart of the asvattha or peepul tree. That tree has red berries like those of the mountain ash, and the latter resembles the sami in the pinnate form of its leaves, which call to mind the feather shot from the soma-bringing falcon. The leaves of the palasa are not pinnate, but the tree is remarkable for the luxuriant abundance of its foliage, a characteristic which belongs also to the mountain ash. On the whole, then, it is clear that not without manifest reason did the mountain ash acquire its high European renown.

But we can connect the rowan still more closely with a tree venerated in India as a soma-bearer.

"Near Boitpoor, in Upper India," says Bishop Heber, "I passed a fine tree of the mimosa, with leaves at a little distance so much resembling those of the mountain ash, that I was for a moment deceived, and asked if it did not bring fruit? They answered no; but that it was a very noble tree, being called the imperial tree, for its excellent properties; that it slept all night, and awakened and was alive all day, withdrawing its leaves if any one attempted to touch them. Above all, however, it was useful as a preservative against magic. A sprig worn in the turban, or suspended over the bed, was a perfect security against all spells, evil eye, &c.; insomuch that the most formidable wizard would not, if he could help it, approach its shade. One indeed, they said, who was very renowned for his power (like Lorinite, in the Kehama) of killing plants and drying up their sap with a look, had come to this very tree and gazed on it intently; but, said the old man, who told me this with an air of triumph, look as he might, he could do the tree no harm. I was amazed and surprised to find the superstition which in England and Scotland attaches to the rowan tree, here applied to a tree of nearly similar form. What nation has in this case been the imitator? Or from what common centre are these common notions derived?"

This imperial tree was most probably the *Mimosa catechu;* but if not, it was at all events of the same genus, and therefore, in a mythical point of view, closely allied to or even identical with it. Now the *Mimosa catechu* was the tree which sprang from the claw lost by the soma-robbing falcon,* along with the feather which became a palasa or parna tree (p. 159). Its younger branches have straight thorns, which afterwards become hooked, and very much resemble a bird's claw.

The asvattha or peepul is often propagated by seeds dropped by apes or birds on housetops or on other trees; and we have seen (p. 23) that a peculiar virtue was ascribed to an asvattha which had come by that means to grow upon a sami. The same superior excellence is attributed at this day in Sweden and Norway to the *flögrönn,* or fly-rowan, which grows upon another tree, or in the cleft of a rock, where the seed has been dropped by a bird—perhaps by a god disguised in that form. "Anybody who ventures out in those countries at night, unprovided with flögrönn to *chew,* must look sharp

* Kuhn, Herab. p. 236.

lest he be robbed of his wits or left unable to stir from the spot."* Manifestly the fly-rowan is chewed for sake of its juice, which must be a most potent antidote to witchcraft. The Swedish author last quoted says, "The belief is almost as general in the efficacy of the flögrönn as a divining rod, for the discovery of hidden treasures, but people can hardly tell nowadays how the matter must be set about. The art is explained, however, as follows, in a manuscript of the beginning of the seventeenth century.

"When you find in the wood or elsewhere, on old walls or on high hills or rocks, a rowan which has grown out of a berry let fall from a bird's bill, you must go at twilight in the evening of the third day after our Lady's day, and either uproot or break off the said rod or tree; but you must take care that neither iron nor steel come nigh it, and that it do not fall to the ground on the way home. Then place the rod under the roof, at a spot under which you have laid sundry metals, and in a short time you will see with astonishment how the rod gradually bends under the roof towards the metals. When the rod has remained fourteen days or more in the same place, you take a knife or an awl which has been stroked with a magnet, and previously stuck through

* Dybeck's Runa, 1845, p. 62.

a great Frö-groda (?), slit the bark on all sides, and pour or drop in cock's blood, especially such as is drawn from the comb of a cock of one colour; and when this blood has dried, the rod is ready, and gives manifest proof of the efficacy of its wondrous nature."

In England and in France the divining rod is known chiefly for its alleged power of discovering mines, buried treasure, and hidden springs of water, and it is named accordingly; but this is a modern and too limited view of its wondrous efficacy, the boundless range of which is duly signified by the German name *wish-rod* (wünschelruthe). That name implies a rod which endows its possessor with all earthly blessings, health, wealth, fortune, favour —with everything, in short, that heart can *wish*. In the Niebelungen Lied it is called, like the bounteous god Odin, simply "wish." "The wish lay thereunder, a rod of gold." In this larger sense the divining or wish-rod corresponds very closely with the Hindu chark, and also with the mandrake.

The mandrake is a root, in shape resembling a human being, and is renowned for its power of bringing wealth and other good things to its possessor. A letter is extant* which was written by a burgher of

* Keysler, Antiqu. Septempt., p. 507.

Leipsic to his brother in 1575, condoling with the latter for the heavy losses he had sustained: his cattle had died, his store of corn and other provisions had been spoiled, his business had all gone wrong and there was great discord in consequence between him and his wife. The writer, therefore, sends him a mandrake or earth-mannikin, because if he keeps it in his house, things will take quite a different turn with him. When he receives it he is to let it rest for three days, and then bathe it in warm water. He is to sprinkle his cattle and the threshold of his house with the water of the bath, and all will go better with him. Be it known to him, moreover, that the bath is singularly good in the case of a woman in childbed; if she cannot be delivered, let her take a spoonful of the water, and she will bring forth with joy and thankfulness. Finally, should he have to go before the court or the council, he has only to stick the mannikin under his right arm, and then he will have judgment in his favour, be his cause right or wrong.

From this letter, and other evidence to the same effect, it is plain that the mandrake, as well as the wish-rod, was credited with the power of conferring good fortune in general, the only apparent difference between the two being that a human form was invariably attributed to the one but not to the other. There is good reason however, according to Dr. Kuhn, to think that anciently they were both alike in this respect. Even now the likeness of a puppet or doll is sometimes given to the wish-rod, it is wrapped in swaddling clothes, a head is stuck upon it, and a baptism is smuggled for it by furtively attaching the puppet to the body of a child that is about to be christened.* In the Oberpfalz, immediately after the wish-rod is cut, it is baptised and given a name, and three signs of the cross are made over it with the hand.† But this is not all. In every instance the divining or wish-rod has a forked end. This is an essential point, as all authorities agree in declaring. Now a forked rod (or "a forked radish") is the simplest possible image of the human figure.

The inference drawn by Dr. Kuhn from all this is that, as the mandrake was conceived to be a superhuman being—god or demigod—so the equally manlike wish-rod was originally understood to be an incorporate god—the god of the lightning, as we have seen with regard to the rowan rod, and as Dr. Kuhn has likewise proved in the instances of the hazel

* Pröhle, Harzbilder, 79.

† Schönwerth, Oberpfälzische Sagen, iii., 216.

and the thorn, the trees from which the wish-rod was most commonly taken. A comparison with ancient Hindu usages fully confirms the truth of this conclusion. The human form is expressly attributed in the Rig Veda and other Sanscrit books to the pieces of asvattha wood used for kindling sacred fire—so many inches for the head and neck, so many for the upper and lower parts of the trunk, the thighs and legs respectively—and the operator is warned to be very careful where he churns, for perdition will issue from most parts of the arani, whereas he who churns in the right spot will obtain fruition of all his wishes; he will gain wealth, cattle, sons, heaven, long life, love, and good fortune. Evidently the tabular part or block of the chark is equivalent to the wish-rod, and the reason of this is that they are both embodiments of the lightning.

So also was the caduceus, or Hermes' rod, which Grimm and all the best authorities after him have identified with the wish-rod; and so were all the plants which popular tradition has gifted with similar virtues. Germany is inexhaustible in legends of the luckflower and the springwort, before either of which hidden doors and rocks fly open, and give admission to vast treasures concealed in the hearts of mountains. Rock, mountain, and cloud are synonymous in all Indo-European mythologies; the luckflower or keyflower is the lightning that opens the clouds, and the treasures it discloses are that primal wealth of the pastoral Aryan, the rain that refreshes the thirsty earth and the sunshine that comes after the tempest. The intimate connection between lightning and human life and happiness may not be very obvious to all minds at the present day, but in primæval times it was a palpable fact intuitively understood, and out of it grew the conception of the magic rod that fulfilled all wishes. In like manner the epic poetry of the Hindus evoked out of the waters of the cloud sea the marvellous cow Kâmaduh, from which all things that could be desired might be milked. It is clear that the supposed attraction of the divining-rod for metals was also a product of the same primitive mode of thought, for "the golden sunbeams" is a current expression in all Indo-European languages that possess an ancient literature.

The adventure with the luckflower is generally described in this way. The fortunate discoverer of the entrance into the treasury-hall, in the heart of the mountain, is a man who has happened to find a beautiful flower, in most instances a blue one, which he sticks in his hat. The mountain suddenly opens to admit him; he enters it, and a white lady bids him help himself freely from the heaps of gold coin he sees before him. He stuffs his pockets full, and is hastening away, when she calls after him, "Forget not the best!" He thinks, as he feels his crammed pockets, that he has nothing to reproach himself with in that respect, and he quite forgets his hat, which he had dropped, with the blue flower stuck upon it. As he hurries out through the doorway the iron door shuts suddenly behind him with a crash of thunder, and cuts off his right heel. The mountain side has resumed its old impenetrable appearance, and the entrance to the golden hall can never be found again.*

It was from stories like this that the little blue flower, Forget-me-not, received its name, which at first was significant of its magic virtue, but afterwards acquired a sentimental meaning.†

The springwort is procured by plugging up the hole in a tree in which a green or black woodpecker has its nest with young ones in it. As soon as the bird is aware of what has been done, it flies off in quest of a wondrous plant, which men might look for in vain, and returning with it in its bill, holds it before the plug, which immediately shoots out

* D. M. 923. † Ibid.

from the tree as if driven by the most violent force. But if one conceals himself before the woodpecker's return, and scares it when it approaches, the bird will let the root fall; or a white or red cloth may be spread below the nest, and the bird will drop the root upon the cloth after it has served its own turn.* This is the German account of the matter, and Pliny tells the same tale, with this notable addition, that the plug is driven out from the tree with an explosion,† caused, as we may safely conclude, by the thunder contained in the plant which is applied to it by a bird already known to us as a lightning-bearer. In the county of Mark, it is believed that the woodpecker drops the springwort upon a red cloth for the purpose of burning it, lest it should fall into anybody's hands, for it mistakes the cloth for a fire.‡ In Swabia, they say the hoopoe brings the springwort, and lets it fall into water or fire to destroy it. To obtain it, therefore, one must have in readiness a pan of water, or kindle a fire, or spread out a red cloth or garment, on which the bird will let the plant

* D. M. 925. Kuhn und Schwartz, Ndd., p. 450.

† Adactos cavernis eorum a pastore cuneos, admotu quodam ab his herba, elabi creditur vulgo. Trebius auctor est, clavum cuneum ve adactum quanta libeat vi arbori, in qua nidum habeat, statim exsilire cum crepitu arboris, cum insederit clavo aut cuneo.—Plin. x., 18.

‡ Woeste, p. 44.

fall, believing it to be a fire.* Evidently the original notion was, that the bird must return the plant to the element from which it springs, that being either the water of the clouds, or the lightning-fire enclosed therein.

The connection between the springwort and the lightning is also expressed in another piece of folk-lore current in the Oberpfalz and in Swabia. It is there said that when the plant is buried in the ground at the summit of a mountain, it draws down the lightning and divides the storm, making it pass off to right and left.

In Normandy, as previously mentioned (p. 102), a story is told of the swallow which has some analogy to that of the woodpecker or hoopoe and the spring-wort. "The swallow knows how to find on the sea-shore a stone that has the marvellous power of restoring sight to the blind. The villagers tell of a sure means of obtaining possession of this stone. You must put out the eyes of one of the swallow's young, whereupon the mother-bird will immediately go in quest of the stone. When she has found it and applied it effectually, she is careful to hide her talisman where it can never be discovered. But if one has taken the precaution to spread a piece of

* Meier, Schwäb. Sagen, No. 265.

scarlet stuff below the nest, the swallow will drop the stone upon it, for, deceived by the colour, she will believe she is dropping it into fire."*

We have not yet adequate data for a full explanation of this curious tradition, but the celestial origin of the talismanic stone can hardly be questioned.

The springwort is generally believed to be an unknown species of plant, and therefore hard to find; but some accounts specify known plants, and among these Grimm mentions the *Euphorbia lathyris*, called by the Italians sferracavallo, because it acts so strongly on metals that horses, if they tread on it, lose their shoes. Now, there is a species of euphorbia, the Sanscrit name of which signifies thunderbolt-thorn, and several others which are all called thunderbolt-wood in the same language.† A story of the Ilsenstein, within which lives an enchanted princess, is related by Kuhn in his North German Legends, and appears to him to throw additional light on the nature of the wishing-rod as well as of the springwort. The story is that "a shepherd, who was driving his flock over the Ilsenstein, having stopped to rest, leaning on his staff, the mountain suddenly opened, for there was a springwort in his staff with-

* Amélie Bosquet, p. 217.

† Vajrakantaka, vajradru, vajradruma.—Wilson, s. v.

out his knowing it, and the princess stood before him. She bade him follow her, and when he was inside the mountain, she told him to take as much gold as he pleased. The shepherd filled all his pockets, and was going away, when the princess called after him, 'Forget not the best.' So, thinking she meant that he had not taken enough, he filled his hat also; but what she meant was his staff, with the springwort, which he had laid against the wall as soon as he stepped in. But now, just as he was going out at the opening, the rock suddenly slammed together and cut him in two." Now, it appears to Kuhn that since shepherds' sticks, as well as wishing-rods, are most commonly cut from the blackthorn or the hazel, it was probably so with the shepherd's staff in this instance; and thus far the story tends to show that the springwort and the wishing-rod are identical.

The hazel was sacred to Thor, as its reddish leaves indicate, and like another of his trees, the rowan, it was regarded as an actual embodiment of the lightning.* Hence the almost universal belief that it is never struck by the thunderbolt, and that it protects from both heavenly and earthly fire.† In some parts of France the people dance three times round the

* Mannhardt, p. 193. † Vernaleken, Alpensage, p. 416.

bonfires on St. John's day with branches of hazel in their hands, and peasant proprietors wave a hazel branch through the flame, and hang it up before the door of their cattle stall.* In the Oberpfalz, hazel twigs are stuck in the window frames during a tempest. Serpents cannot approach the tree,† and in Sweden it is believed that the touch of a hazel-rod deprives them of their venom.‡ In a popular story given by Panzer, the hero cuts off the seven heads of a dragon with a hazel-rod.§ The mythic dignity of the hazel is evidenced by two facts mentioned by Grimm: it was a law of the Ostrogoths that anybody might hew down what trees he pleased in the common wood, except oaks and hazels; those trees had peace, *i. e.*, they were not to be felled;‖

* Mannhardt, p. 201.

† Menzel, Odhin, p. 155.

‡ Dybeck, Runa, 1848, p. 38.

§ Panzer, Beitr., i., 193.

‖ "Reference is supposed to be made to some old law in the following :—

'The oak, the ash, the elm tree,
They are hanging a' three.'

That is, it was a capital crime to mutilate these trees.

"Another version of the rhyme runs thus :—

'The oak, the ash, the elm tree,
Hang a man for a' three,
And ae branch will set him free.' "

Robert Chambers, "Popular Rhymes."

The coincidence is worth noting, although it is quite as possible that the Scotch law or practice was dictated by motives of thrift as by mythical considerations.

and it is a common saying in modern Germany, that the oak and the hazel dislike each other, and cannot agree together any more than the haw and the sloe (whitethorn and blackthorn). This looks as if the oak and the hazel were rivals for supremacy, like those old competitors for kingship, the eagle and the wren, and upon similar grounds.

As for the white and the black thorn, theirs was a family quarrel, most probably provoked in the first instance by the circumstance of their being both of them European representatives of the sacred thorn-tree of India, the *Mimosa catechu* (p. 167), and endowed like it with supernatural properties. The wood of the thorn (ramnos) was used by the Greeks for the drilling-stick of their pyreia, and it was held by them to be prophylactic against magic, as the whitethorn was by the Romans,* among whom it was used for marriage torches. Both trees have enjoyed a similar repute among the German nations, and wishing-rods have been made of the white as well as of the black thorn.† In Germany the Easter fire was anciently called "buckthorn,"‡ simply, because that was the fuel of which it always consisted, as it

* Sic fatus, spinam, qua tristes pellere posset
A foribus noxas, hæc erat alba, dedit.
Ov. Fast. vi., 130.

† Leoprechting, Lechrain, p. 29.

‡ M. 583 n.

does to this day at Dassel, in Westphalia. It is probable that the tree itself (bocksdorn) was so called from the sacrificial buck goat which was burned upon its wood in heathen times. A paschal buck goat for the baptism of the first infant continued to be a church offering in Schillingen, near Trêves, until the year 1712.*

Thorn-trees are reverenced also by the Celts. "The whitethorn is one of the trees most in favour with the small people; and both in Brittany and in some parts of Ireland it is held unsafe to gather even a leaf from certain old and solitary thorns, which grow in sheltered hollows of the moorland, and are the fairies' trysting places. But no 'evil ghost' dares to approach the whitethorn."† The author of this passage derives the supposed virtues of the whitethorn from the general belief of the Middle Ages that our Lord's crown of thorns was made of its branches, though, as he observes, "we now know that it cannot have been so." More than that, we know that the whitethorn was a sacred tree before Christianity existed, so that we must needs invert the statement of the writer in the *Quarterly*, and conclude that the

* Kuhn, Westf. ii., 135.

† "Sacred Trees and Flowers," Quarterly Review, July, 1863, pp. 231-2.

ancient sanctity of the aubépine or whitethorn was what gave rise to the mediæval belief. The passage which the reviewer himself has quoted from Sir John Mandeville bears on its front the unmistakable impress of pagan tradition :—

"Then was our Lord ylad into a gardyn . . . . and there the Jewes scorned hym, and maden hym a croune of the braunches of Albespyne, that is whitethorn, that grew in the same gardyn, and setten yt on hys heved . . . . And therefore hath the whitethorn many virtues. For he that beareth a braunche on hym thereof, no thondre, ne no maner of tempest may dere (hurt) hym ; ne in the hows that yt is ynne may non evil ghost entre."

The old traveller is here an unconscious witness to the enduring vitality of the Aryan tradition, that invested the hawthorn with the virtues of a tree sprung from the lightning.

To return to the hazel. Its relation to the clouds and the lightning explains its supposed virtue as a promoter of fruitfulness, and its consequent use in divinations relating to love and marriage. When Loki, transformed into a falcon, rescued Idhunn, the goddess of youthful life, from the power of the frost-giants, it was in the shape of a hazel nut that he carried her off in his beak. In Altmark, nuts are scattered at marriages, as they were in Rome. In the Black Forest the leader of a marriage procession carries a hazel wand in his hand, and in Westphalia and other parts of Germany a few nuts are mingled with the seedcorn to make it prolific. Peas, another of Thor's fruits, are also used for the same purpose.* In Hertfordshire and other parts of England, as well as in Germany, a certain relation is believed to exist between the produce of the hazel bushes and the increase of the population, a good nut year always bringing—*tant bien que mal*—an abundance of babies. Among the sports of Allhallow-e'en, as described in Brockett's Glossary, and by Burns in his poem on that night, the burning of nuts is of great importance as affording omens concerning marriage. The persons engaged in the ceremony give the name of a lad and a lass to each pair of nuts as they lay them in the fire; and as the nuts burn quietly together, or start away from each other, so will be the course and issue of the courtship. The custom, as practised in England, is thus described by Gay in his "Spell"—

> Two hazel nuts I threw into the flame,
> And to each nut I gave a sweetheart's name.
> This with the loudest bounce me sore amazed,
> That in a flame of brightest colour blazed.

* Mannhardt, p. 199.

As blazed the nut so may thy passion grow,
For 'twas thy nut that did so brightly glow.

"It is a custom in Ireland, when the young women would know if their lovers are faithful, to put three nuts upon the bars of the grate, naming the nuts after the lovers. If a nut cracks or jumps, the lover will prove unfaithful; if it begins to blaze or burn, he has a regard for the person making the trial. If the nuts named after the girl and her lover burn together, they will be married."*

In Bohemia, on Christmas Eve, girls fix coloured waxlights in the shells of the first parcel of nuts they have opened that day, light them all at the same time, and set them floating on water, after mentally giving to each the name of a wooer. He whose lighted bark first approaches the girl will be her future husband. If an unwelcome suitor seems likely to be first in, a head wind is directed against his vessel from the fair one's lips, until the favourite has won the race. But woe to him whose light is extinguished, for it portends his death.†

Hazel nuts are believed in Sweden to have the power of making invisible. What that implies will be seen in the next chapter.

The preceding data will enable the reader to con-

* Brand, "Pop. Antiq."   † Reinsberg-Düringsfeld, p. 550.

jecture rightly the cause to which the mistletoe owes the sanctity in which it was held from the earliest times by the German as well as the Celtic nations. It possesses in a high degree all the virtues proper to botanic lightning, as implied in its Swiss name, *donnerbesen*, "thunder besom," and its mode of growth is conformable in all particulars to its exalted mythical character. It is a parasite, and, like the asvattha and the rowan, it is everywhere believed to spring from seed deposited by birds on trees. When it was found upon the oak, the Druids ascribed its growth directly to the gods; they *chose* the tree;* and the bird was their messenger, perhaps a god in disguise. The oak mistletoe is held in the highest repute in Sweden, and is commonly seen in farm-houses, hanging from the ceiling to protect the house and homestead from injuries in general, but especially from fire. In England the Christmas frolics under the mistletoe are a relic of the old faith in the potency of the plant in affairs of love and marriage. Like the rowan-tree, the mistletoe makes cattle

* Nihil habent druidæ (ita suos appellant magos) visco et arbore in qua gignatur (si modo sit robur) sacratius. Jam per se roborum eligunt lucos, nec ulla sacra sine ea fronde conficiunt, ut inde appellati quoque interpretatione græca possint druidæ videri. Enimvero quicquid *adnascatur illis e cœlo missum putant*, signumque esse *electæ ab ipso deo arboris.*—Plin. 16, 44.

fruitful, being given to them in a drench for that purpose, and according to Celtic tradition the plant was a safeguard against poison, and a remedy for all diseases, "They call it in their own tongue 'heal-all' (omnia sanantem)," says Pliny. In Sweden its virtues in this respect still rank very high in popular esteem; persons afflicted with the falling sickness provide themselves with a knife having a handle of oak mistletoe, as a means of warding off attacks of the malady. For other complaints a piece of the plant is hung round the patient's neck, or a ring made of it is worn on the finger. This healing virtue, which the mistletoe shares with the ash, is a long-descended tradition, for "the kushtha, the embodiment of the soma,"* a healing plant of the highest renown among the Southern Aryans, was one of those that grew beneath the heavenly asvattha. In fine, Swedes and Carinthians ascribe to the mistletoe the powers of the springwort and of the wish-rod. Nature has given it the essential form of the latter in the regular forking of its branches, whilst this form is only to be found in the rowan and the hazel by diligent search.

* Rig Veda, ii., 164.

CHAPTER VII.

THE DIVINING OR WISH-ROD CONTINUED—TRADITIONS OF IT IN GREECE AND ROME—FERN—INVISIBILITY—CRAZING AND DEADLY POWER OF LIGHTNING PLANTS, TREES, RODS, ETC.—MAGIC CUDGELS.

IT is remarked as a matter of special significance in the old sacred books of India, and by their Sanscrit commentators, that the palasa (p. 158) is triple-leafed, that is to say, its leaves consist, like those of the clover, of three distinct lobes springing from one stalk. There can be no doubt as to what this form of leaf was understood to typify, for a trident,* and a cross or hammer with three points, are among the oldest Indo-European symbols of the forked lightning from which sprang the palasa, and which is called *trisulcum*, "three-pronged," by Ovid and Varro.

The herald rod of Hermes (κηρύκειον) was taken from a tree leafed like the palasa; it was "a rod of prosperity and wealth," a real wish-rod,

* Poseidon was the Zeus of the sea, and his trident was equivalent to his brother's fulmen trisulcum.

"golden, triple-leafed,"* and was given to him by Apollo, the Grecian Rudra (p. 18). It had served Apollo as a herdsman's staff when he tended the cattle of Admetus, a fact which again assimilates it to the palasa, the sami, and the rowan rod (p. 159 ff.). In later times it was represented as having two serpents coiled round it, with necks and heads curving towards each other at its upper end, appendages which were either mere artistic variations of its originally forked form, or which stood for the serpents that were connected with the world-tree. Hermes himself possesses among his multifarious attributes and functions some that connect him in a very marked manner with Agni. Repeatedly in Vedic hymns and prayers is Agni invoked as the messenger of the gods, and the mediator who carries up to them the offerings of men in wreaths of smoke from the altar fires. He is styled priest of sacrifice and prayer-speaker. Hermes too is priest of sacrifice, prayer-bearer (precum minister),† and messenger of the Olympic gods, especially of Zeus (Διὸς ἄγγελος). This very title of his, angelus, messenger, angel, for which no Greek root can be found, has been traced back by Roth to Angiras,‡

* Homer, Hymn. in Merc. 529.

† Preller, Griech. Myth. i., 258.

‡ Böhtlingk-Roth, Wörterb. s. v. Angiras.

a name frequently given in the Vedas to Agni himself, as well as to one of the priestly families attendant upon himself. Hermes is in fact an old fire-god, and Callimachus actually ranks him with the fiery Cyclops. The poet says in his hymn to Diana that among the gods, when a girl is fractious, her mother calls out for the Cyclops Arges and Steropes, and then Hermes makes his appearance, coming forth from the innermost part of the house (where the hearth stood) *begrimed with soot.* Above all, Hermes was commonly credited with the invention of the pyreia, or fire-kindling machine, which Diodorus ascribed to Prometheus (p. 44). All things considered, therefore, we must conclude that the staff of Hermes could have been nothing else than that ligneous receptacle of transformed lightning, the drilling-stick of the pyreia.

Dr. Kuhn has not been able to ascertain whether or not there were any certain plants known to the Greeks and Romans as substitutes in ordinary life for the staff of Hermes; but that they had their wish-rods like ourselves, or at least traditions of such instruments, is plain from sundry passages in their writers. One of them, which the author of Charicles has cited from Arrian, is this: "He has a bad father, but I have a good one, and that is the staff of

Hermes. Touch what you will with it, they say, and it turns to gold." Another is the well-known passage in Tully's Offices: "But were all the necessaries of life supplied to us by means of a divine rod (virgula divina) then," &c.

"Ex quovis ligno non fit Mercurius:" it is not every forked hazel twig that is fit to make a divining-rod, nor can so precious an instrument be manufactured at all seasons and at a moment's notice. Had the Antiquary been half as well skilled in magic lore as he was in the art of discovering Roman camps and Latin inscriptions, he might have convicted Dousterswivel on the spot as an impostor, when the fellow pretended to cut a divining-rod in the broad glare of day, and with as little ceremony as one might cut a walking-stick. The success of such an operation is dependent upon many special conditions. It must always be performed after sunset and before sunrise, and only on certain nights, among which are specified those of Good Friday, Epiphany, Shrove Tuesday, St. John's day, the first night of a new moon or that preceding it. In cutting it one must face the east, so that the rod shall be one which catches the first rays of the morning sun; or, as some say, the eastern and western sun must shine through the fork of the rod, otherwise it will be good for nothing. Such also were the directions given in the Vedas with respect to the sami branch and the arani. They were to be cut at new moon or on the night before it, and none were to be chosen but such as grew towards the east, the north, or straight upwards. This last peculiarity has also been recognised as proper to the wishing or divining rod, to which a mediæval poet of Germany compares the form and carriage of the Greek Helen,

> "Fair as a wish-rod came she gliding upright." *

The summer solstice is a favourite season for gathering plants of the lightning tribe, and particularly the springwort and fern. It is believed in the Oberpfalz that the springwort, or St. John's wort (johanniswurzel) as some call it, can only be found among the fern on St. John's night. It is said to be of a yellow colour, and to shine in the night like a candle; which is just what is said of the mandrake in an Anglo-Saxon manuscript of the tenth or eleventh century. Moreover, it never stands still, but hops about continually, to avoid the grasp of men. Here then, in the luminosity and the power of nimble movement attributed to the springwort, we have

* D. M. p. 926.

another remarkable tradition signifying the transformation of the lightning into the plant. It is also a highly significant fact that the marvellous root is said to be connected with fern; for the johnsroot, or john's hand, is the root of a species of fern (*Polypodium Filix mas*, Lin.) which is applied to many superstitious uses. This fern has large pinnate fronds, and is thus related to the mountain ash and the mimosæ. In fact, says Kuhn, it were hardly possible to find in our climate a plant which more accurately corresponds in its whole appearance to the original signification of the Sanscrit name parna, as leaf and feather. Nor does the relationship between them end here, for fern, Anglo-Saxon *fearn*, Old German *faram, farn*, and Sanscrit *parna*, are one and the same word. It is also worthy of note that whereas one of the German names of the rowan means boar-ash (eberesche), so also there is a fern (*Polypodium Filix arboratica*), which is called in Anglo-Saxon *eoferfarn, eferfarn*, that is, boar-fern. In all the Indo-European mythologies the boar is an animal connected with storm and lightning.

As to another large fern (*Pteris aquilina*), eagle fern, a wide-spread belief prevails, that its cut stalk presents the figure of an eagle, some say a double-headed eagle; and, in fact, such a figure may generally be made out with more or less distinctness in the section. The plant itself, with its two great feathered fronds, has the look of a bird with its wings spread; and, as if to confirm the likeness, the young shoots, just rising out of the ground with their downy covering, may be aptly compared to unfledged nestlings. Pteris, the Greek name of this fern, is an old feminine form of *pteron*, a wing, and it seems to have been given to the plant with reference to more than its general appearance. The scholiast on Theocritus says that this fern was used for rustic beds, not only for its softness, but also because its smell drove away serpents. This last quality brings it into the same mythical category with the ash and the hazel. It is believed in Thuringia, that if any one carries fern about him, he will be pursued by serpents until he throws it away. In Sweden the plant is called "snake-bane."

The luck-bringing power of the fern is not confined to one species, but belongs to the tribe in general. It resides in the fullest perfection in the seed, the possessor of which may wish what he will, and the devil must bring it him.* In Swabia they say that fern-seed brought by the devil between

* Panzer, Beitr. ii., 73, 272, 306.

eleven and twelve on Christmas night enables a man to do as much work as twenty or thirty ordinary men.* Such a talisman must be proportionately hard to find, and only on Midsummer eve can it be gathered from

The wondrous one-night-seeding ferne.†

On that one night it ripens from twelve to one, and then it falls and instantly disappears. "Much discourse," says Richard Bivot, "hath been about gathering of fern-seed (which is looked upon as a magical herb) on the night of Midsummer eve ; and I remember I was told of one who went to gather it, and the spirits whisk't by his ears like bullets, and sometimes struck his hat and other parts of his body; in fine, though he apprehended he had gotten a quantity of it, and secured it in papers, and a box besides, when he came home he found all empty." ‡

Brand was told by a respectable countryman at Heston in Middlesex, that, when he was a young man, he was often present at the ceremony of catching the fern-seed at midnight on the eve of St. John Baptist. The attempt he said was often unsuccess-

* Meier, Schuäbische Sagen, No. 267.

† Browne, Britannia's Pastorals.

‡ "Pandæmonium." London : 1684 ; p. 217. Scott's "Minstrelsy of Scottish Border."

ful, for the seed was to fall into the plate of its own accord, and that too without shaking the plant.* One of the statements made by the Slovacks agrees with Bivot's. They say that whoever comes too near the flowers of fern will be overcome with sleep, and that supernatural beings repulse all who dare to lay hand on the plant.†

Fern-seed has the wonderful property of making people invisible—

> We have the receipt of fern-seed, we walk invisible.
>
> Shaks., Henry IV., part 1, sc. 1.

> I had
> No medicine, sir, to go invisible,
> No fern-seed in my pocket.
>
> Ben Jonson, New Inn.

The people of Westphalia tell of a curious thing that once befell a man in those parts. He happened on Midsummer night to be looking for a foal he had lost, and passed through a meadow just as the fern-seed was ripening, so that it fell into his shoes. In the morning he went home, walked into the sitting-room and sat down, but thought it strange that neither his wife nor any of the family took the least notice of him. "I have not found the foal," said he. Everybody in the room started and looked alarmed, for they heard the man's voice but saw

* Brand, i. 315. † Vernaleken, Alpensagen, p. 374.

nobody. His wife called him by his name, thinking he must have hid himself. Thereupon he stood up, planted himself in the middle of the floor and said, "Why do you call me? Here I am, right before you." Then they were worse frightened than before, for they had heard him stand up and walk, and still they saw nothing. The man now became aware that he was invisible, and it struck him at once that he might possibly have fern-seed in his shoes, for he felt as if there was sand in them. So he took them off and shook them out, and as he did so, there he stood, plain to be seen by everybody.*

No mythical gift can be less ambiguous in its origin than is that of the power of becoming invisible at will. The thing that confers it is always to be understood as pertaining to the mists or clouds. The poets of Greece and Rome constantly represent the gods as concealing themselves and their attendants from mortal eyes in a cloud. The northern nations turned this cloud into a mantle or cap of darkness, the latter commonly called a mist-cap (nebelkappe). The king of the Greek realm of the dead had likewise his dark helmet, which symbolised the concealing clouds of which his world was made, and for that very reason was he called Aïdes, the

* D. M. 1160.

"invisible."* The German dwarfs, those thievish elves and mist-brewers, who are notoriously addicted to stealing the husbandman's peas in the field, are always furnished with such a cap when they are committing theft, and on many other occasions also.† The fern-seed derives its power of making invisible from the cloud that contained the heavenly fire from which the plant is sprung.

A man may make himself invisible whenever he pleases if he is possessed of a "raven-stone," a talisman which is procured in New Pomerania in the following manner. When you have discovered a raven's nest you must climb the tree, and take your chance that the parent birds are at least a hundred years old, for otherwise you will have your trouble for nothing. You are then to kill one of the nestlings, which must be a male bird, and not more than six weeks old. Then you may descend the tree, but be very careful to mark well the spot where it stands, for by-and-by it will become invisible, as soon as the raven comes back, and lays a raven-stone in the throat of its dead nestling. When it has done this, you may go up again and secure the stone.‡ In mythical language, stone and cloud are convertible terms; and here we have the cloud of darkness

* Schwartz, p. 67. † Ibid., p. 247. ‡ Kuhn, Westf. ii., 76.

brought down by the storm-bird which was sacred both to Apollo and Odin, the Greek and German representatives of Rudra (p. 18). The raven's hue is that of the storm-cloud, but it was not so until angry Apollo turned it from white to black, like the swan-white clouds of fair weather that darken as the tempest gathers. Once upon a time, so runs the Grecian story, Apollo sent his feathered attendant to a fountain to fetch water for sacrifice. The raven found a fig-tree with fruit nearly ripe, and waited till they were quite so, that he might satisfy his appetite. Then, having to devise some excuse for his delay, he took the water-snake out of the fountain, brought it with the pitcher to Apollo, and told the god that the snake had daily drunk the fountain dry. But Apollo, who was not to be imposed upon, turned the disobedient raven black, besides condemning it to be always plagued with thirst at the same season of the year, and to give token of its punishment by its painful croaking.*

To return from this digression to the fern-seed, one method prescribed for obtaining it is, in Dr. Kuhn's opinion, particularly worthy of notice. At the summer solstice, if you shoot at the sun when it has attained its midday height, three drops of blood

* Eratosth. Cat. xli. Schwartz, p. 199.

will fall. They must be gathered up and preserved, for that is the fern-seed.* According to Dr. Kuhn, this thoroughly heathen account of the heavenly origin of fern-seed is certainly very ancient; so also is the conception of the Freischütz or dead-shot, for it coincides with that of the Cabdavedhî of the Hindu epic poems. The latter has only to name the object he wishes to hit, and the thing is done. In the Mahâbhârata one of these fatal marksmen wounds an enemy who has made himself invisible by magic art. A German freischütz did almost as well, for he fired out of the back door of a farm-house, and shot a kite that was making havoc among the poultry in front of the house.†

Besides the powers already mentioned, fern has others which distinctly mark its affinity with thunder and lightning. "In the place where it grows the devil rarely practises his glamour. He shuns and abhors the house and place where it is, and thunder, lightning, and hail rarely fall there."‡ This is in apparent contradiction with the Polish superstition, according to which the plucking of fern produces a violent thunderstorm; but it is a natural supposition, that the hitherto rooted and transformed thunderbolt

* Bechstein, Deutsche Sagenbuch, No. 500.

† Leoprechting, p. 61.

‡ D. M. 1161.

resumes its pristine nature, when the plant that contained it is taken from the ground. In the Thuringian forest fern is called *irrkraut*, or bewildering weed (from *irren*, to err, go astray), because whoever treads on it unawares loses his wits and knows not where he is. In fact, he is in that condition of mind which we English call "thunderstruck," and which Germans, Romans, and Greeks have agreed in denoting by exactly corresponding terms.* He has been crazed by a shock from the lightning with which the fern is charged like a Leyden jar. Instances of a similar phenomenon occur in the legends of India and Greece. When Cyavana, an Indian personification of lightning, was pelted with clods by the sons of Saryâta, he grew wroth with them, and immediately their souls were so bewildered that father and son, brother and brother, began to fight one with the other. Saryâta could not explain to himself how the fray had broken out; but when he asked his herdsmen, and they told him in what way it had begun, he understood the whole matter, and exclaimed, "It is Cyavana!"† The madness of Lycurgus was doubtless the effect of a like electric force inherent in Dionysos or Bacchus, the fire-born

* Viz., pidonarot, angedonnert, attonitus, εμβροντητός.

† Çatapatha-brâhmana IV., i., 5.3. Kukn, Herabk. p. 223.

god (pyrigenés), whom one legend describes as having come down with the levin from heaven. "Does not this lightning birth," asks Dr. Kuhn, "also explain why it was that, as Plutarch relates, men durst not swear by Dionysos under a roof, but only in the open air?"

The power of disordering the wits which is evinced by fern in Thuringia is ascribed in Aargau to the plantain or waybread, which is there called *irrwurzel*, a name equivalent to *irrkraut.** Moreover, it is related of this plant by Paracelsus, that its root is changed every seven years into a bird.† From these data it is to be inferred that plantain is one of the forms in which lightning has assumed a vegetative existence, that it first came down to earth as a bird, and that its septennial metamorphosis is a return of that lightning-bringer to its former shape. It becomes a question, therefore, of much interest, whether or not we can ascertain the bird's name; but for the present, I fear, we must leave that point undecided. The writer in the *Quarterly Review*, indeed, to whom we have already referred more than once, asserts that the bird is either the cuckoo or the hoopoe (German, wiedhopf). This would be wel-

* Rochholz, Aarg. Sag. i., 79. Kuhn, Herabk. p. 223.
† D. M. 1165.

come information, capable of throwing much light on the whole mythical character of both birds, if it could be relied upon; but, unfortunately, the reviewer cites no authority for a fact which is not mentioned by Grimm, or by any other German mythologist whose works we have consulted. His words are :—

". . . The plantain or waybread, said to have been once a maiden, who, watching by the wayside for her lover, was changed into the plant which still loves to fix itself by the beaten path. Once in seven years it becomes a bird, either the cuckoo or the cuckoo's servant, the 'dinnick,' as it is called in Devonshire, the German 'wiedhopf,' which is said to follow its master everywhere (Grimm, D. Myth. p. 787). The latter part of the belief is a piece of Devonshire folk-lore."

The reference to Grimm in this extract applies accurately only to the first sentence. The transformation of the plantain into a hoopoe could hardly have been known to Grimm, for had it been so he would not have failed to notice it. He says, indeed (p. 646), that the hoopoe is a transformed being, but does not tell us what it was before it became a bird. I have searched in Paracelsus for the passage concerning plantain, but have not been able to find it.

The edition of that writer's collected works to which Grimm refers is not in the British Museum.

At all events there are apparently good grounds for including the hoopoe among the fire-bringers, since, like the wood-pecker, it is said to know how to find the spring-wort (p. 175); and, if this fact may be regarded as proved, it increases the probability that the hoopoe's master belongs also to the same class.

Analogy would lead us to expect that the plants which were supposed to be incorporations of the thunderbolt should be able to evince their destructive powers in other ways besides that of paralysing the mind. They ought to be able to destroy life itself, and some of them did in fact give marvellous proof of their power to blast and kill. It was manifested in the groans and shrieks of the mandrake when it was pulled out of the ground—sounds so horrible that neither man nor beast could hear them and live. Extraordinary precautions were therefore necessary in gathering the plant. It was not to be touched with iron, but a circle was to be cut round it with that metal that it might not run away, and the ground was to be dug and loosened with an ivory tool, until the root remained attached only by a few fibres. This being done, the daring operator, whose ears had previously been well stopped with wool or wax, tied one end of a string round the plant, and the other round the neck or tail of a black dog that had not a single white hair, and that had been brought fasting to the spot. The man then moved away to some distance, showed the dog food, and ran for his life. The dog ran after him, pulled up the root, and fell dead, killed in an instant by the unearthly yell of the mandrake as if by a stroke of lightning.*

The death-dealing power of the mistletoe is seen in the legend of the bright day-god Baldr. Freyja had taken an oath of all created things that they would never hurt that "whitest" and most beloved of the gods; but there was "one little shoot that groweth east of the Valhalla, so small and feeble that she forgot to take its oath." It was the mistletoe, and with a branch of that feeble plant, flung by the hand of the blind Hodr, was Baldr struck dead.

That such death-dealing power belonged to the lightning plants from the earliest times appears from a Vedic incantation which Kuhn has translated.† It is addressed to a branch of an asvattha which had grown upon a khadira, or *Mimosa catechu*, and

* D. M. 1151-5.

† It is found in the Atharvaveda, iii., 6.

which was intended for hostile purposes. The incantation runs thus :—

"A man from man has it sprung, an asvattha upon the khadira ; may it kill my foes whom I hate, and who hate me. Do thou, O asvattha, tear to pieces the foes . . . thou who art the companion of the Vritra-slayer Indra, of Mitra and Varuna. As thou, O asvattha, dost smash and shatter in the great sky sea, so smite all those whom I hate and who hate me. Thou who marchest victorious as a strong steer, through thee, asvattha, may we vanquish the foes ; may Nirriti bind, O asvattha, with the indissoluble bonds of death my foes whom I hate and who hate me. As thou, O asvattha, ascendest the trees and makest them subject to thee, so cleave my foes' heads and be victorious. Down may they go like a ship torn from its mooring, chased away . . . may they not return. Forth I drive them with mind, and with thoughts, and with prayer, forth drive we them with branch of the asvattha tree."

There cannot be the least doubt that the power here ascribed to the asvattha was derived from the lightning it contained ; and hence the whole passage has served perfectly, in Dr. Kuhn's hands, to explain for the first time a very remarkable legend and custom of ancient Scandinavia. At the battle of

Fyrisvall, King Erich turned towards Odin's temple, and prayed for victory over his opponent Styrbjörn, in return for which the god should have his life after ten winters. When that term had elapsed the king would cheerfully quit the earth for Valhalla. Soon afterwards there appeared a stalwart man, easily known as Odin by his one eye and his broad-brimmed hat, who put a reed * into Erich's hand, and bade him hurl it over the heads of the enemy, with the words, "Odin have you all!" The king did so, the reed became a spear as it flew through the air, and Styrbjörn and his men were struck blind. From this event arose the Norse custom of devoting the enemy to death by hurling over their heads a spear consecrated to Odin, or received from him, and crying out, "Dismayed is your king, fallen your duke, sinking your banner, wroth with you is Odin." †

The analogy between this Norse usage and the ancient Roman mode of declaring war has been remarked by Simrock and others. The Roman fetialis advanced to the enemy's boundary, and along with the declaration of war he hurled across

* In the original, reyrsproti, 'reed-sprout.' "One is almost tempted," says Kuhn, "to read 'reynisproti,' a rowan twig."

† Mannhardt, p. 162.

it a bloodstained spear, burned at the further end or tipped with iron. It is to be inferred that this spear must have been one dedicated to Jove the Thunderer, for that god was specially invoked on the occasion along with Janus Quirinus (the commoner reading is Juno, Quirine). The other attributes of the fetialis also point the same way, particularly the Jupiter lapis, or Jove-stone, which was plainly the thunderbolt, for so was the Thunderer's weapon often represented among the Romans as well as among the Germanic nations. The same inference is increased in force by an ancient war custom of the Greeks.* Instead of trumpeters they employed in early times priests of Ares, called "fire-bearers" (πυρφόροι). These men advanced from either army into the space between, each bearing a lighted torch which he flung forwards, and then retired out of danger. This torch was another and still more self-evident symbol of the lightning.

In Odin, the old storm-god, are combined the characteristics of Rudra, the father of the Maruts or winds, and of Indra. His ashen spear Gungnir, like Indra's asvattha spear, returns of itself to his hand every time he throws it. Its nature is that of the lightning, a fact which was fully manifested

* Described by the Scholiast on Euripides. Phœn. 1386.

when it smote Styrbjörn and his army with blindness.

Human sacrifices were offered to Odin, and hanging was a favourite mode of despatching the victims. Vikarr, king of Agdhir, being wind-bound on a cruise, his followers cast lots that they might learn the will of Odin. The god required that one of the warriors should be sacrificed to him, and the lots being cast again, the choice fell upon King Vikarr. That night Odin, in the form of an old man who called himself Hrossharsgrani (*i. e.*, Horsehair-beard) commissioned the gigantic hero Starkadhr to accomplish his will, and gave him his spear, which to human eyes appeared but a reed. Next morning the king's councillors resolved to proceed to the sacrifice, but to perform it only in a typical and harmless fashion. Starkadhr fastened one end of a calf's gut to the top of a pine sapling that grew near an old stump, and telling the king that the gallows and the noose were ready, begged he would mount the stump; no harm would happen to him. The king complied and put the noose round his own neck, whereupon Starkadhr hurled the reed at him, exclaiming, "Now give I thee to Odin." Instantly the reed became a spear and pierced Vikarr through and through; the old stump broke down under his feet; the sapling shot up into a tall tree, dragging the king with it; the calf's gut turned into a stout rope; and thus Odin received his victim. From this mode of sacrifice, and from the fact that Odin himself hung for nine days and nights on Yggdrasil, he was surnamed god of the hanged, gallows lord, gallows ruler. Hence also the superstition, very common in Germany, and not extinct in England, that every suicide by hanging produces a storm. Odin comes with his wild host to carry off the soul of his self-immolated victim.

Odin's spear figures in popular tales, retaining its marvellous qualities, but its form is necessarily changed; for the spear has long been an obsolete weapon, and the costume and stage properties, so to speak, of popular tales are always those of the narrator's own times. Thus the spear of the ancient god becomes for later generations a stick which can send heads flying from their bodies at a touch, or make whole armies come and vanish in a moment. This is still grand enough, and some at least of the actors in such tales are persons of royal race; but in the course of time the story descends from tragedy or heroic drama to low comedy and farce. The actors in it are ordinary workmen and peasants who want no armies to settle their quarrels with one another. A good sound cudgelling does the business quite well enough, and so the divine spear is found in its last stage of transformation as the "stick out of the bag" of a well-known story.* A lad sets out on a journey, having in his possession three wonderful things,—a buck-goat that spits gold, a hen that lays golden eggs, and a table that covers itself, without anybody's help, with the choicest food. A rascally innkeeper steals these treasures from the lad, and puts worthless trash in their place; but a stick, that jumps out of a bag in which it is usually concealed, goes to work of its own accord upon the innkeeper's back, and with such effect that the lad gets his own again. The stick then returns of itself to its owner's hand.

The table in this story is the all-nourishing cloud. The buck-goat is another emblem of the clouds, and the gold it spits is the golden light of the sun that streams through the fleecy coverings of the sky. The hen's golden egg is the sun itself. The demon of darkness has stolen these things; the cloud gives no rain, but hangs dusky in the sky, veiling the light of the sun. Then the lightning spear of the ancient storm-god Odin leaps out from the bag that concealed it (the cloud again), the robber

* Wolf, I., p. 12.

falls, the rain patters down, the sun shines once more.

The asvattha rod of the Atharvaveda incantation and its equivalent, the spear of Odin, are in fact wish-rods especially adapted for bringing victory to their possessor. They have also another comic counterpart in a sort of wish-rod, which serves for administering a drubbing at a distance. With such a hazel implement, cut and prepared with the proper formalities, one has only to lay an old garment on a molehill or on a threshold, name the person intended, and whack away. He will feel every blow as sorely as though he were actually under the stick, and if the old garment is beaten into holes, so will it be with the skin of the absent sufferer.

CHAPTER VIII.

MYTHICAL DRINKING VESSELS, SIEVES, CAULDRONS, AND OTHER UTENSILS —WITCHES—COWS—HARES—CATS—NIGHTMARES.

THE train of thought by which the Aryans and the Greeks were led to the discovery of casks and wine-butts in the clouds (p. 36) could not fail to provide the denizens of the sky with many other utensils, such as urns and pitchers, cups, drinking-horns, cauldrons, and even sieves. The Grecian Naiads were originally cloud-nymphs, who poured out the rain-water from their urns; and the sieves in which the Danaids were ultimately condemned to draw water in Tartarus were those which they had used of yore to pour down the mild rain upon the earth. Originally the daughters of Danaus were cloud-goddesses, and were honoured for having enriched Argos with springs, and changed its arid territory into a well-watered land (p. 142).* The goddess Holda has been seen in the Harz going up a steep hill with a bottomless pail of gold from which water

* Strabo, p. c. 371.

flowed incessantly; and Meister Pfriem is described in one of Grimm's popular tales as entering heaven, where he finds two angels engaged in drawing water in a perforated vessel. There was even a tribe of water-spirits, the Draci of Languedoc, old cloud-gods, like the rest of their order, whose hands were said to be perforated like colanders.* Water poured through a sieve was so obvious and apt an image of the rain, that other primitive peoples, as well as the Aryans, could hardly have failed to seize it. The Finnish goddess Untar sends all kinds of fine vapours down upon the earth through a sieve.

The connection of the sieve with the clouds and the rain accounts for much that even Grimm was forced to leave unexplained, when he summed up the mythology of the subject with the unsatisfactory remark, that "the sieve appears to be a sacred archaic implement to which marvellous powers were attributed."† It possessed those powers because, like the chark, it was invented and used by gods. The Greeks, Romans, Germans, and Slaves employed it in divination and in solemn ordeals. "The vulgar in many parts," says Brockett,‡ "have an abominable practice of using a riddle and a pair of scissors

* Liebrecht, p. 135. † D. M. 1066.
‡ Glossary of North Country Words, s. v.

in divination. If they have had anything stolen from them the riddle and shears are sure to be resorted to. A similar mode of discovering thieves or others suspected of any crime prevailed among the Greeks (Potter's Gr. Antiq. i., 352). In Northumberland, young people turn the riddle for the purpose of amusing themselves with the foolish idea of raising their lovers. It is done between open doors at midnight, and in the dark."

There was extant in Pliny's time a spell (precatio) by means of which Tuccia, an unchaste vestal, carried water in a sieve. In one of Grimm's popular tales a good boy performs the same feat without spilling a drop; and it is a Hindu belief that an innocent person can confute his accusers by holding water in his hand in the shape of a solid ball.*

The ancient Poles presaged victory from water carried in a sieve. When Conrad made war upon his brother Wlodislas in 1209, the latter had with him a wise woman—a pythoness, the chronicler calls her—who marched before his troops carrying in a sieve water drawn from a river. It did not run through, and from that portent she promised them victory. But it was a false prophecy, and she herself fell at the first onset.†

* D.M. p. 1066. † Ibid.

A sieve, as a symbol of the clouds, is used as an appropriate vehicle by witches, nightmares, and other elfish beings in their excursions over sea and land. "But in a sieve I'll thither sail," says the first witch in "Macbeth" (act 1, sc. 3). Stories of voyages performed in this way are still common enough in Germany. A man, for instance, was going through a field of corn, found a sieve on the path, and took it with him. He had not gone far when a young lady hurried after him, and hunted up and down as if looking for something, ejaculating all the time, "How my children are crying in England!" The man thought he would lay down the sieve and see what would follow; but hardly had he done so ere sieve and lady had vanished.* In the case of another damsel of the same species the usual exclamation is thus varied: "My sieve rim; my sieve rim! how my mother is calling me in England!"† At the sound of her mother's voice the daughter immediately thinks of her sieve, as an earthly lady would call for her carriage when she was in haste to set out on a journey.

Seeing that the nectar and ambrosia of the Olympic gods were what mortals call rain-water,

* Kuhn, u. Schwartz, Ndd. 262.

† Wolf, Zeitschrift, ii., 141.

we know what to think of the golden urns and beakers of their cupbearers Ganymede and Iris. These vessels must have come from the same workshop, and been of the same material, as the golden cup which was given to Hercules by the sun-god Helios, and which also served the hero as a ship to convey him across the ocean, in like manner as the Apas (p. 21) and other heavenly navigators were borne in their cloud-ships over the waters on high. Out of the same plastic material were formed the horn of the river-god Acheloos, and the magic horn of the nymph Amaltheia, for which Acheloos is said to have exchanged his own when the latter was broken off in his combat with Hercules. According to another legend, Amaltheia's horn was one which had been lost by the goat of that name that had suckled Zeus, and the god made it a cornucopia. Both legends amount to the same thing, the essential fact being that the one horn or the other passed into the possession of the Naiads or rain-goddesses, in whose hands it became a horn of abundance, for out of it they poured down the rain which is the source of all wealth and plenty.

The Wishmays or Valkyries, the manes of whose horses dropped dew upon the earth, filled the drinking-horns for the gods and the warriors in Odin's hall; and, like them, white maidens, elves, and witches offer full goblets and horns to thankless mortals, who usually run away with the beaker after spilling its contents on the ground. A Count of Oldenburg, when out hunting one day, left his retinue far behind, and pulled up at a mountain called Osenberg. His hard ride had made him thirsty, and as luck would have it, as he stood before the mountain he saw it open, and out came a damsel who presented him with drink in a splendid horn. The Count took the horn in his right hand, tossed its contents over his shoulder, and, vaulting into the saddle, galloped away at full speed. When far off he could still hear the damsel's wailings, and when he looked back he saw the mountain open again and the damsel disappear within it. Some of the drink he had thrown away had fallen on his horse, and all the hair was singed off the spot it had touched. The Count took the horn home, and after being long preserved in Oldenburg in memory of the wonderful adventure, it was at last transferred to the Hanoverian Museum. One thing especially curious in this horn was, that its point was broken off, and all the gold and silversmiths tried in vain to mend it, for it was of a metal unknown to any man.*

* Kuhn und Schwartz, Ndd. p. 280.

The liquid that singed off the horse's hair must have been strong drink, brewed in the storm, and with a good dash of lightning in it. A Danish ballad tells how Svend Fälling drank from a horn presented to him by elfin women, and found himself, in consequence of the draught, possessed of the strength of twelve men,* and with an appetite in proportion.

It is related by William of Newbridge that a countryman belonging to a village near his own birthplace was returning home late at night, and tipsy, from a visit to a friend in a neighbouring village, when he heard a sound of singing and merriment within a hill. Peeping through an open door in the side of the hill, he saw a numerous company of both sexes feasting in a large and finely-lighted hall, and a cup was handed to him by one of the attendants. He took it, threw out the contents, and made off with the cup, pursued by the whole party of revellers; but, like Tam o' Shanter, he was saved by the speed of his mare, and got safe home with his booty. The cup, which was of unknown material and of unusual form and colour, was presented to King Henry the First.

The most celebrated of these elfin drinking vessels is the Luck of Edenhall. "It is still currently

* D.M. 345, n.

believed that he who has the courage to rush upon a fairy festival, and snatch from them their drinking cup or horn, shall find it prove to him a cornucopia of good fortune, if he can bear it across a running stream. A goblet is still carefully preserved in Edenhall, Cumberland, which is supposed to have been seized at a banquet of the elves by one of the ancient family of Musgrave, or, as others say, by one of their domestics in the manner above described. The fairy train vanished, crying aloud:

> 'If that glass do break or fall,
> Farewell the luck of Edenhall!'"*

The Luck is described by Mr. Walter White as a tall enamelled glass, apparently of Venetian workmanship of the tenth century. It is supposed to have been a chalice belonging to St. Cuthbert's ruined chapel in the neighbourhood of the hall.

The reason why fairies, white women, and witches offered drink to mortals has been clearly explained by Grimm.† It was for the purpose of making those who drank it remain with them and forget all other women. The fairy beverage was the same as that quaffed in Valhalla, and which was called, among

* Sir W. Scott's "Minstrelsy," ii., 130.
† D. M. p. 1055.

other names, *ominnisöl*, *i. e.*, the ale or drink of forgetfulness, for the mortal who has tasted it at once forgets the earth. The hero Sigurd received from Grimhild a draught of ominnisöl, and forthwith forgot Brynhild, and Godrun had to drink of the same oblivious potion before she could forget Sigurd and choose Atli. The affinity of meaning between the words ominnisöl and nectar has been pointed out by Kuhn.* *Nectar* signifies a destroyer of earthly recollection and earthly existence,† for which very reason it is equivalent to ambrosia (Sanscrit *amartyâ*, immortal), and the two words are used interchangeably. The termination of earthly life is the beginning of immortality. Thetis (Iliad xix., 38) preserved the body of Patroclus from decay with nectar and ambrosia. In like manner it is said of the haoma plant (p. 137), "Where grows the hom, the preparer of corpses, with which corpses are put in due order, and the subsequent bodies are made."‡

The identity of the heavenly soma with the cloud-water, and the close connection in which fire and

* Herabk. 175, n.

† Νέκταρ is formed from the same root as νεκ-ρός, νέκ-υς, Lat. nex, nec-is, nec-are.

‡ Spiegel, Pârsigramm. 170, 6. Kuhn, Herab. p. 175.

soma are brought in various Aryan legends, prove that the drink of the gods was conceived to be a product of the storm. It appears also that the earthly soma was boiled or brewed before it was fermented,* whence it must have followed as a matter of course that its divine counterpart should be supposed to undergo the same process. Hence it is manifest that we cannot claim for any of the later ages the credit of having invented the metaphor involved in the common saying, "It's brewing a storm." In that phrase, as in many others, we only repeat the thoughts of our primæval ancestors. In Germany the mists that gather about the lofty mountain-tops before a storm are accounted for in like manner, as if they were steam from the brewing or boiling in which dwarfs, elves, or witches were engaged. Such modes of expression, according to the dictionary of the brothers Grimm, are of extreme antiquity; and Kuhn has identified the word *brew* itself with the Sanscrit *brajj*, which is applied in the Rig Veda to the roasting of barley for an ingredient in soma-wort, and is very closely related to the word Bhrigu (p. 44). On tracing the word *brajj* still further back, Dr. Kuhn finds reason to think that it originally comprised within its meaning the

* Rig Veda, iv., 27, 7.

action of the beings who brewed and lightened in the storm, namely the Bhrigus, the genii of the lightning, who in one passage of the Veda are expressly designated as yielders of soma.

If the Bhrigus or their associates were brewers they must needs have had brewing utensils, at the very least they must have had a brewing-pot, and therefore we are justified in referring back the origin of the witch's cauldron to the remotest antiquity. Perhaps the oldest example of such a vessel of which there is any distinct record is the cauldron which Thor carried off from the giant Hymir, to brew drink for the gods at Oegir's harvest feast. It was five miles deep, and modern expounders of the Eddic myths are of opinion that it was in fact the vaulted sky.

Cauldrons or brewing-pans figure very prominently in tales of the elfin race. When the departing Zwergs pay their boat fare or bridge toll in money, or when they are caught stealing peas in a field and have to pay ransom, the coin is almost always dropped by them into a large brewing-pan which is placed expressly for the purpose. Not far from the village of Scharfenberg, near Brilon, is the Hollenhoel, a cave formerly inhabited by the Hollen or Holden (p. 135). There they had all sorts of utensils which they readily lent to the people of the village. Among other things they had a large brewing-pan, which the villagers often borrowed when they wanted to brew beer, and when they brought it back they just left a little beer in it by way of thanks. It happened one day that some unmannerly fellows saw the cauldron in the cave, where it had been left by one who had borrowed it. They drank up the beer, and, not content with that, they defiled the cauldron in a most abominable manner. From that time forth no one got the loan of the cauldron again; the Holden vanished soon after, and not a trace of them remained.*

The same tale is told of another Holden cave at Velmede, in Westphalia; and there is a parallel for it in the story of Ludlam's Hole, near Farnham, in Surrey. "Mother Ludlam or Ludlow, a white witch" (the inhabitant of the cave), "kindly assisted her poor neighbours in necessities, by lending them such culinary utensils and household furniture as they wanted for particular occasions. The business was thus transacted: the petitioner went into the cave at midnight, turned three times round, and thrice repeated: 'Pray, good Mother Ludlam, lend me such a thing' (naming the utensil), 'and I will

* Kuhn, Westf. p. 213.

return it within two days.' He or she then retired, and coming again early the next morning found at the entrance the requested movable. This intercourse continued a long time, till once a person not returning a large *cauldron* according to the stipulated time, Madam Ludlow was so irritated at this want of punctuality that she refused to take it back when afterwards left in the cavern; and from that time to this has not accommodated any one with the most trifling loan. The story adds that the cauldron was carried to Waverley Abbey, and, after the dissolution of that monastery, deposited in Trensham church."*

The human witches of Northern Europe are degenerate and abhorred representatives of the ancient goddesses and their attendants, who were themselves developments of the primitive conception of the cloud-women; but witches, even in their degraded state, exhibit a multitude of characteristics by which we can recognise the originals of whom they are but loathsome caricatures. Their alleged Mayday meetings for instance on the Brocken, the Blocksberg, and at Lucken Hare in the Eildon Hills, are not, as commonly supposed, merely reminiscences of certain popular gatherings in heathen times, but

* Wonderful Magazine, v. 202.

were originally assemblies of goddesses and their retinues, making their customary progress through the land at the opening of the spring, and visible to their believing votaries in the shifting clouds about the summits of the mountains. Even the Mayday night dances of the witches, with the devil for a master of the ceremonies in the shape of a buck-goat, are but coarse representations of weather tokens of the early spring; they are analogous in all but their ugliness to the dances of the nymphs, led by the goat-footed Pan at the same glad season of the year, amongst the clouds on the windy mountain tops of Arcadia.*

The witch's broom, or besom, appears to be not less ancient than her cauldron, for it is known in the folk-lore of the Hindus as well as in that of the West. "The Asiatic as well as the European witches practise their spells by dancing at midnight, and the principal instrument they use on such occasions is a broom."† Hence it is tolerably clear that the broom must originally have been supposed, like the sieve, to be used for some purpose or other in the economy of the upper regions. Now it seems that in modern times, besides serving the

* Schwartz, p. 222.

† Asiatic An. Regist. 1801. Miscell. Tracts, p. 91.

witch as a nag, the implement is intended for sweeping the sky; for that is a work assigned to its riders, as may be inferred from the prevalent belief in the Harz, that on the 1st of May the witches must dance away all the snow upon the Blocksberg.* The besom is a type of the winds, and therefore an appropriate utensil in the hands of the witches who are wind-makers and workers in that element. They say in the Mark that if you want a wind you must burn an old broom; and it is a nautical tradition in Hamburg, that if you have long had a contrary wind, and meet with another ship, you must throw an old broom before it. The wind will then chop round and become a good one for you, and a bad one for the other ship.†

The traditional sanctity of the besom is indicated by sundry other superstitions and customs of the Germans and Slaves. For instance:—

It is well known in England, and also in Germany, that no witch can step over a besom laid along the threshold of the house door on the inside. She will kick it or push it aside before she can enter your house, and by this token you may know her for what she is.‡ An axe (Thor's weapon) and a broom

* Kuhn, u. Schwartz, Ndd. p. 376.

† Ibid. p. 454.

‡ Kuhn, Westf. p. 28.

are laid crosswise on the inner side of the threshold over which the nurse has to step when she goes out with an infant to have it christened. This is done that the babe may be safe from all the devices of the powers of evil.* When the cattle are first driven out to pasture in the spring, a besom made in "the twelve days" is laid on the threshold of their stall, or of the gate of the cattle-yard, and they are made to step over it, by which means they are secured against witchcraft throughout the year.†

At Theden, on the Lenne, on Mayday, birches are set up before the houses, and besoms are fastened to them which are made quite white by peeling them.‡ In several other parts of Westphalia, at the beginning of Shrovetide, white besoms with white handles are tied to the cows' horns. The house is afterwards swept with them, and then they are hung up over or near to the cowhouse door.§

The custom of going about with burning besoms at Michaelmas is mentioned by Schmitz, pp. 43, 44.‖ The St. John's fires in the Harz are accompanied with burning besoms which are swung in the air.¶ In Voigtland fires are seen on Walpurgis night on

* Kuhn, Westf. p. 34.

† Kuhn, u. Schwartz, Ndd. pp. 410, 447.

‡ Kuhn, Westf. p. 156.

§ Ibid. p. 167.

‖ Ibid. p, 99.

¶ Ibid. p. 135.

most of the hills, and children run about with burning besoms.* In the Altenburg territory people go up a hill on Walpurgis night with all the old besoms they can gather, which they then set on fire, and run about with them, playing all sorts of tricks upon each other.† The Czechs of Bohemia do the same thing on St. John's day, and young men and lads are busy for weeks beforehand in collecting all the worn-out besoms they can beg or steal for the occasion. They dip them in tar, light them, and run with them from one bonfire to another, jumping over each of the latter. The burnt stumps of the broom handles are stuck in the cabbage gardens, to preserve the plants from flies and caterpillars. In some places the lads and lasses toss their burning besoms into the air, and sing a rhyme, in which they ask for a token how many years they have to live. If the besom is still alight when it comes down, and continues to burn on the ground, they expect to live through the year, and they count upon another year of life for every time the experiment is repeated with success.‡

The reason is plain why the plague of witches is by all accounts more severely felt in the dairy than

* D.M. p. 594. † Kuhn, u. Schwartz, Ndd. p. 377.
‡ Reinsberg-Düringsfeld, pp. 307—311.

in any other department of rural economy. The Aryan idea, that the rain-clouds were cows, has been well preserved among the Northern nations. Hence it is a common superstition in Germany, that a fire kindled by lightning can only be extinguished with cow's milk, cow's hair, or cow dung. Read in its natural sense, the proposition is, that flames kindled by heavenly fire can only be quenched by the waters of heaven. It is also a very common opinion that rain and dew, the milk of the heavenly cows, are capable of increasing the milk of earthly cows; hence a dewy May morning is welcomed as giving promise of a good dairy year. On such a morning witches go into the fields, brush the dew from the grass, and collect it in linen cloths, which they squeeze into their milk churns, to the manifest increase of the butter. In North Germany it is customary, when the cows are driven out to pasture for the first time in spring, to tie a green maybush to the tail of the foremost cow, that she may gather up the dew with it, and so yield plenty of milk.* On the same occasion the farm-wives in Aberdeenshire tie a red thread (p. 146) round the cows' tails, to preserve the animals from witchcraft, and German herdsmen lay a woman's red apron, or a broad axe

* Mannhardt, p. 89.

covered with a woman's red stocking, before the threshold of the cow-house, and make the animals step over it.

But it is no easy matter to guard against the secret practices of the witch. There was a farmer in Caseburg whose cows gave no milk, though he fed them ever so well, so that at last he sent for a wise man to see what he could do with them. The wise man went into the cow-house, looked at the cows, and saw at once what was the matter. They were bewitched. So he went about the village to look for the witch, and at last he found the neighbour's wife standing in her own cow-house, at the wall nearest to the farmer's. She had stuck a broom handle into the wall, with a bucket hanging from it, and was milking the broom stick, which gave milk like a natural udder. Thus, then, this witch was caught in the fact. The wise man threatened her terribly, and from that day forth the farmer had no cause to complain of his cows.* In Scotland, "witches were supposed to have the power of supplying themselves with milk from their neighbours' cattle by a very simple though insidious process. Procuring a small quantity of hair from the tail of every cow within her reach, the vile wretch twisted it up into a rope,

* Kuhn und Schwartz, Ndd. p. 24.

on which she tied a knot for each cow. At this she tugged in the usual manner of milking a cow, pronouncing at the same time some unhallowed incantation, at which the milk would stream abundantly into her pail. The following is a verse said to have been used on such occasions, though it seems of larger application:—

> 'Meares' milk and deer's milk,
> And every beast that bears milk,
> Between St. Johnston and Dundee,
> Come a' to me, come a' to me.'

It was believed that some cows of uncommon sagacity knew when this process was going on, and would give warning of it by lowing. An acute old woman could easily distinguish this low from any other, as it bore a peculiar expression of pain. The proper antidote was to lay a twig of rowan-tree, bound with a scarlet thread, across the threshold of the byre, or fix a stalk of clover, having four leaves, to the stall. To discover the witch, the goodman's breeks might be put upon the horns of the cow, one leg upon each horn, when for certain, she, being let loose, would run straight to the door of the guilty party."*

As Indra used to milk the cloud cows and churn the milk lakes and fountains with the thunderbolt,

* Robert Chambers, "Pop. Rhymes," p. 111.

so did Thor. The German god's fiery weapon was often represented as an axe,* and hence it is a customary thing with witches to draw milk from the handle of an axe stuck in a doorpost.† They stir the waters of a fountain about with a stake, and bring out of it pats of the finest and sweetest butter; or, if they like, they can produce thunder and lightning by the same process. A little girl was seen paddling with a stick in a fountain, and was asked what she was doing. "Oh," said she, "I am doing what mother does, you know. She takes a stick and turns it round and round in the fountain, and then there comes a storm."‡

When cows go dry, their udders are stroked with a belemnite that they may fill again.§ Belemnites are well-known fossils of a conical form, and are called thunderbolts by the country people in Germany, as well as by the workmen in the chalk-pits of Lewes and Dover; for it is an old tradition that they are actually missiles shot down from the thunder-cloud. In Sweden they are called *smördubbar, i. e.*, butter-beater. Their Greek name

* An Anglo-Saxon poem, quoted by Kemble, says that the thunder threshes with a fiery axe:

Se thunor hit thryscedh mid thære fyrenan æcxe.

† D.M. 1025. ‡ Mannhardt, p. 195. § Ibid.

signifies a missile, and was applied to certain stones (fossils?) resembling arrow-heads. In Swabia and Switzerland the cows are milked through a perforated stone, which is believed to have fallen from the clouds, and is therefore called cowstone (*kuhstein*). In Holstein the churn-dash is made of rowan wood, and in Carinthia a red cloth is laid under the churn when it is in use, to prevent the milk from being bewitched and yielding no butter. For witches are not content with stealing the produce of their neighbours' cows, but delight in turning good milk into blue or bloody, and their glosing speeches when they enter a house endanger all the work of the dairy, and hinder the butter from coming in the churn.* There are certain Sundays and holidays when these wicked hags go to church, and though they seem to be dressed like other women, people who are in possession of certain talismans, such as an egg laid on "Green Thursday" (formerly sacred to Thor), may see that they wear churns or milk-pails on their heads. The fact is well known in Denmark and in Germany.†

Giraldus Cambrensis‡ says that in Wales, Ireland, and Scotland, it was an old complaint, and a common

* D.M. 1025.

† D.M. 1032. Kuhn, u. Schwartz, Ndd. p. 378.

‡ Topogr. Hiber. 2, 19.

one in his own day, that certain old crones turned themselves into hares, and in that shape sucked the cows. The same complaint is still rife in those three countries. A certain Scotch witch "has been seen a hundred times milking the cows in the shape of a hare."* This sort of thing appears to be peculiarly Celtic; at least I cannot call to mind any record of its occurrence among other races, although witches of German, as well as those of Celtic, descent are known to affect the forms of hares and cats above all other animals. The goddess who represents Freyja in Lower Saxony is attended by hares (p. 129), two of them acting as her trainbearers, whilst others carry lights before her. Another form of Freyja walks the fields in Aargau at night, accompanied by a silver-grey hare.† Mannhardt even asserts that this animal is reputed to be a fire and soul bringer, that many "baby fountains" (kinderbrünnen) are named after it, and that in some places children are said to come out of the hare's form.‡ The hare is no doubt mythically connected with the phenomena of the sky, but upon what natural grounds it has been credited with such meteoric relations is a point not yet determined. I incline

* Athenæum, Nov. 1846.

† Mannhardt, p. 303.

‡ Ibid. p. 283.

to think it will be found to lie, in part at least, in the habits which the animal displays about the time of the vernal equinox, and which have given rise to the popular saying, "as mad as a March hare."

There are some local customs that seem to indicate, however obscurely, that the hare, like the serpent among the Celts, was anciently regarded as a prominent actor in the celestial changes peculiar to that season. At Easter, in Swabia and in Hesse, a nest is made of moss, a hare is set upon it, and the children are sent to look for the eggs that the hare has laid.* Now it was the custom of the Parsees to distribute red eggs at their spring festival;† the Easter eggs of the Germanic and Slave nations are indisputably emblems of the renovated sun, and when we find them thus associated with the hare, we may be sure that there once was a reason for the venerable joke. "Last year," says Schwartz,‡ "I heard them say in the Saxon mountains, 'the Easter hare brings the Easter eggs,'" and Friedreich§ states that in many districts these eggs are made into cakes in the form of a hare. Leoprechting mentions the same practice as common in the Lechrain.‖ In England,

* Meier, Gebräuche, No. 65. Wolf, Zeitschrift, i. 175.

† Schwartz, p. 229.

‡ P. 229.

§ Symbolik der Natur, p. 692.

‖ P. 175.

too, we find some evidence of a connection between Easter hares, and Easter eggs. "They have a singular custom at Coleshill, in the county of Warwick, that if the young men of the town can catch a hare and bring it to the parson of the parish, before ten o'clock on Easter Monday, the parson is bound to give them a calf's head, a hundred of eggs for their breakfast, and a groat in money."*

The question why the chariot of the goddess Freyja was drawn by cats, and why Holda was attended by maidens riding on cats, or themselves disguised in feline form, is easily solved. Like the lynx, and the owl of Pallas Athene, the cat owes its celestial honours above all to its eyes, that gleam in the dark like fire, but the belief in its supernatural powers may very probably have been corroborated by the common observation that the cat, like the stormy boar, is a weatherwise animal. Pigs, as everybody knows, see the wind; in Westphalia they smell it.† Good weather may generally be expected when the cat washes herself, but bad when she licks her coat against the grain, or washes her face over her ear, or sits with her tail to the fire. In Germany, if it rains when women have a large washing on hand, it is a sign that the cats have a spite against them, because they

* Brand.

† Kuhn, Westf. ii. 93.

have not treated the animals well; an enemy to cats may reckon upon it that he will be carried to his grave in wind and rain;* and in Holland, if the weather is rainy on a wedding-day, the saying is that the bride has neglected to feed the cat.† Seeing that these sly creatures know so much of the weather, and are more than suspected of having a share in making it, nothing can be more unwise than to provoke them, as English sailors know very well. They do not much like to see cats on board, but least of all do they like to see them unusually frisky, for then they say "the cat has a gale of wind in her tail." An infallible recipe for raising a storm is to throw a cat overboard.‡ The presence of a dead hare on board ship is also said to bring bad weather.§

Cats, though inveterate milk-stealers, very rarely rob the dairy in any but the natural way; on the other hand, witch-cats have a great hankering after beer, a liquor into which no canny puss will dip her whiskers. Witches are adepts in the art of brewing (p. 221), and therefore fond of making parties to taste what their neighbours brew. It appears that on these occasions they always masquerade as cats, and what they steal they consume on the spot.

* Mannhardt, p. 90. † "Notes and Queries," x. 184.
‡ "Choice Notes," p. 160. § Ibid.

There was a countryman whose beer was all drunk up by night whenever he brewed, so that at last he resolved for once to sit up all night and watch. Well, as he was standing by his brewing copper, up came a great lot of cats, and he called to them, "Come, puss, puss, come warm you a bit." So they all squatted in a great ring round the fire as if to warm themselves. After they had sat there for a while, he asked them if the water was hot. "Just on the boil," said they, and as they spoke he dipped his long-handled pail in the wort, and soused the whole company with it. They all vanished at once; but on the following day his wife had a terribly scalded face, and then he knew who it was that had always drunk up his beer.*

This story appears to be widely spread. I know it to be current among the Flemish-speaking natives of Belgium.

The nightmare, also, often appears as a cat. A joiner in Bühl, who was much plagued with the nightmare, at last saw it steal into his room in that shape about midnight. Having stopped up the hole through which the cat had come in, he caught the animal, and nailed it by one paw to the floor. Next morning, instead of a cat, it was a handsome naked

* Kuhn u. Schwartz, Ndd. p. 287.

woman he found, with a nail driven through her hand. He married her, and they had three children; but one day he uncovered the hole he had stopped up; she escaped through it instantly in the shape of a cat, and never returned.*

There are a great number of cases on record in which German nightmares have been caught by stopping up the hole through which they had entered, and either striking a light or waiting till day, when the nightmare is always found in human form, and naked, like Tamlane in the old ballad. The sequel of the story is almost always the same as in that of the joiner of Bühl, except that the departing *mahrt*, or *mårte*, often makes some exclamation about England, and that in many instances she comes back every Saturday evening, but invisible, and brings clean linen for her husband and children.

In a village near Riesenburg, in East Prussia, there was a girl, who, unknown to herself, was every night transformed into a black cat. In the morning she used to feel exhausted as after a heavy dream; but the fact was that in her transformed state she used to go to her betrothed lover and scratch and torment him. One night he caught the cat and tied it up in

* Baader Volkssagen, No. 136.

a sack, in which he found next morning no cat, but his naked sweetheart. The parson of the parish cured her.*

In standard German the nightmare is called Alp, *i. e.*, Elf. It has many German provincial names, the most current of which is Mahrt, Mårte, or Mahr, different forms of a word which has no relation to the equine species, but is identical with the Sanscrit Marut (p. 17). Sometimes the nightmare appears as a mouse, a weasel, or a toad, but never, I believe, as a horse or mare, except in Fuseli's well-known engraving, which must have been designed after one of those suppers of half-raw pork from which the artist was wont to draw inspiration. It is a bit of false etymology embodied in a corresponding style of art.

The nightmare, or night-hag,† is equestrian, not equine. It is an old story in England, and still is common in Germany, that they infest stables at night and mount the horses, which are found sweating in their stalls in the morning as after a hard ride.‡ These riders, in all other respects iden-

* Tettau und Temme, Ostpreussen, p. 274.

† Hag, Anglo-Saxon *hægesse*, is the German *hexe*, witch, a word as applicable to a young and comely woman as to an ugly old crone.

‡ Brand, iii. 147.

tical with the Mahrts, are in some parts of Germany called Walriderske, *i. e.*, Valkyrs. In some of the tales that are told of them, they still retain their old divine nature; in others they are brought down to the common level of mere earthly witches. If they ride now in stables, without locomotion, it is because they swept of old through the air on their divine coursers. Now they steal by night to the beds of hinds and churls; but there was a time when they descended from Valhalla to conceive, in the embrace of a mortal, the demigod whom they afterwards accompanied to the battle-field, to bear him thence to the hall of Odin.

CHAPTER IX.

THE WEREWOLF.

THE werewolf is so called from the Anglo-Saxon *wer* (Lat. *vir*) "man" and *wolf*. The word corresponds exactly to the Greek *lycanthropos*, Italian *lupo mannaro*, Portuguese *lobis-homem*, and means a wolf who is properly a man. *Loup-garou*, the name given by the French to the same fearful being, is a pleonastic compound, which they have made out of their Romance appellation for the wolf and their old Frankish word *gerulf*, *i. e.*, werwlf, werewolf. The people of Bretagne have just such another mongrel term, *bleiz-garou* (from bleiz, wolf); but they have also the purely Celtic terms *denvleiz* and *grekvleiz*, meaning man-wolf and woman-wolf.

The werewolf tradition has not been discovered with certainty amongst the Hindus, but there is no European nation of Aryan descent in which it has not existed from time immemorial. Hence it is certain that the tradition itself, or the germs of it more or less developed, must have been brought by them all from Arya; and if Dr. Schwartz has not actually proved his case, he seems at least to have conjectured rightly in assigning, as one of those germs, the Aryan conception of the howling wind as a wolf.* The Maruts and other beings who were busy in the storm assumed various shapes. The human form was proper to many or all of them, for they were identical with the Pitris or Fathers (p. 15), and it would have been a very natural thought, when a storm broke out suddenly, that one or more of those people of the air had been turned into wolves for the occasion. It was also a primæval notion that there were dogs and wolves among the dwellers in hell, and Weber, who has shown that this belief was entertained by the early Hindus,† is of opinion that these infernal animals were real werewolves, that is to say, men upon whom such a transformation had been inflicted as a punishment.

The oldest werewolf story on record is that of Lycaon, king of Arcadia, in which however the legend of the werewolf proper is mixed up with another, and apparently a less ancient one, relating to the practice of sacrificing human victims, which seems to have prevailed more extensively and to a

* Ursprung, p. 118.

† Indische Studien, i. 412.

later period in Arcadia than in other parts of Greece. Lycaon is said to have been turned into a wolf by Zeus Lycaios, as a punishment for having offered a human victim to the god; and after Lycaon's time, according to a tradition recorded by Pausanias, Plato, and Pliny, similar transformations continued to be things of common occurrence on the same spot. One of the race of Anthos (probably a priestly family) was periodically chosen by lot and taken to an Arcadian lake, where he hung up his clothes on an oak. Then he swam across the lake, was changed into a wolf, and roamed the wilderness for nine years in company with other wolves. At the end of that time, if he had not tasted human flesh in the interval, he swam back again, found his clothes where he had left them, and recovered his original form, only with this difference, that it was nine years older.

It is certain that in Greece as well as in Arya the wolf was in early times a symbol of the stormy winds. It was sacred above all other animals to Apollo, who was surnamed after it Lycaios, or the wolf-god. This fact has much perplexed many learned men, and given them a world of trouble in striving to explain why an animal that figures so often and so naturally as a type of winter, night, and death, should have become the favourite of the radiant god of day. But all this labour would have been spared had it been borne in mind that even in Homer's time Apollo had not yet become the sun-god. Originally he was the god of the summer storms, and in that capacity he himself appeared as a wolf on sundry occasions, as, for instance, in Rhodes, when he slew the Telchins, a dwarfish race of magicians, smiths, and weather-makers, like the German Zwergs and the Panis of India. In the spring time, the appropriate season for the birth of such a god, Apollo's mother, "the dark-robed Leto," or Latona (*i. e.*, the dark storm-cloud), escorted at Jove's command by the Northwind, came as a she-wolf from Lycia to the place where she was delivered of her twins. The Zeus Lycaios of the Arcadians was evidently Zeus *plus* Apollo, the thunderer, considered with special reference to the winds that accompany the thunder. In mythical language, Apollo was the son of Zeus; that is to say, he was Zeus in another form. The two gods were in fact, like Indra and Rudra (p. 18), only different personifications of the same cycle of natural phenomena.

In Greece the tradition of the werewolf appears to have run the usual course of myths. Beginning as a figurative explanation of meteoric facts, it next became a hieratic mystery, and then descended from the domain of religion to that of magic and popular story. In this last stage it is the subject of a ludicrous tale told by Æsop. A thief hung about a tavern for some days without being able to steal anything. At last he saw the host sitting before the door in a handsome new garment, and going up to him he began a conversation, in the course of which he fell to yawning and then howling like a wolf. "What's the matter with you?" said the host. "I'll tell you directly," said the thief, "but first let me beg you will take care of my clothes, for I will leave them here. I cannot tell how it is this yawning comes upon me; whether it be for my sins or for any other cause is to me unknown; but so sure as ever I yawn three times I change into a wolf that devours men." So saying he yawned a second time and howled as before. The host started up and would have made off, but the thief held him fast by his tunic, saying, "Stay where you are, I beseech you, and take care of my clothes, that I may not tear them all to bits." With that he yawned a third time, and the host, in mortal terror, ran and hid himself in the innermost nook of his tavern, leaving his tunic in the hands of the thief, who vanished with it instantly.

Herodotus was informed that the Neurians passed for wizards among the Scythians and the Greeks who were settled about the Black Sea, because each of them, once a year, became a wolf for a few days, and then returned to his natural shape.

The transformation of men into wolves is known in Roman literature only as a work of magic. Virgil is the first Latin author who mentions this superstition. He is followed by Propertius; and Petronius gives the following circumstantial story as related by Niceros at Trimalchio's banquet:—

"It happened that my master was gone to Capua to dispose of some second-hand goods. I took the opportunity, and persuaded our guest to walk with me to the fifth milestone. He was a valiant soldier, and a sort of grim water-drinking Pluto. About cockcrow, when the moon was shining as bright as midday, we came among the monuments. My friend began addressing himself to the stars, but I was rather in a mood to sing or to count them; and when I turned to look at him, lo! he had already stripped himself and laid down his clothes near him. My heart was in my nostrils; and I stood like a dead man; but he made a mark round his clothes (*circumminxit vestimenta*), and on a sudden became a wolf. Do not think I jest; I would not lie for any man's estate. But to return to what I was saying. When he became a wolf he began howling, and fled into the woods. At first I hardly knew where I was, and afterwards, when I went to take up his clothes, they were turned into stone. Who then died with fear but I! Yet I drew my sword, and went cutting the air right and left, till I reached the villa of my sweetheart. I entered the court-yard. I almost breathed my last, the sweat ran down my neck, my eyes were dim, and I thought I should never recover myself. My Melissa wondered why I was out so late, and said to me,—'Had you come sooner you might at least have helped us, for a wolf has entered the farm and worried all our cattle; but he had not the best of the joke, for all he escaped, for our slave ran a lance through his neck.' When I heard this I could not doubt how it was, and as it was clear daylight, I ran home as fast as a robbed innkeeper. When I came to the spot where the clothes had been turned into stone, I could find nothing except blood. But when I got home I found my friend the soldier in bed, bleeding at the neck like an ox, and a doctor dressing his wound. I then knew he was a turnskin; nor would I ever have broke bread with him again, no, not if you had killed me."

The werewolf is here called a turnskin (versipellis), there being no special name for the thing in Latin.

It was an old belief in the North that transformations of all kinds were commonly effected by means of an appropriate garment of fur or feather, which could be put on or laid aside at pleasure (pp. 21, 22). The oldest Norse legends of the werewolf make the change of form depend upon the putting on of a wolf-skin shirt. Thus it was, according to the Volsunga Saga, that the heroes Sigmundr and Sinfjötli became wolves for nine days out of ten. It was only on the tenth day that they could put off the wolf-skins; and when, after a long course of adventures, they desired to abandon the wolfish shape for ever, they effected their purpose without difficulty or inconvience by burning the skins. The Berseker of historic times were also men who had acquired superhuman strength by transformation. It is said of King Harald Harfagr, that he had among his retainers a corps of berseker who were called *úlfhednar*, that is to say, "wolf-frocked." "The Saga itself," says Maurer,* "seems to indicate that this epithet is to be understood as signifying that the warriors in question wore coats of wolf-skin over their armour; but this is manifestly a mistake of

* Bekehrung, ii. 109. Hertz, p. 57.

later times, for the original conception was that of men who possessed *ulfahamir*, wolf-shirts, and were in fact werewolves." This view of the matter is corroborated by the etymology lately assigned to the word *berseker* by Egilssohn in his Poetical Lexicon of the Icelandic tongue. According to that weighty authority the word means one who has a bear-skin shirt (*berr*, bear, *serkr*, sark, shirt), and possesses the strength of a bear through its transforming power. King Harald's warriors differed from those ursine heroes in having the skins and the fierceness and force of wolves.

"Even now in Norway it is matter of popular belief that Finns and Lapps, who from time immemorial have passed for the most skilful witches and wizards in the world, can at will assume the shape of bears; and it is a common thing to say of one of those beasts, when he gets unusually savage and daring, 'that can be no Christian bear.' On such a bear, in the parish of Oföden, after he had worried to death more than sixty horses and six men, it is said that a girdle of bear-skin, the infallible mark of a man thus transformed, was found when he was at last tracked and slain." *

The Russians also are held by their Swedish

* Dasent, Introd. D. M. 1051.

neighbours to be very potent wizards. In the last war between Sweden and Russia, when the province of Calmar was overrun with wolves, it was generally believed that the Russians had turned the Swedish prisoners of war into wolves, and sent them home to ravage the country. It is also related of a soldier in the Calmar regiment, that, having been transformed into a wolf, he made his way from Finland over the Aland islands to Smaland, impelled by his desire to see again his home and his wife and children. He was shot by a hunter, who brought the dead wolf into the village; and when it was flayed a shirt was found beneath the skin, which was recognized by the soldier's wife as one she had made for her husband before he went to the war.—A Swedish bridegroom and his friends were riding through a wood when they were all turned into wolves by evil spirits. After the lapse of some years the forlorn bride was walking one day in the same wood, and in anguish of heart, as she thought of her lost lover, she shrieked out his name. Instantly he appeared in human form and rushed into her arms. The sound of his christian name had dissolved the devilish enchantment that bound him.

The baptismal name has not quite lost in Protestant lands the virtue which belonged to it in Catholic times as the name of one's patron saint. I have been told by an Essex woman, that when she was a child she had orders from her mother, who was very subject to nightmare, not to call her "mother," when she groaned at night, but to address her by her christian name.

It is a belief peculiar to Denmark that if a woman uses a certain charm to secure ease and safety in childbirth, every boy she will henceforth bear will become a werewolf, every girl a nightmare.

Gervase of Tilbury testifies that werewolves were common in England in his time; and, though Celtic witches generally prefer to disguise themselves as hares, mention is made of a wolfwoman in the Mabinogion. Camden reports a story current in the county of Tipperary of men who were every year turned into wolves, but declares that he does not believe it; and Giraldus Cambrensis gives an older instance of the same superstition. A priest, he says, on his way from Ulster to Meath, was addressed one night by a wolf in the following terms: "We belong to a certain Ossyrian sept (Ulster), two of whom, male and female, are every seven years compelled, through a curse laid upon us by a certain saint, to wit, Abbot Natalis, to depart both from their natural form and from their native soil; for, wholly putting off the human form, they put on that of wolves. But after the space of seven years, if they be still alive, two others take their places under like conditions, and the first pair return to their pristine nature and country." Having said this, the wolf led the priest to his companion in misfortune, that he might give her the holy viaticum, for she lay at the point of death; and, to prove that she was a human being, he stripped off the wolf-skin with his paw from her head to her middle, and thereupon the perfect form of an old woman was plain to be seen. The priest gave her the sacrament, and then the wolf drew back the skin over her head. The coincidence between this Celtic story and the Arcadian legend of Lycaon and his successors, with respect to the continuance of the transformation for a stated number of years, is worthy of note.

Stories about werewolves are still current in Germany, especially in the north and east. The transformation is in most cases effected by a girdle which has taken the place of the old wolf-shirt. It is made of the skin of a wolf, or of a man who has been hanged, and is fastened with a buckle having seven tongues. When the buckle is unclasped, or the girdle is cut, the charm is dissolved. There was a werewolf in the village of Hindenburg in Altmark so terribly strong that he could carry off an ox in his mouth. He worried cattle and devoured human beings, but never hurt his wife, because she could *ban* him with magic words which he had taught her for the purpose. Then she used to unbuckle his belt, and he became a rational man again. The girdle transforms everybody who puts it on, whether he does so with that intention or not. A sale was made, by order of the authorities, of a heap of old things that lay in a room in the Erichsburg. Among them were old implements of the chase which had been taken from poachers, and also some werewolf girdles. The amtmann's man, having a mind to try the effect of the latter, buckled one of them on, was immediately turned into a wolf, and started off for Hunnesrück. The amtmann rode after him, and cutting at his back with a sword, severed the girdle, whereupon the man resumed his proper shape.—A man in the neighbourhood of Steina having forgotten to lock up his wolf-girdle, it was found by his little boy, who put it on and was transformed. He looked like a bundle of peastraw, and lumbered off with the clumsy gait of a bear. His father overtook him, and unfastened the girdle before any mischief was done. The boy afterwards stated that, the moment he put on the girdle, he was seized with so ravenous a hunger that he could fain have devoured everything that came in his way. Of all the German tales of werewolves, the most widely difused is that of the mower, herdsman of horses, or charcoal-burner, who, believing that his two comrades are asleep in the meadow, fastens a strip of wolf-skin about him, becomes a wolf, and eats up a whole foal. All this has been observed by one of his comrades, and on the way home, when he complains of pain in his body, "That is not to be wondered at," says the man, "when a fellow has got a whole foal in his belly." "Had you said that to me out yonder," replied the werewolf, "you would never have reached home again;" and with these words he vanished, never to return.

In Germany, as already mentioned, the skin of a man that has been hanged makes as good a werewolf girdle as the skin of a wolf, and this for a reason derived, apparently, from old judicial usages. The Northern nations used of old to class the proscribed murderer and robber with the wolf, and make that animal the symbol of his crime and outlawry. In the old Norse tongue the common appellation for such a man was *vargr*, wolf; the man who had broken the peace of the temple by an act of violence was called *vargr i veum*, "wolf in the sacred place." The phrase "lupinum enim gerit caput, quod Anglice wulfes heafod dicitur," is found in the laws of Edward the Confessor; and in the Tale of Gamelyn (ascribed to Chaucer, 1387) it is said, "When that Gamelyn their lorde wolves hede was cried and made." In old times a wolf was hung by the side of thieves and robbers; and *varagtreo*, *i. e.*, wolf-tree, is the old Saxon name for the gallows.

Wounding a werewolf severely either forces him to resume his natural form on the spot, or leads to his speedy detection. A farmer and his wife were haymaking near Caasburg. After a while the wife declared that she felt an unconquerable restlessness; she could stay there no longer; and away she went, after making her husband promise that if any wild beast came near, he would throw his hat to it and run away. She had not long been gone when a wolf swam across the Swine, and rushed at the haymakers. The farmer threw his hat at the beast, which tore it to bits; but meanwhile a man stole round with a pitchfork and stabbed the wolf from behind. The form changed instantly, and all present were horrified at seeing that the man had slain the farmer's wife.—A farmer of Malchin, when driving through a wood, suddenly alighted, telling his wife to drive on, and if anything attacked her, she was to throw her apron to it. Presently up came a wolf, and tore the apron to pieces; but the wife knew who it was after her husband's return, when she saw some threads of the apron sticking between his teeth. In a similar case which occurred at Gross Schnee the wife was struck with death by the horrible discovery.

The last three instances exemplify that inborn or imposed necessity which some persons feel at particular seasons to become wolves, and rend or devour something human or pertaining to the persons of human beings. A still more horrible example of this necessity is seen in the following story from Ottensee, near Altona. A farmer there had made a contract with the evil one, which secured to him an unfailing supply of money, on condition that on the last day of every month he should become a wolf, and should each time kill a human being. This he did punctually for a long time, but at last an old woman whom he attacked jammed him so hard between a door and a doorpost that he had to crawl home severely injured. That night the devil came to fetch him because he had broken his contract, and to redeem himself he was forced to devour his own little daughter. About a year afterwards he fell upon his maid-servant in the field, but she called him three times by his christian name, and he stood in his proper shape before her. Thereupon she went away to Hamburg, without saying a word to anybody. That night the devil came again to fetch away the farmer, and again he purchased his life by eating his only remaining child. It was then suspected that he was a werewolf; his wife deserted him, and the neighbours shunned him; so he stole away to Hamburg, where he thought to continue his cannibal practices in an inn, but he was recognized by his former maid-servant, and given up to justice.*

A farmer's wife in Hesse used to put flesh-meat on the table at every meal, but for a long time she would not tell how she procured it. At last she promised to let her husband see how it was done, on condition that, whilst she was about it, he should not call her by her christian name. They went together into a field where sheep were feeding. There the woman threw a ring over her; in a moment she was a wolf amongst the flock, and in another she was off with a sheep in her mouth. The husband was petrified; but when the shepherd and his dogs pursued the wolf, the danger in which he saw his wife made him forget his promise, and he cried out, "Oh, Margaret!" At the word the

* Hertz, p. 83.

wolf had vanished, and his wife stood naked in the field.

Mere recognition of the werewolf, without directly naming the person, often has the same disenchanting effect. An old she-wolf met a farmer in the field, and sprang again and again at his horse's neck. The farmer thought he should know the wolf's voice, its tone seemed so familiar to his ears, and he cried out, "Is that you, my old mother, or is it not?"—when behold! there she stood before him in her proper shape, but unable to move a limb. He laid her on the cart and took her home, but she did not live long after.

Another way of unmasking the werewolf or other transformed persons is by casting iron or steel over them. The skin splits crosswise on the werewolf's forehead, and the naked man comes out through the opening. If a sword be stuck in the ground with the hilt downwards and the point turned towards the werewolf, he is "banned," and must stay there until the time comes when he must appear again as a man.

It frequently happens that the werewolf is "frozen," that is to say, invulnerable by ordinary weapons or missiles. In that case he must be shot with elder-pith, or with balls made of inherited silver.

The change of a werewolf back again to human form does not always take place so quickly as to prevent the pursuers from descrying in the man some vestige of the bestial shape. A villager of Elmenhorst had from his birth the gift of changing himself into a wolf. In that form he was once chased into his bedroom by two Hamburg butchers armed with great whips. They found him in bed with his wife, but not yet completely retransformed, for the wolf's tail still hung out from under the quilt.

Distinct from the ordinary werewolf which we have hitherto been considering is another kind which is near akin to the vampyre, for it is not a transformed living man, but a corpse that has risen from the grave in the form of a wolf. The belief in this kind of werewolf still prevails in Prussia, as it did formerly in Normandy. In that province, down to the close of the last century, a change of this nature not uncommonly befell the remains of one who had died in mortal sin. First, the corpse began to gnaw and tear the cloth that covered its face. Then fearful sounds of wailing were heard issuing out of the ground; the coffin was burst open; the earth that lay upon it was rent, and flames of hell broke forth. Whenever the watchful priest of the parish became aware of those well-known tokens, he had the corpse dug up, and then cutting off its head with the sexton's spade, and bidding defiance to the hell-hounds that strove against him, he carried the head to the nearest stream and cast it in. It sank at once; but this was not all; for, weighted with its doom, it pierced the bottom of the river, and pressed slowly downwards through the earth to the place of its everlasting torments.*

King John of England is said to have gone about as a werewolf after his death. An old Norman chronicle avers that the monks of Worcester were compelled by the frightful noises proceeding from his grave, to dig up his body and cast it out of consecrated ground. "Thus the ill presage of his surname Lackland was completely realised, for he lost in his lifetime almost all the domains under his suzerainty, and even after death he could not keep peaceful possession of his tomb."

Trials of alleged werewolves (loups-garous) were very numerous in France in the sixteenth century, and many of the accused were condemned to the flames. Boquet, in his *Discours des Sorciers*, relates the following facts as having occurred in 1588, near Apchon, in the mountains of Auvergne:—A gentleman looking out one evening from a window of

* Mdlle. Bosquet.

his château, saw a hunter whom he knew, and asked the man to bring him something on his return from the chace. The hunter was attacked in the plain by a great wolf, and after a sharp conflict cut off one of its fore-paws with his hunting-knife. On his way back he called at the château, and putting his hand into his game-bag, to show the gentleman the wolf's paw, he drew out a human hand with a gold ring, which the gentleman at once recognized as his wife's. He looked for her, and found her in the kitchen with one arm concealed under her apron, and on uncovering it he saw that the hand was gone. The lady was brought to trial, confessed, and was burnt at Ryon. Boquet says he had this story from a trustworthy person who had been on the spot a fortnight after the event.

In Eastern Europe the werewolf appears in his most appalling aspect, as a being whose nature is blended with that of the vampyre. The same word is used to designate both in the languages of most branches of the Slave stock; but this appears to be a comparatively modern trait, for there is no sign of it in the ancient tradition of the Neurians, of which we have already spoken. In Poland there are traces of the old belief that werewolves were bound to assume that form at certain periods in every year; in the

Middle Ages it was twice a year, at Christmas and St. John's Day; but in later legends the *wilkolak*, or werewolf, is generally the victim of a spiteful sorceress's vengeance. Once upon a time, when some young people were dancing on the banks of the Vistula, a wolf broke in among them and carried off the prettiest girl of the village. The young men pursued, but they were unarmed, and the wolf escaped with his booty to the woods. Fifty years afterwards, whilst the villagers were again making merry on the same spot, there appeared among them a woebegone, ice-grey man, in whom an aged villager recognized his long-lost brother. The latter narrated how he had long ago been turned into a wolf by a wicked witch; how he had carried off the beautiful girl during the harvest feast, and how the poor thing had died of grief a year after in the forest. "From that time forth," he said, "I flung myself with ravenous hunger upon every human being that came in my way;" and he showed his hands, which were still all smeared with blood. "For the last four years," he continued, "I have been going about again in human shape, and I am come to look once more upon my native place, for I must soon become a wolf again." Hardly had he uttered the words ere he sprang to his feet in the form of a wolf, and ran off howling, never to be seen again.

It is related of another Pole that he was turned into a wolf by a witch whose love he had despised. In spite of his bestial form he loathed raw flesh, and lived on milk, bread, and other food, which he snatched from the labourers in the field. Living in this way he wandered about for many a long year without sleeping, until a great weariness at last overcame him, and he fell asleep. On awaking, he found himself again a man, and ran naked as he was to his village; but there he found everything changed.

A peasant had been seven years a werewolf, when the witchery suddenly ceased, and he hastened home; but finding that his wife was married to his man, he cried out in his wrath, "Oh, why am I no longer a werewolf, that I might punish this base woman!" No sooner had he uttered the impious words than, again become a wolf, he sprang at his wife, devoured the child she had borne to his man, and wounded herself mortally. The neighbours hastened to the spot and killed him; but when light came, they saw, instead of a dead wolf, the body of the man they had well known.

A witch came to a wedding, rolled her girdle

together, laid it on the threshold, and poured on the floor a drink brewed from linden wood. After this, when the new-married couple and their friends stepped over the threshold, they were turned into wolves on the spot, and in that form they prowled for three years about the witch's house with hideous howlings. On the day when the enchantment expired, the witch came out with a fur cloak, wrapped it, with the hairy side out, round one werewolf after another, and thereby restored them to their natural shape ; but the bridegroom's tail, which she had left uncovered by the cloak, stuck to him for the rest of his days. This happened in the year 1821 or 1822.

Of another wedding party of Poles it is related that they became werewolves through a spell laid on them by a soldier upon whom the bridegroom had set his dogs. Some years afterwards three werewolves were killed in a great hunt, and under the skin of one of them was found a fiddle, under those of the other two were the wedding dresses of the bride and bridegroom.*

* The examples of the werewolf tradition in this chapter are taken for the most part from Dr. Hertz's treatise.

CHAPTER X.

THE WILD HUNT—THE TWILIGHT OF THE GODS.

WHEN the Romans and the Germans became acquainted with each other's gods, both sides agreed in identifying the Odin, Woden, or Wuotan of the one with the Mercury of the other. Tacitus, in his work on the Germans, written in the first century of our era, says that above all the immortals they worshipped Mercury, and propitiated him with human sacrifices. We are told also in the legendary history of our own country that when Hengist and Horsa arrived with their Saxons in Britain, and were asked by King Vortigern what gods they adored, "We sacrifice," said they, "chiefly to Woden, whom you call Mercury, and to his wife Frea." Hence, when the planetary week of seven days was adopted by the Germans in the fourth century, the Roman dies Mercurii (French Mercredi) became their Woden's-day, in English, Wednesday.

There were two principal reasons for this agreement between the two races: one was that both gods were givers of wealth and good fortune; the other, that whereas it was Mercury's office to conduct the shades to Hades, so Woden rode with the wild host of the dead and led them to Walhalla.

The name of Woden or Wuotan denotes the stormy or furious goer, being derived from a verb which is closely related to the Lowland Scotch word *wud*, mad or furious.* The verb itself survives in English, but greatly tamed down and restricted in meaning, for it now signifies nothing more violent than to walk through shallow water, to *wade*. Originally it meant to go like one that is "wud," to go as the winds go when they rend the forests in their furious course. So went Woden or Odin, whose original nature was that of a storm-god;† and that is the character he sustains at this day in the popular legends of Germany. They picture him as sweeping through the air in the roaring winds, either alone or with a great retinue consisting of the souls of the dead, which have become winds, and have, like the Maruts, taken the shape of men, dogs, boars, &c. In some parts of Germany the hunt is called Heljagd or dead hunt, in others the English hunt (die engelske

* "The women are a' gane wud."—Jacobite song of the '45. "Dinna put a knife in a wud man's hand."—Proverb.

† Wâta, the Sanscrit name of the wind, is radically the same as Wuotan.

jagd), which means the same thing (p. 123), England being another name for the nether world.* The apparition is known under two forms and by corresponding names, as the Wild Hunt and as the Furious Host. The former occurs chiefly in North and the latter in South Germany.

Mounted on his white or dappled-grey steed, the wild huntsman may always be recognized by his broad-brimmed hat and his wide mantle, from which he is surnamed Hakelbärend or Hakelberg, an old word signifying mantle-wearer. The hooting owl Tutursel flies before him, and ravens, birds peculiarly sacred to Woden, accompany the chase. Whoever sees it approach must fall flat on the ground, or shelter himself under an odd number of boards, nine or eleven, otherwise he will be borne away through the air and set down hundreds of miles away from home, among people who speak a strange tongue. It is still more dangerous to look out of the window when Odin is sweeping by. The rash man is struck dead, or at least he gets a box on the ear that makes his head swell as big as a bucket and leaves a fiery mark on his cheek. In some instances the offender has been struck blind or mad. There are certain places where Woden is accustomed to feed his horse

* Kuhn, Westf. ii. 13.

or let it graze, and in those places the wind is always blowing. He has also a preference for certain tracks, over which he hunts again and again at fixed seasons, from which circumstance districts and villages in the old Saxon land received the name of Woden's Way. Houses and barns in which there are two or three doors opposite each other are very liable to be made thoroughfares by the wild hunt.

The wild huntsman's hounds can talk like men. A peasant caught one of them, a little one, and hid it in his sack. Up came the wild huntsman and missed it. "Where are you, Waldmann?" he cried. "In Heineguggeli's sack," was the answer. When the hounds are running aloft their hair drops rain; when they light upon the earth they sniff about the people they meet, and greedily devour whatever comes in their way. It is recommended, as a means of safety, to give them a bag of meal, that they may eat the contents as they fly through the air. When Woden rides through a house he often leaves one of his hounds behind him. It lies down on the hearth, and there it remains for a whole year, howling and whining and living upon nothing but ashes, until the god returns, when it jumps up, wags its tail, and joins the pack again. There is only one way of ridding the house sooner of the unwelcome guest, and that is to brew beer in eggshells. The hound watches the operation and exclaims

> Though I am now as old as the old Bohemian wold,
> Yet the like of this, I ween, in my life I ne'er have seen ;

and away it goes and is seen no more. On Christmas evenings especially, that is to say, at the season of the winter solstice, it is very unsafe to leave linen hanging out of doors, for the wild huntsman's hounds will tear it to pieces.

When Woden rides at the head of a full field the object of the chase is generally a boar or a horse. When he rides with his hounds alone, it is in pursuit of a woman with long snow-white breasts. Seven years he follows her; at last he runs her down, throws her across his horse, and carries her home. In Central Germany the wild hunt chases a whole flock of elfish beings, the Moss-wifekins and Wood-maidens, whose lives are bound up with those of the forest trees. If any one adds his voice by invitation to the cries of the wild hunters, the god throws him down, as his share of the booty, a horse's haunch that turns to gold. But if any one dares to bawl out "halloa!" and "hurrah!" in mockery when the hunt passes by, Woden shouts to him in a voice of thunder,

> You that helped to chase the game
> Eat your share now of the same;

and down comes a horse's leg, or a moss-wifekin's foot with the green shoe upon it. The stench of it is suffocating, and it sticks fast to the mocker's back or to his dwelling, and do what he will he cannot remove it. The wild hunt comes out from the hills and mountains, and disappears in them again, or in ponds or lakes, when the hunt is over.

The Furious Host is also a cavalcade of the dead, but not for purposes of the chase. Sometimes it gallops through the stormy air as a herd of wild boars; but the spirits of which it consists generally appear in human form. They are of both sexes and of all ages, souls of unchristened babes being included among them; for Holda or Bertha often joins the hunt. At the end of the last century a woman was delivered of a still-born child. Soon afterwards she heard that the furious host had passed over the village, and in her anguish at the thought of her child, now doomed to sweep through the stormy air with the unblest spirits until the day of judgment, she was seized with a violent malady and died. In Tyrol, according to the testimony of Baron von Alpenburg, it is no uncommon thing for mothers, who have lost a child, to seek the aid of the wizard, with the hope that he may be able to reanimate the little corpse for a moment, so that it may receive baptism and its soul be rescued from the furious host, or from Bertha. Was it the tradition of the furious host—not unknown in England—that suggested to Shakespeare the image of

> Pity, like a naked new-born babe,
> Riding the blast!

I cannot find any mention of the wild hunt or the furious host among the superstitions of Ireland; but there is one element of that tradition which certainly exists there. "The ideas of the Irish peasantry respecting the state of departed souls are very singular." So says a writer in the *Athenæum* (Jan. 1847). "According to the tenets of the church to which the majority of them belong, the souls of the departed are either in paradise, hell, or purgatory. But popular belief assigns the air as a third place of suffering, where unquiet souls wander about until their period of penance is past. On a cold or wet or stormy night the peasant will exclaim with real sympathy, 'Musha! God help the poor souls that are in the shelter of the ditches, or under the eves this way!' And the good 'chanathee,' or mother of a family, will sweep the hearth, that the poor souls may warm themselves when the family retires. The conviction that the spirits of the departed sweep along with the storm or shiver in the driving rain, is singularly wild and near akin to the Skandinavian myth."

The first token which the furious host gives of its approach is a low song that makes the hearer's flesh creep. The grass and the leaves of the forest wave and bow in the moonshine as often as the strain begins anew. Presently the sounds come nearer and nearer, and swell into the music of a thousand instruments. Then bursts the hurricane, and the oaks of the forest come crashing down. The spectral appearance often presents itself in the shape of a great black coach, on which sit hundreds of spirits singing a wondrously sweet song. Before it goes a man, who loudly warns everybody to get out of the way. All who hear him must instantly drop down with their faces to the ground, as at the coming of the wild hunt, and hold fast by something, were it only a blade of grass; for the furious host has been known to force many a man into its coach and carry him hundreds and hundreds of miles away through the air.

The legend of the furious host has taken a peculiar shape in the Bernese Oberland, the Grisons and

Wallis, where it is known as the Nightfolk or Dead Folk, and is described as a ghostly procession, the appearance of which betokens an approaching mortality. The skeleton Death himself marches at its head playing the fiddle, and it bears along, with low mutterings and music, the corpses of those who are next to die. If the Nightfolk knock at the door of a house, whoever answers the summons must go along with them and die. Two children were lying down on a crossway, the one asleep, the other awake. The latter heard a rattling of bones, and several voices praying. It was the Nightfolk. Presently one said, "Shall we wake the children?" "No," replied another, "one of them will soon come with us." The child had seen nothing. It died soon after.

Most of the legendary details in the foregoing sketch may be traced back to their origin, and found to resolve themselves into figurative, and sometimes highly poetical descriptions of natural phenomena. As the man of southern climes prostrates himself before the simoom and the sirocco, so did the man of Northern Europe before the storm-god. The wild huntsman loves to ride through houses that have two outer doors directly opposite each other: that is to say, in plain prose, there is always a thorough draught, more or less strong, from one such door to the other. Woden's hounds are human souls that have become air, and as winds they tear the linen that is hung out to dry, eat meal, or blow and scatter it out of sight, and feed upon the ashes that are swept up from the hearth by the gusts that are always stronger there than in any other part of the room—a fact which is typified by the continual howling of the hound left behind by the wild hunt. Woden's mantle is the speckled sky, and his broad hat the cloud. His grey horse, again, is the wind-driven cloud (p. 7), which the storm-god rides or hunts, when he is not chasing the woman. There are legends which combine both images, for they tell how women who have sinned with priests become the horses of the wild huntsman, who stops from time to time, by night at a forge, and has them shod with red-hot iron. The moss-wifekins and wood-maidens are female elementary spirits brought down to the earth from the clouds to become genii of the forest, and when they are chased *in whole flocks*—or, in other words, when the leaves are blown off the trees—this is but a modification of the older conception of the flying cloud. The fetid leg of a horse or foot of the wood-nymph signifies the sulphurous lightning which Woden casts down from the clouds; and the red gleam of the lightning is seen in the horse's leg that turns into gold.

The woman chased by the wild huntsman is the light whirlwind which precedes the great storm, and which is called in Germany the wind's bride (Windsbraut).* The dancing, pirouetting movements of the one, and the stern rush of the other, sufficiently explain the genders respectively ascribed to them. This bride is Freyja, the wife of Odin. The seven years during which the spell-bound storm-god has hunted her without being able to run her down, are the seven winter months during which the storm has lost the peculiar character that belongs to it in summer, and is comparatively inert, and, as it were, "enchanted." In mythical language, the phrase "seven years" has almost always the meaning we have here assigned to it. Thus, gold-guarding dragons come forth and subterranean treasures sun themselves every seven years—that is, after winter is past; and Thor's lightning hammer, buried during the winter in the earth, comes to the surface in seven years, seven days, and seven hours.

The coach of the furious host is the cloud driven along by the storm, and its marvellous music is the

* Schwartz, p. 6.

strain that was sung of old by the Maruts (p. 15). Its boars are winds (p. 7), and their white flashing tusks were also looked upon by the southern Aryans and the Greeks, as well as by the Germans, as images of the lightning. The cloud-water may easily be recognized in the pond, lake, or river in which the wild hunt and the furious host disappear, or over which they are ferried. Many legends tell how the spirits of the furious host slaughtered and ate up a cow, which they brought to life again out of the hide. This cow is the cloud which the souls consume, as spirits of the winds, by pouring down its rain upon the earth. Only a little remnant of cloud, the hide, remains, and it grows again into a new cloud. In Vorarlberg, for instance, one Sunday during mass, the Nightfolk came to a peasant's house, took a cow out of the stall, killed, roasted, and ate it, making a great uproar all the time. The peasant's children were allowed to share in the repast, but were ordered not to gnaw or destroy any of the bones. Before the Nightfolk went away they gathered up the bones, and wrapped them in the cow's hide; but one little bone was missing; the children had thrown it away. "There's no help for it," said the spirits; "the animal must go lame." And sure enough, when the people of the village came out of church, there stood the cow in the stall, as well as ever, only that one foot was crippled.

Out of the same conception of the clouds as cows arose the belief that Woden and his host carried cows with them up into the clouds, and brought them back three days afterwards, milked dry, or never brought them back at all. If the cow is not given up willingly, the god comes and takes it. The people of the Hellhouse, in Ostenholz, a village between the Weser and the Elbe, were obliged, year by year, on every Christmas Eve, to turn out a cow for the Hellhunter (the wild huntsman). As soon as the animal was let out of the stall it disappeared. Everybody knew perfectly well beforehand what cow was to be taken, for when Martinmas or Michaelmas was come, the cow whose turn it was had manifestly grown fatter than any of the rest. Once the people ventured to keep the animal shut up in the stall, but there was such an uproar and din about the house as never was heard before. The cow plunged about in the stall as if she was mad, pulled up the stakes out of the ground, and would never be quiet until they let her out, when she instantly vanished.

We are too much accustomed to think of the chief gods of Greece only as they appear in the more finished theogony of that people,—immortal and victorious over all enemies; but the earlier legends represented them as subject to defeat and even to death. They tell how Apollo was slain by the Python, and even the grave of Zeus was to be seen in Crete.* Such legends belong to a time when the gods were still understood to be elementary beings, part and parcel of nature, and subject to all its changes. Their death was therefore regarded as a trance, a sort of enchanted sleep, from which they awoke to fresher life and vigour. So was it also with the wild huntsman. Wherever the name of Hackelberg (p. 268), or of one of his legendary representatives, is known, it is coupled with this story:—He heard once at midnight a voice asking from the neighbouring thicket if the *stumpy-tail* was ready that was to kill him; and that same night he dreamed of perishing by the tusks of a furious wild boar with a short tail. A great hunt had been appointed for the next day, but in consequence of his dream his wife implored him to remain at home. He went to the hunt nevertheless, fell in with the boar he had seen in his dream, and killed it after a hard struggle. Elated with his victory, he kicked the dead boar, saying, "Rip me up now if you can!

* Spannheim z. Callim. h. in Jovem, 8; in Dianam, 89. Schwartz, p. 96.

You were to have taken my life, and you are dead before me." But the kick he gave was so violent that the boar's sharp tusk pierced his leg through his boot, and he died of the wound. Before his death he gave orders that he should be laid in his coffin, unwashed as he was, and buried in the spot to which his dappled grey steed should draw him. This was done, and he lies buried on a wild mountain spot, the way to which no one can find twice. Some have come upon it by chance, but have never been able to discover it again.

The meaning of the story is this. The storm-god pursues the fierce whirlwind—the boar—that ravages the woods and fields, but its death in the last storms of autumn is soon followed by that of the hunter himself. During the winter Hackelberg-Woden is dead, or asleep, or enchanted in the cloud mountain.

In some places local tradition makes Hackelberg a mere man; in others an enormous giant. At Rocklum, near Wolfenbuttel, the existence of a group of hills is accounted for by saying that they are composed of the gravel which Hackelberg once threw out of his shoe as he passed that way with the wild hunt. Similar traditions are not unknown in England. "There were formerly three huge upright stones near Kennet, not far from Abury; the country people called them from time immemorial 'the devil's coits.' They could be playthings, it might be readily imagined, for no other busy idler. But the good folks of Somersetshire, by a sort of refinement of such hackneyed traditions, hold that a great stone near Stanton Drew, now called '*Hackell's Coit,*' and which formerly weighed thirty tons, was thrown from a hill about a mile off by a mortal champion, Sir John Hautville." *

Woden and his hunting train still haunt Dartmoor. One of that god's many names was Wunsch (p. 169), Anglo-Saxon, Wisk, English, "wish," and this name "is retained in the Devonshire term 'whishtness,' used to signify all unearthly creatures and their doings. The spectral pack which hunts over Dartmoor is called the 'wish-hounds,' and the black 'master' who follows the chace is no doubt the same who has left his mark on Wistman's Wood"—a very ancient forest of dwarf oaks overhanging the West Dart. †

When the name of the wild huntsman ceased to be generally remembered as that of a god, the people substituted for it various names of historical or

* Knight's "Old England," p. 14.

† Quarterly Rev., July, 1836, p. 219.

legendary personages, such as Theodorick, the great King of the Goths, or as he is popularly called in Germany, Dietrich of Bern (*i. e.*, Verona). In the French province of Perigord, the wild hunt is called La chasse Hérode, from a confusion of the name of Herodias, the murderess of John the Baptist, with Hrôdso (*i. e.*, renowned), a surname of Odin. The "Grand Veneur" hunts in the forest of Fontainebleau, Hugh Capet about Tours. In the department of the Pyrenees, Lower Normandy, and Guienne, the leader of the wild hunt is the Arthur of British and Armorican romance. "Very often," says Gervase of Tilbury, "have knights been seen hunting with hounds and horns in the woods of Great or Little Britain at noonday and by the light of the full moon; and when the foresters asked who they were, they said they belonged to the company and household of Arthur." * In Scotland also,

> Arthour knycht he raid on nycht
> With gylden spur and candel lycht. †

In these two notices we miss one portion of the original tradition—the stormy nature of the wild hunt—for the spectral Arthur and his companions pursue their game in calm weather, by torchlight or under the unclouded moon. By the middle of the

* G. T. p. 12. † "Complaynt of Scotland."

eighteenth century the legend had become still more incomplete in Scotland, for whilst the hunt was still known there, the name of its leader had faded away from popular recollection. How completely it was forgotten is plain from the following lines in a poem called Albania, which was first published in 1742.*

> There since of old the haughty thanes of Ross,—
> So to the simple swain tradition tells,—
> Were wont with clans, and ready vassals throng'd,
> To wake the bounding stag or guilty wolf,
> There oft is heard at midnight or at noon,
> Beginning faint, but rising still more loud
> And nearer, voice of hunters and of hounds,
> And horns hoarse-winded, blowing far and keen.
> Forthwith the hubbub multiplies; the gale
> Labours with wilder shrieks and rifer din
> Of hot pursuit, the broken cry of deer
> Mangled by throttling dogs, the shouts of men,
> And hoofs thick beating on the hollow hill.
> Sudden the grazing heifer in the vale
> Starts at the noise, and both the herdsman's ears
> Tingle with inward dread. Aghast he eyes
> The mountain's height, and all the ridges round,
> Yet not one trace of living wight discerns,
> Nor knows, o'erawed and trembling as he stands,
> To what or whom he owes his idle fear,
> To ghost, to witch, to fairy, or to fiend;
> But wonders, and no end of wondering finds.

But the Scottish Arthur still represents the storm-god, though not in combination with the wild huntsman, for what says the rhyme?

* It was reprinted by Leyden, in his "Scottish Descriptive Poems," 1803.

Arthur o' Bower has broken his bands,
And he's come roarin' ower the lands.
The king o' Scots and a' his power
Canna turn Arthur o' Bower.*

Woden was the god chiefly honoured of yore in the festivities of Spring, and the people of Edinburgh still go out and gather the May-day dew on Arthur's Seat—at least they did so twenty years ago.† In another act of the Hackelberg-Wuotan drama, of which we have now to speak, we shall again see the British Arthur distinctly representing the god of his foes, the heathens of Germany and Scandinavia.

Germany and Denmark abound in legends wherein the winter trance of Woden is enacted by various popular heroes. Charlemagne slumbers in many places with his enchanted army—in the Desenberg near Warburg, in the castle of Herstalla on the Weser, in the Karlsburg on the Spessart, the Trausberg and the Donnersberg in the Pfalz, &c.; and the Emperor Henry the Fowler is entranced in the Sudemerberg, near Goslar. But the best known of all these slumbering heroes is he of the red beard, the Emperor Frederick Barbarossa. He was drowned when far from home on a crusade, but, just as it was in Portugal after King Sebastian

* Robert Chambers, Pop. Rhy. p. 41.
† Chambers' Ed. Jour., April 30, 1842.

had perished in Africa, the lower classes of Frederick's subjects would not believe the story. They would have it that the Emperor was alive, and would return to his dominions, and so stubbornly did they hold fast by that opinion that several pretenders took advantage of it to pass themselves off as the true Barbarossa. The German people still maintain the same faith, for their hero has been seen by many of them in the Kyffhäuser mountain, in the old palatinate of the Saxon imperial house. There, in a cavern, with all his knights and squires around him, he sits to this day, leaning his head upon his arm, at a table through which his beard has grown, or round which, according to other accounts, it has grown twice. When it has thrice encircled the table, he will wake up to battle. The cavern glitters with gold and jewels, and is as bright as the sunniest day. Thousands of horses stand at mangers filled with thorn-bushes instead of hay, and make a prodigious noise as they stamp on the ground and rattle their chains. The old Kaiser sometimes wakes up for a moment and speaks to his visitors. He once asked a herdsman who had found his way into the Kyffhäuser, "Are the ravens" [Odin's birds] "still flying about the mountain?"

The man replied that they were. "Then," said Barbarossa, "I must sleep a hundred years longer."

That Frederick and all the rest of the caverned princes and warriors are no other than Woden and his wild host, is clear from many details of the legends concerning them.* People who visit the Emperor in the Kyffhäuser receive just such presents as are given by the wild huntsman,—horses' legs or heads that afterwards turn into gold ; and there is a lady in the Kyffhäuser, who is variously called the Princess, the Kaiser's housekeeper, Mademoiselle or Jungfer, and sometimes even Frau Holle (Holda), who is beyond all doubt Woden's wife Fria.†

"Arthur too, the vanished king, whose return is expected by the Britons, and who rides at the head of the nightly host, is said to dwell with his men-at-arms in a mountain ; Felicia, Sybilla's daughter, and the goddess Juno, live with him, and the whole army are well provided with food, drink, horses, and clothes." Such was the belief of mediæval Germany, as stated by Grimm ;‡ for the legend of the British Arthur overspread all Christendom, and was even localized in Sicily, where, as Gervase of Tilbury was

* D. M. p. 912. Mannhardt, p. 138.

† Ndd. p. 495.

‡ On the authority of the Wartburg Krieg. D. M. p. 912.

told by the inhabitants, the departed hero had his dwelling in Ætna.* To the same legend belongs a tradition of Thomas the Rhymer, the favourite of the Fairy Queen, which is current on the Scottish border, and which has been related by Sir Walter Scott.† It is that "of a daring horse-jockey having sold a black horse to a man of venerable and antique appearance, who appointed the remarkable hillock upon Eildon hills, called the Lucken hare, as the place where, at twelve o'clock at night, he should receive the price. He came, his money was paid in ancient coin, and he was invited by his customer to view his residence. The trader in horses followed his guide in the deepest astonishment through several long ranges of stalls, in each of which a horse stood motionless, while an armed warrior lay equally still at the charger's feet. 'All these men,' said the wizard in a whisper, 'will awaken at the battle of Sheriffmoor.' At the extremity of this extraordinary depôt hung a sword and a horn, which the prophet pointed out to the horse-dealer as containing the means of dissolving the spell. The man in confusion took the horn and attempted to wind it. The horses instantly started in their stalls, stamped,

* Liebrecht.

† "Demonology and Witchcraft," p. 133, and Notes to "Waverley."

and shook their bridles, the men arose and clashed their armour, and the mortal, terrified at the tumult he had excited, dropped the horn from his hand. A voice like that of a giant, louder even than the tumult around, pronounced these words :—

> Woe to the coward that ever he was born,
> That did not draw the sword before he blew the horn !

A whirlwind expelled the horse-dealer from the cavern, the entrance to which he could never find again."

"This legend," Sir Walter adds, "with several variations, is found in many parts of Scotland and England ; the scene is sometimes laid in some favourite glen of the Highlands, sometimes in the deep coal-mines of Northumberland and Cumberland, which run so far beneath the ocean. . . . . But it is a circumstance worth notice, that although this edition of the tale is limited to the year 1715, by the very mention of the Sheriffmoor, yet a similar story appears to have been current during the reign of Queen Elizabeth, which is given by Reginald Scot."

Sir Walter takes it for granted that Thomas the Rhymer was himself the leader of the army for which he purveyed horses, but this is a gratuitous and improbable assumption. The very passage which he has quoted from Leyden's "Scenes of Infancy" shows that according to other versions of the story the cavérned warriors are King Arthur's knights:

> Say who is he, with summons long and high,
> Shall bid the charmed sleep of ages fly,
> Roll the long sound through Eildon's caverns vast,
> While each dark warrior kindles at the blast;
> The horn, the falchion grasp with mighty hand,
> And peal proud Arthur's march from Fairy-land?

Although Scott confessed his inability to account for the incident of the horn and sword, its meaning is not at all dubious. The caverned heroes, as we have said, under whatever name they are known, and wherever they repose, are all representatives of Odin and his host. The great battle to which they will at last awake is that which will be fought before the end of the world, when heaven and earth shall be destroyed and the Æsir gods themselves shall perish, and their places shall be filled by a new creation and new and brighter gods. The sword concealed in the heart of the Eildon hill is that of Heimdallr, the Sverdâs or Sword-god, and warder of Bifrost bridge, and his is the Gjallar horn with which he will warn the gods that the frost giants are advancing to storm Valhalla.*

* Kuhn u. Schwartz, Ndd. p. 496.

The gods will answer to the call, but we know their doom. By what miracle did the Germans and Norsemen, alone among pagans, become possessed with an idea apparently so antagonistic to the very spirit of paganism? How came that rude and bloodthirsty race, in times when they were as yet so little given to abstract speculation, to conceive the thought of a great consummation, in which all nature should be destroyed by fire, the gods themselves, whom they had made after their own likeness, should perish, and their own highest ideal of life, human and divine, should give place to something ineffably purer and better? Scarcely can we imagine by what impulse they were prompted for once to strain their thoughts so far beyond the ordinary reaches of their souls, but at least we can trace the line along which they moved in that astonishing flight.

Their whole religion was essentially a personification of the processes of nature. For themselves, they were before all things warriors; and such as their own habits of life were their views of nature, and the language in which they clothed them. War, elemental war, was the constant occupation of their gods; and when the usual tendency of polytheism to rise towards monotheism led them to choose a supreme deity, their choice could not be doubtful.

They raised to that rank the storm-god Odin, who better represented the national character than did any of the others, not even excepting Thor, and whose death in Autumn and resurrection in Spring corresponded to the beginning and end of nature's two greatest annual vicissitudes. Thus the annual death of nature and of its supreme god became dominant and inseparable points in their theology, just as in that of the Egyptians; but unlike the Egyptians they had among them some man of genius who was able to push the same theory to its extreme limits, and to impose his own views upon his countrymen. "Life and death," such a man would have argued, "run the round of the year, and seven months of death are a necessary preparation for five months of life. What if the death were longer, and also more profound and unbroken; for now it is suspended for twelve nights at the winter solstice, when the gods revive and visit the earth. What if the universe and the gods were once for all to die outright? Would not that perfect death be followed by a perfect life, infinitely transcending all that has come of the petty deaths of all the years since the ash-tree first became a man?"

CHAPTER XI.

THE HEARTH FIRE—MARRIAGE—BOUNDARY OAKS—RED HAIR—PEAS.

AGNI, beloved as the hearth fire, is styled in the Vedas "the guest," but he is also worshipped as lord of the house, the family, and the tribe, and god of domestic life and of marriage. In these attributes he corresponds exactly with Thor.

The ceremonies constituting the nuptial solemnity in India are thus described by Colebrooke :*—"The bridegroom goes in procession to the house where the bride's father resides, and is there welcomed as a guest. The bride is given to him by her father in the form usual at every solemn donation, and their hands are bound together with grass. He clothes the bride with an upper and better garment, and the skirts of her mantle and his are tied together. The bridegroom makes *oblation to fire,* and the bride drops rue on it as an oblation. The bridegroom solemnly takes her hand in marriage. She treads

* Miscell. Essays, i. 224.

on a stone and mullar. They *walk round the fire.* The bride steps seven steps, conducted by the bridegroom, and he then dismisses the spectators, the marriage being now complete and irrevocable. In the evening of the same day the bride sits down on a bull's hide, and the bridegroom points out to her the polar star as an emblem of stability. They then partake of a meal. The bridegroom remains three days at the house of the bride's father; on the fourth he conducts her to his own house in solemn procession. She is then welcomed by his kindred; and the solemnity ends with *oblations to fire.*"

Burning torches were carried in bridal processions at Rome, and the bride always wore the flammeum or flame coloured veil, "for good omen's sake," as Festus says. Her shoes were also of the same colour. The Hindu bride wore a red girdle, the *cautuka,* a name which in later times designated also the bridal ring.

In Scandinavia the union of man and wife was anciently consecrated by laying Thor's symbol, the hammer, in the bride's lap; and Thursday is still regarded as an auspicious day for marrying. In Germany, where Christian tradition has partially identified Thor with the devil, it is held unlucky to marry on that day. In that country, in old times, when the bride first entered her husband's house, she was led three times round the hearth fire. Among other old customs, some of which are not yet extinct, was the carrying of a red banner in marriage processions. In some places, when the bridal pair are setting out for church they are made to step over a firebrand laid on the threshold of the house they are leaving. In other places, after the bride has been formally received in the house where the wedding is to be celebrated, she takes a pair of tongs and a firebrand in each hand, and carries them to the gate of the forecourt, where her friends are waiting to form the wedding procession. In times within living memory the bride wore a lofty head-dress of a peculiar form, never used on any other occasion. A band of red silk wound round it was an indispensable part of its adornment. The bridal nosegays of rosemary were always tied with red thread, as they are still in Havelland. In a wood near Dahle there was formerly a great oak tree (now reduced to a stump) to which new married couples used to repair, dance round it three times, and cut a cross upon it. This cross betokened of yore Thor's hammer, the consecrator of marriage.*

Thor's wife was Sif, whose name, signifying "kin,"

* Kuhn, Westf. ii. 44.

is the Scottish *sib*,* and is found in the English *gossip*, *i.e.*, god-sib, this word having originally denoted the spiritual relationship between the godfathers and godmothers of the same child. The god of the house-fire and guardian of the household and its belongings was the natural protector of the aggregate of families forming the *gens* or tribe, the village, town, commune, or nation, and of the soil occupied by each of them. Possession was taken of unoccupied or newly purchased land with a hammer, which the new owner cast out as he drove over the ground in a cart, or, in Scandinavia, by kindling a fire upon it;† and the oak, Thor's tree (p. 49), was planted on the boundaries of lands, and lordships great and small. To this usage our English parishes owe their gospel oaks, so called from the custom of having the gospel read under or near them by the clergyman attending the perambulation of the parish boundaries, which took place annually on Ascension day or Holy Thursday, the high festival of Thor in pagan times, when his rites were doubtless celebrated beneath his sacred tree. "It is possible that many of the more famous oak trees yet standing in

* "It's guid to be sib to siller." Scots Proverb.

† Mannhardt, pp. 197, 227.

England may date from the days of at least Saxon heathendom. . . Nearly all are boundary trees, marking the original limit of shire or of manor. Such was the great 'Shire-oak' which stood at the meeting place of York, Nottingham, and Derby, into which three counties it extended its vast shadow. Wider spreading than the chestnut of the 'Centi Cavalli' on Mount Etna, the branches of the Shire-oak could afford shelter to 230 horsemen. Such, too, is the 'Crouch' oak at Addlestone, in Surrey, under which Wickliffe preached and Queen Elizabeth dined—one of the ancient border-marks of Windsor Forest, whose name, according to Mr. Kemble, refers to the figure of the cross anciently cut upon it. Trees thus marked are constantly referred to as boundaries in Anglo-Saxon charters."* The writer of this passage is not quite accurate in saying that "the cross withdrew the oak from the dominion of Thor or Odin." More or less it did so in Christian times, but previously to them the cross as well as the tree may have belonged to Thor.

Indra's beard was golden ; Agni is invoked in the Vedas as the god with the golden beard and golden teeth. Fire and the "red gold" are associated ideas

* Quarterly Rev., July, 1863, p. 222.

in all Indo-European languages. Thor's beard was red, and it thundered and lightened when he blew in it. His hair too was red, and that such hair and beards were much admired when he was there to set the fashion, may be inferred not only from general considerations, but more particularly from the extreme aversion which was conceived for them when Christianity came in. *Rother-bart, Teufelsart,* "Redbeard, devil-steered," is a German proverb; and the more to insult the memory of the fallen god, it was fabled that he and the vilest of men, the arch traitor Judas, had hair and beards of the same colour. "His very hair," says Rosalind, pouting because Orlando has not kept his appointment with her—

> "His very hair is of the dissembling colour.
> *Celia.* "Something browner than Judas's; marry, his kisses are Judas's own children.
> *Ros.* "I' faith, his hair is of a good colour.
> *Celia.* "An excellent colour; your chestnut was ever the only colour."

The tradition about the colour of Judas's hair did not come from the East, but is of German origin. No allusion to it is found in the works of the fathers of the church or of other early ecclesiastical writers.

As Odin was identified with the Roman Mercury, so Thunar, Donar, or Thor, was called in Latin by the name of his brother thunderer, Jupiter. There is a plant popularly called in Germany Donner-bart (thunderbeard), in England Jupiter's beard, in France Joubarbe, *i.e.*, Jove's beard, which is set on the roofs of houses to preserve them from lightning. Whether these names properly belong to house-leek, which bears a pink blossom, or to stonecrop, which has numerous yellow flowers (yellow is one of the lightning colours), or whether they are common to both plants, I am unable to say, for the authorities on the subject are ambiguous. Mannhardt maintains the latter opinion,* Kuhn asserts that the donner-bart is our English house-leek, that it is a sedum, and that sedum, according to Festus, was planted on housetops by the Romans as a preservative against lightning.† House-leek can by no stretch of fancy be likened to a beard; stonecrop has some resemblance to a crisp and curly yellow beard.

The mythology of peas is very curious, but still somewhat obscure. This much, however, is certain, that the plant and its fruit are in some way or other related to celestial fire. It may be that they were regarded in this light because they belong to the class of creeping and climbing plants to which such

* P. 191. † Kuhn, Westf. ii. 90.

relations were pre-eminently attributed (p. 45); at all events, the fact that they too represented something in the vegetation of the sky is substantiated by numerous details in their mythical history. The dragons that poison the air and the waters (p. 57) carry peas in their flight, and let them fall in such quantities that they fill up the wells to the brim, and their smell is so foul that the cattle refuse to eat them.* These peas are the lightning, that seemed, as appears from a multitude of traditions, to fall in drops or pellets, and their smell is the sulphurous stench that clings to whatever else the dragon brings, and to the gifts thrown down by the Wild Huntsman. The Zwergs, who are closely connected with Thor, and who forged for him his lightning hammer, are exceedingly fond of peas, as many a husbandman knows to his cost, whose pea-fields they plunder under cover of their caps of darkness. Peas were sacred to Thor himself, and even now in Berlin, peas with sourcrout are a standing dish on Thor's own day, Thursday.* That they are typical of lightning is further proved by their being used in the same manner as the thunderbolt and as hazel nuts to promote the fertility of seedcorn (p. 183). In Swabia and elsewhere peas

* Kuhn u. Schwartz, Ndd. p. 4. † Mannhardt, p. 190.

are boiled over the St. John's fire, and eaten dry out of the hollow of the hand. They are thought to be good against all sorts of complaints, and particularly against wounds and bruises.* It is also recommended that children in the measles should be washed with water in which peas have been boiled.†

The use of peas in divination concerning love matters is accounted for by the fact that they are sacred to the patron of marriage. In the Leitmeritzer district of Bohemia the girls go into a field of peas, and make there a garland of five or seven kinds of flowers, all of different hues. This garland they use as a pillow, lying down with their right ear upon it, and then they hear a voice from underground, which tells them what manner of man they are to have for a husband.‡

In England, when the kitchen-maid shells green peas, if she chance to find a pod with nine peas she hangs it over the kitchen door, and the first rustic who comes in is infallibly to be her husband, or at least her sweetheart. The village girls in Hertfordshire lay the pod with nine peas under a gate, and believe they will have for husband the first man that passes through, or one whose christian name and

* Mannhardt, p. 201. † Ibid. 197.

‡ Reinsberg-Düringsfeld, p. 312.

surname have the same initials as his. A Cumbrian girl, when her lover proves unfaithful, is, by way of consolation, rubbed with pea-straw by the neighbouring lads; and when a Cumbrian youth loses his sweetheart by marriage with a rival, the same sort of comfort is administered to him by the lasses of the village.*

"Winter time for shoeing, peascod time for wooing," is an old proverb found by Sir Henry Ellis in a MS. Devon glossary. A peascod wooing was performed, according to Brand, "by selecting one growing on the stem, snatching it away quickly, and, if the good omen of the peas remaining in the husk were preserved, then presenting it to the lady of their choice." An example of this practice is tenderly recounted by Touchstone :—

> "I remember when I was in love, I broke my sword upon a stone, and bade him take that for coming a-night to Jane Smile; and I remember the kissing of her batler, and the cow's dugs that her pretty chapped hands had milked; and I remember the wooing of a peascod instead of her, from whom I took two cods, and giving her them again said, with weeping tears, 'Wear these for my sake.'"

* Brand, ii. 99.

INDEX.

CPSIA information can be obtained
at www.ICGtesting.com
Printed in the USA
LVHW100440110522
718424LV00003B/175

9 783375 006273